SUMMER NIGHTS IN PINE HARBOR

TAMMY ROBINSON

B

Boldwood

First published in Great Britain in 2026 by Boldwood Books Ltd.

Copyright © Tammy Robinson, 2026

Cover Design by Debbie Clement

Cover Images: Shutterstock and Alamy

The moral right of Tammy Robinson to be identified as the author of this work has been asserted in accordance with the Copyright, Designs and Patents Act 1988.

Every effort has been made to obtain the necessary permissions with reference to copyright material, both illustrative and quoted. We apologise for any omissions in this respect and will be pleased to make the appropriate acknowledgements in any future edition.

A CIP catalogue record for this book is available from the British Library.

Paperback ISBN 978-1-80600-117-0

Large Print ISBN 978-1-80600-116-3

Hardback ISBN 978-1-80600-115-6

Trade Paperback ISBN 978-1-80656-169-8

Ebook ISBN 978-1-80600-118-7

Kindle ISBN 978-1-80600-119-4

Audio CD ISBN 978-1-80600-110-1

MP3 CD ISBN 978-1-80600-111-8

Digital audio download ISBN 978-1-80600-114-9

This book is printed on certified sustainable paper. Boldwood Books is dedicated to putting sustainability at the heart of our business. For more information please visit https://www.boldwoodbooks.com/about-us/sustainability/

Boldwood Books Ltd, 23 Bowerdean Street, London, SW6 3TN

www.boldwoodbooks.com

This book is dedicated to Vicki Marsdon and Emma Beswetherick.
Thank you both for continuing to believe in me.

1

TAYLOR

Normally, the open road and the wind on my face would be enough to put me in a good mood. A night owl by habit, I craved moments like this. The stars overhead. My headlight highlighting the curves of the road.

Just a few short hours ago, I'd climbed into my beloved king-size bed with the luxurious linen I'd splurged on from that expensive shop on Lexington Ave, thinking it was just the end of another, ordinary day. Tired but satisfied. Ready to do it all again tomorrow. Instead, as tomorrow dawned, I found myself riding through the night to answer a call for help.

Even when dawn eventually came, chasing away the dark and bathing the sky in delicate shades of pink, yellow and orange, it did nothing to improve my mood. I was too annoyed. Annoyed with idiot drivers on the road who failed to give way and cut corners too close to the line. With my mother for her middle-of-the-night phone call, but most of my annoyance was directed towards my great-uncle Ray, whose carelessness had necessitated the call. Ninety-four or not, the man should have taken more care with his foot placement. If he had, I wouldn't be in this predicament.

The highway narrowed the closer I got to the coast. The corners tightened. The pine trees that gave my hometown its name lined up like soldiers on the hills both sides of the road, their tall, sturdy silhouettes achingly familiar.

Pine Harbor.

Apart from the odd weekend visit home, made solely with the purpose of appeasing my mother, I'd barely spent any time there in years. This trip was different. It would be my first extended stay since I'd left fourteen years before, a skittish newlywed clutching a suitcase, heading out into the unknown, certain only that what was out there had to be better than what I was leaving behind.

'*Please*, Taylor,' my mother had begged the night before over the phone, which had immediately put me on high alert. My mother hated begging. *Never beg for anything you can take care of yourself,* she'd always told us growing up. 'There's no one else I can trust to look after him while I'm gone,' she'd continued. 'You know I wouldn't ask unless I was desperate.'

I'd shrugged out of the sheets and rolled to one side, perching on the edge of the bed as the circulation had returned to my extremities. My bedroom windows were open but the air refused to move, and the summer heat was stifling. 'Gone where?'

She'd sighed, the sound loud through the phone. It was a sigh well-honed by practice. 'I knew you'd forget. I'm going on the cruise, remember?'

I'd squeezed my eyes shut. Right. The cruise. Not *a* cruise, *the* cruise. The one my mother had been looking forward to since she booked it a year ago. Almost three weeks around the Caribbean with four of her friends, the plan concocted over drinks after the funeral of Ellen's husband, Frank. They'd decided life was short. That they must seize the day. Apparently, this meant cocktails around a pool and casino nights on board a floating palace.

'I haven't forgotten,' I'd lied.

'I just can't in good conscience leave him home by himself,' she'd fretted. 'It was a dubious enough idea before, but now? What if he falls again and lies undiscovered for days? Dying alone, of starvation and neglect?'

'Or,' I'd offered a different perspective, 'what if he's fine?'

'I can't take the risk.'

'Can't you pay someone to do it? A nurse or someone?'

'He doesn't like strangers.'

'He doesn't like anyone.'

'Taylor.'

'Especially me.'

'Taylor.'

'Mom.'

'You know I wouldn't ask if there was another option. Maybe if I wasn't leaving tomorrow I could figure something else out, but I have a matter of hours to sort something. You're my only hope.'

I'd pinched the skin between my eyebrows and accepted my fate. She didn't ask for much, my mother. I could hardly turn her down in her hour of need. 'Fine. I guess I'm done sleeping anyway. I'll have a coffee and get on the road.'

'How long will it take you to get here?'

'Seven hours.'

'It's too much. Why can't you move home now that you and...' She didn't need to finish.

'New York is home now. My business is here.'

'So? You could just move your business here. There's a few vacant shops in town that would be perfect.'

'It's not as simple as that. I've built up a following here. You know that.'

She'd given up, changed tack. 'I don't suppose there's any chance Adam might come with you?'

'Who?'

'Be as obtuse as you like, Taylor. He's still your husband.'

'No, Mother. Adam will not be coming with me.'

'Are you sure you two can't work things out?' The hope in her voice did something to my heart. 'This is where you fell in love,' she'd added. 'Maybe being back here, around familiar surroundings, will remind you both of that.'

'It's not me who needs reminding,' I'd pointed out. 'And considering the fact that I haven't seen Adam in eight months, and the last I heard he was still very much with that skank—'

'*Taylor.*'

'Sorry, *slut*, from the gym.'

She'd tutted.

'Considering all that,' I'd continued, 'I'd say it's very unlikely he will be accompanying me.'

'You were just so good together. Everyone thought so.'

I'd felt the words land like a kick in the guts. *Not everyone.*

2

JACK

The table was sticky with spilled beer and lobster-shell detritus. After eight months, I still found it entertaining to watch people who'd never demolished a whole lobster before give it a try. It wasn't so entertaining when you were the one who had to clean up after them. Bits of shell and flesh went everywhere, even the walls. I finished clearing and wiping down the table, restocking the cutlery and napkin holder, then picked up the tray loaded with dirty dishes. It was only as I headed towards the kitchen that I realized Hannah had come downstairs and was sitting on a barstool, watching me. She'd helped herself to a bottle of wine from behind the bar and had poured a glass, twirling the stem between her fingers. A sure sign that she was feeling either sad or bored.

'Are you almost finished?' she asked, as I drew near her.

'Not for a while yet.'

She sighed. 'I'm bored.'

Bingo.

'Well, you know what I'm going to say to that.'

'Set a table,' she said, mimicking my voice. 'Wipe down the bar. Take an order.' She blew her hair out of her eyes. 'Newsflash, it's too hot to do any of those things.'

'You don't have to do all three,' I pointed out, smiling. 'Just pick one and start there.'

She gestured around the room to where various staff were carrying out their duties. 'That's what these guys are paid to do.'

'That doesn't mean you can't help out.'

'*You* shouldn't even be doing that,' she replied, gesturing towards the tray I was holding. 'You're the manager. It's not a good look.'

'This isn't like one of your fancy restaurants you're used to back home,' I reminded her. 'And you know I'm not the kind of manager to stand around in a penguin suit acting like I'm better than anyone else.'

'That's a shame. You look cute in a penguin suit.'

'Hannah.'

'What?' she said petulantly. 'It's a compliment. Am I not allowed to compliment you any more?'

I checked to make sure no one was within earshot. The rumor mill was already in overdrive – no need to add fuel to it. 'I just want to keep things professional.'

She sighed. 'Whatever. At least you referred to L.A. as home, I suppose. You haven't done that in a while. I was beginning to think you were starting to like it here.'

'I do like it here.'

'But you prefer L.A.'

I pulled a face. 'I don't know. This place isn't so bad.'

'What do you mean, you don't know?'

'Does it matter?'

'Yes. It matters a lot actually.'

I put the tray on top of the bar while I considered my reply. 'OK, well, this place is growing on me, I guess. The slower pace of life. The nature right on the doorstep. I've even made some friends.'

Her eyes narrowed. 'What are you saying?'

'It's really not that bad. You'd probably like it too if you spent more than a few weeks at a time here.'

'A few weeks is more than enough for me,' she retorted. 'Even that's too much, sometimes.'

'Well, then I guess you've got yourself a bit of a problem, haven't you?' I shifted the tray to balance the weight. 'Seeing as you bought yourself a business here.'

'I don't have to be here full-time for this place to work.'

'I know that. Even when you're here *part-time* this place works just fine without you. It's not like you lift a finger to do anything around here.' My tone was mild, not betraying how irked I really was.

She held up one hand and showed me her long, perfectly manicured pink nails. 'You want me to risk breaking one of these? When there isn't a decent manicurist in this town capable of fixing it?'

'Have you even given the local salon a chance? Because I've heard nothing but good things. The woman who owns it, Addison, comes in for happy hour every Friday and seems nice.'

She shuddered. 'My girl in the city would kill me if I went to someone else. Literally.'

'Not literally.'

'OK maybe not literally. But I certainly wouldn't be able to show my face there ever again.' She pouted. 'I'd be a social outcast, and you don't want that, do you?'

I had to laugh. She was spoiled, but I'd known that from the moment I'd met her. I couldn't be mad at her now when it was just the way she'd always been. It was me who had changed, not her.

'I don't have time to stand around chatting,' I told her briskly. 'Either make yourself useful or entertain yourself.'

'Fine, I will,' she sniffed. 'There's a new romance on Netflix I wanted to watch anyway. I just came down for a bottle of wine, and to tell you that I'll be heading back to L.A. tomorrow.'

'Again? You've only been here a week.'

'Eight days, actually.'

I tried not to show the flicker of annoyance I felt. 'Fine. Drive safe to the airport.'

'Come with me?'

'I can't.'

'Why not?'

'Because I have this place to run,' I reminded her. '*Your* business.'

'As your boss I hereby grant you the time off to come back to the city with me. It'll be fun. We can catch up with friends.' Her voice softened. 'Do some of the things we used to enjoy doing.'

'No.'

'Don't just say no. Sleep on it. Let me know in the morning.'

'I don't need to.' I picked up the tray again. 'The answer will still be no.'

'*Please* come. You're no fun any more. Don't you think we deserve to have fun after everything we've been through?'

It was a dirty tactic, and I resented her for resorting to it. 'Do whatever it is that makes you happy. But don't get mad at me if I'd rather stay here and work.'

She stood up abruptly, picking up the glass and the bottle of wine. 'I wish I'd never bought this place.'

I took a step backwards so she could pass. 'Well you did. And you asked me to manage it for you. I'm just doing what you wanted, Hannah. For your future. You might not be able to appreciate it now, but hopefully one day you will.'

'Don't count on it,' she retorted, then flounced off past me towards the stairs that led to the apartment upstairs. I watched her leave, feeling drained and frustrated.

3

TAYLOR

As I rode through the town, the nerves in my stomach kicked up a notch at the sight of so many familiar places. Every street corner, every bench seat, the sidewalks, the wharf, they all held memories. Memories I'd spent a long time trying to forget.

It was summer, the sweltering heat relentless, and the ferry had just come in, purging another batch of sandal-clad tourists to swarm through the picturesque town and historical paths around the island. You could drive across the bridge to Pine Harbor, as I'd just done, but most tourists preferred the scenic trip on the old ferries that shuffled between the mainland and the numerous islands off the coast of Maine.

Settled in 1786, Pine Harbor was originally founded by seafarers and loggers from Massachusetts and Nova Scotia, who'd been drawn to the area because of the harbor and the forests of white pine trees that surrounded it. Originally a ship-building town, the last yard had closed in the nineteen sixties, but the lobster fishermen still thrived, as well as the oyster farmers. I rode through town slowly, checking out what had changed – not much – and what was new. Again, not a hell of a lot. With its old buildings, manicured town green and picturesque wharf covered with colorful lobster buoys, the place looked as picture-perfect as ever.

My family lived on the other side of town. Ten minutes along the coast, towards the northern point of the island. My mother, no doubt alerted by the sound of my bike coming down the long, treelined driveway, was waiting for me beside the old garage before the noise of the engine had even died away. As I slowed down and parked, I took a moment to surreptitiously study her through the visor of my helmet. In two months, she'd be turning fifty-six, but she looked at least a decade younger. Thanks to the yoga she did every morning and the fact that she never sat still, she had a figure most twenty-year-olds would envy, and the cute little strapless playsuit she was wearing to combat the summer heat showed off her toned and tanned legs. Only the fine lines around her eyes and the graying-silver streaks in her hair gave away her true age.

'Sorry,' I pre-empted, pulling my helmet off. 'I know I'm late, but I had to sort out cover at work and organize someone to water my plants.' This wasn't true. I'd actually forgotten about my plants until I was halfway here. I'd stopped buying myself houseplants years ago because, despite my best intentions, the damned things were more fragile than a new-born baby and had a tendency to die on me, despite my best efforts. Occasionally someone who didn't know me well enough would gift me one. If it thrived on neglect, it was welcome to stay. If not, it soon joined its predecessors in the bin.

'I can't believe you rode that thing here,' she tutted. 'I can't believe you're still riding it at all.'

I slung my helmet over the handlebars and started peeling off my gloves. Now that I'd stopped riding, the lack of a breeze to cool me down meant my bike safety clothing suddenly felt oppressively heavy, and I could feel sweat pooling in the curve of my lower spine. 'Bit of an expensive garage ornament if I don't.'

'You know how I feel about it.'

'I do.'

'Come here.' She pulled me in for a hug and I held my breath against the onslaught of her perfume.

'You're too thin,' she said.

'Is there such a thing?'

'Yes.' She pulled back, holding me at arm's length and looking me up and down. 'It's not healthy. And look at those shadows underneath your eyes. You look tired. I thought it was sorted.'

'It is,' I lied. 'But someone woke me up in the middle of the night, remember?'

'If I knew you were going to ride this thing here I would have gone with another option.'

'I thought you said you had no other option.'

'There's always another option.'

I picked my helmet back up. 'In that case, I'll see you later. Enjoy the cruise.'

'Don't be silly.' She took it off me. 'You're here now.'

'Where is he?' I asked her, as we linked arms and walked side by side along the track that led to the house. The trees were tall, even more so than I remembered. But then a decade worth of growth would do that.

'Inside, settled into his armchair with the fan on.'

'What's the damage?'

'Bruises, mostly. Tenderness. Damaged pride.'

'Can't imagine that's helped his mood any.'

'He says he doesn't need a babysitter.'

'We're in agreement then.'

'I told him you're just here to keep him company.'

'How did that go down?'

'Not well,' she admitted.

I shook my head. 'This is going to be a hell of a long three weeks. I hope you've left the key for the liquor cabinet somewhere handy.'

She snorted. 'Good luck finding anything in there. There's only your father's old spirit bottles, and they're mostly full of water now.'

'Ah.' My face crinkled up sheepishly. 'You knew about that?'

'That you and your brother used to siphon off the spirits and water down what was left? Of course I knew.'

'You never said anything.'

'Would it have stopped you?'

'Probably not.'

'Exactly.' She smiled, squeezing my arm. 'It's good to have you home, baby girl. Despite the circumstances.'

'This is just temporary,' I reminded her.

'I know.'

'Then don't smile like that.'

'Like what?'

'Like you know something I don't. Like you're plotting something.'

'Me? Plotting?'

'Mom.'

She stopped walking and put her hands on her hips. 'I didn't push Ray down the stairs in order to get you here, if that's what you're insinuating.'

'I know you wouldn't stoop that low.'

'Good. All I'm saying is that this place...' She lifted her face to the sky and breathed the salty air in deeply, smiling as she exhaled again. 'It gets under your skin. Reminds you what's really in your heart.'

I groaned. 'That's... wow. I forgot how cheesy you can be.'

'Am I cheesy though? Or am I just right?'

'Definitely cheesy. Hallmark card cheesy.'

'Nothing wrong with a good Hallmark card.'

We'd reached the end of the driveway and emerged onto the large lawn that surrounded the house. A load of washing flapped in the breeze on the washing line on the back lawn. There was the sweet smell of rose in the air from the pink flowers blooming near the deck. Despite myself, I felt a jolt of happiness. My childhood home. She'd had it repainted since the last time I was here. The walls were a crisp, clean white, the shutters around the windows navy blue. Built in the nineteen forties, the six-bed, four-bath house was two stories high, and just over three thousand square feet in total. Sitting on four and a half acres, most of which was covered in trees, the house perched right above the beach. This far out of town and with the nearest neighbor two acres away, we were lucky enough to have it to ourselves. The beach itself was sandy, but the shoreline was rocky. At low tide, it was dotted with rock pools and a natural swimming hole. I could smell the water, hear it lightly lapping against the rocks. Inexplicably, I felt the need to feel it on my skin, even though I hadn't swum in the ocean in years.

'House looks good,' I told her.

'Thanks. I had Hudson and his boy paint it two summers ago. They replaced a few worn boards, tidied the whole thing up for me.'

Hudson's 'boy', Owen, was my age. 'How is Owen?'

'Good. Married. Couple of kids.'

'Who'd he marry?'

'Out-of-towner.'

'She nice?'

'I haven't had a lot to do with her, but seems so. Stays at home with his kids.'

'Her kids too, I'd imagine.'

'Obviously not a career woman.'

'Because there're so many careers on offer here,' I drawled sarcastically.

'Life is what you make of it, Taylor.'

'You sound like Forrest Gump.'

'He's a very wise man.'

'He's a character in a movie, Mom.'

'Whatever. Anyway, they're always advertising for new realtors. And like I said, there are plenty of empty shops in town.'

'And the fact that they're empty isn't a giant red flag to you?'

'No. Just people bringing the wrong businesses to town. Like the lady who opened that...' She waved a hand in the air as she tried to think of the words. 'I told you about it – she had crystals and those little stone buddha statues. Dragons. Angels. Books about mythical creatures and self-help books written by ladies with too much money. No call for any of that around here. Three months she lasted before she upped up and left in the middle of winter.'

'I don't blame her. Winter here can suck the life out of you.'

'Don't be so dramatic. Anyway, she didn't leave because of the weather.'

'Whatever her reasons, good on her for trying.'

'Now, an art gallery/tattoo studio,' she said pointedly. 'That'd go down well with the tourists *and* the locals.'

I smiled at her sweetly. 'The second you're back, I'm leaving.'

'We'll see.' She checked her watch. 'I need to finish packing.'

'You're not packed?' I fished my phone out of an inside pocket on my jacket and checked the time myself. 'Jesus, Mom. Talk about leaving it to the last second.'

'Don't stress. It's just a couple of last-minute things.'

'It's not me who'll be stressing if you miss your flight.'

We both turned at the sound of a car horn as a silver Nissan pulled up at the garage. My mother's friends, colorful in the loose, gaudy clothing they'd chosen in preparation for the cruise and an unlimited buffet, spilled out and hurried along the path towards us.

'Brace yourself,' my mother said, smiling brightly at them.

'Taylor!' Angela said, ignoring my body language and pulling me in for a hug. My mother's perfume was joined by hers, something bold and in your face, a bit like she was. She pulled back and held me at arm's length. Looked me up and down. 'You're too thin.'

Mom nodded, pleased to have it confirmed. 'That's exactly what I said. Give me a second, girls, I just need to say goodbye to Ray and grab my things.'

'OK, Moira,' Margaret said, with the look of someone who knew my mother and her timekeeping all too well. 'But don't take too long. We have a long drive ahead of us and you know I like to check in early.'

'Yes, Margaret,' my mother replied, rolling her eyes at me before running up the stairs at the side of the house. 'While you wait, help me convince Taylor she needs to move back here.'

I gaped after her, open-mouthed, although really, I shouldn't have been surprised she'd thrown me under the bus. When it came to getting her own way, my mother could be ruthless.

'You *should* move back here,' Ellen said. 'They clearly don't have proper food in the city, and men like a bit of meat on a woman.'

'Not Adam,' I told her. 'His new girlfriend lifts weights. She's very... sinewy.'

'It's terrible what happened there,' Margaret said, shaking her head. 'Just terrible.'

'I mean, it wasn't *great*,' I agreed. 'But I think there are probably worse things that happen in the world every day.'

'Don't give up hope,' Angie said. 'He still might come back to you.'

It was my turn to snort. 'I bloody hope not.'

'You don't mean that.'

'Hell yes, I do. Why would I want him back?'

'Because he's your husband, and because you two were always so good together.'

'People really need to stop saying that.'

'Why? It's true.'

'You guys have no idea.'

'So tell us.'

I squeezed my eyes shut, decided it was time to play a little dirty myself. 'You know Mom hasn't actually finished packing, right?'

It worked. As Margaret squealed indignantly and headed inside to corral my mother, followed by the others, I took a deep breath, stared up at the house and braced myself. *I can do this,* I told myself. But the nerves were back in full force.

4

JACK

Less than ten minutes after locking up the restaurant, my truck was bouncing down the driveway that led to the cabin where I'd been living the last five months, the smell of pine filling the cab through the open windows. When I first moved to Pine Harbor eight months ago, I'd lived in a room above the restaurant. There was a whole apartment up there. Two bedrooms, each with their own bathroom, a kitchen, large living area with a deck that gave incredible views over the town and harbor. The whole building belonged to Hannah, and even though she wasn't there full-time, flitting between the city and the bay as needed, it didn't feel right sharing the apartment with her.

'You're abandoning me now too?' she'd accused me with tears in her eyes when I'd informed her that I was moving out.

'That's not fair,' I'd chided her. 'The only reason I'm here in Pine Harbor is for you, remember? You're still going to see me every day. I just think we could both do with our own space.'

'You're not even going to ask me how *I* feel about it? You've already made your mind up?'

I'd nodded. 'Signed the lease today.'

'I don't want you to go.'

'I really think it's for the best.'

'For you, maybe,' she'd shot back, and in the morning, she'd been gone. I never knew how long she'd be gone, but she always came back eventually, acting like nothing had happened, and I was happy to play along with that. It was easier than always fighting.

At the top of the driveway, I swung around the last corner and my headlights illuminated a couple of branches that had come down across the track. Big trees dotted the property and were prone to dropping a few branches every time we had high winds, as we'd had the night before. I left the truck running while I dragged them off the drive and piled them up in the undergrowth. Tomorrow I'd bring the saw and chop them into firewood for Moira for next winter. The lawns needed mowing again soon too. It wasn't part of the deal, property maintenance, but I liked doing it, and I knew Moira appreciated it.

The cabin was warm and homey and just as you'd imagine an oceanside cabin in Maine to be. It came fully furnished, and although some of the furnishings wouldn't have been my own choice – like the old duck decoys in rows on top of the beams in the roof, or the shower curtain with its moose pattern that matched the moose lamps and moose kitchen utensil holder – I was just grateful I didn't have to bother with any of it myself. Interior design had never been a passion of mine, and the furnishings from the apartment I'd left behind in the city to move here had all fitted into the back of a truck. I'd donated them to goodwill, severing all ties with the life I had left behind.

It was ten-thirty, too late for a beer, but too early for bed. Even if I was tired, the heat was still stifling, and I knew from experience I would only toss and turn for hours if I tried. It always took me a while to switch my brain off enough from work to be able to fall asleep anyway. Luckily, my first run on the beach after I had moved in here, I had found the perfect spot to cool off and destress. I grabbed my towel and headed out the door.

Following the trail down to the beach, I dodged the various tree roots that emerged through the soil ready to twist an unsuspecting ankle, feeling the moment the ground underfoot changed from the gritty dirt of the forest floor to the sandy beach, the sand still warm from the sun. Stiff grasses brushed up against my legs. The cicada chorus was loud in the quiet of the night, the only other noise the gentle swooshing of the waves meeting the shore. The moon and stars overhead were bright enough that I didn't need a torch, although I carried one with me as usual, just in case. I was still getting used to how many stars there were here, away from the bright lights of the city.

I made my way along the beach to the rocks at the end of the small bay, clambering up them to the edge of the swimming hole that had been carved into the rocks over time. At high tide, the ocean flooded the pool with clean, fresh Atlantic salt water. At its deepest point it was just over six feet, and at its widest point about nine. I dropped my towel and the torch onto a ledge and reached for the ties on the front of my board shorts.

'I wouldn't do that if I were you,' the voice in the dark said idly. 'Not unless you want to add public indecency to the trespass charge you're already facing,' she added.

'Who's there?'

'I could ask you the same question.'

'You could,' I agreed. 'But I asked first.'

There was a splashing sound. 'Would you believe me if I said I was a mermaid?'

'That depends. *Are* you a mermaid?'

'No.' She sounded regretful. 'But I used to spend a lot of time while growing up imagining that I was. Imagine having the freedom to go wherever you wanted in the world. All the amazing sights you would see.'

Scanning the pool, I made out the outline of her head at the other end of the pool, silhouetted against the sky. 'This is private property. How did you even get here?'

'The same way as you did, I walked. The difference is, I'm allowed to be here. *You're* the one who's trespassing.'

'No, I'm not.'

'Yes, you are.'

'I'm not,' I insisted.

'Whatever. You can argue about it with the cops. I've already called them and they're on their way under lights and sirens. We tend to take trespassers pretty seriously around these parts.'

I smirked. In all the months I'd lived here, I'd never seen the cops in a hurry to get anywhere. 'Oh really? What did you call them on, your mermaid shell-phone?'

I heard a snort of laughter. 'No. Just my regular old mobile.'

'Well, I hope it's Gerry who shows up. I haven't seen him around for a few weeks. I know he's pretty busy though. Marianne must be about ready to drop the baby any day now.'

There was a long pause. 'You know Gerry?' she asked, her tone suspicious.

'I do. Do *you* know Gerry?'

'I almost broke his arm in the fifth grade when he pulled my hair in class, so yeah, you could say I know Gerry.'

'You're a local.' I'd met a lot of people through the restaurant since moving here, but her voice wasn't ringing any bells. I felt around for the torch I'd put down on a rock nearby.

'You're pretty smart for a trespasser.'

'Thanks, but like I keep telling you, I'm not trespassing.' I found my torch and clicked it on, beaming the light in her direction.

She recoiled under its bright glare. 'Jesus Christ. Are you trying to blind me?'

'I'm trying to identify you.'

'Well, could you maybe not shine it directly into my eyeballs? I kind of like my retinas working, so I'd prefer it if you didn't burn them with that damn light.'

'Sorry.' I turned the torch to the side so it wasn't directly aimed at her any more. 'Look, why don't you just leave quietly and I won't take this any further.'

'Or,' she replied idly, swimming across from one side of the pool to the other. 'How about *you* leave and *I* won't take it any further.'

Realizing we were at a stalemate, I changed tack. 'OK, seriously, now, who are you? And no, I don't for a second believe you're a mermaid.'

'I'm not telling you.'

'You're refusing to tell me your name?'

'That's what I said, wasn't it? Did I not say it out loud?'

I aimed the light in her face again and waited.

'Ugh,' she sighed. 'Fine. Turn the light off and *then*, if it'll shut you up, I'll tell you my name. I'm trying to enjoy the night sky here, and you're ruining it.'

'Deal.' I clicked the torch off. 'Name.'

'Taylor.'

'You got a last name, Taylor?'

'You sound an awful lot like a cop – anyone ever tell you that?'

'Once or twice.'

'Calderwood,' she said. 'My name is Taylor Calderwood.'

It took a few moments for it to register why her name sounded so familiar. 'Wait, Calderwood as in…?'

'The lady who owns that big old house up there? Yeah. That Calderwood.'

'So, she's your…?'

'Mother. Yep.'

I connected the dots. 'You're the daughter who got married and moved to the city years ago.'

'How do you know that?'

'She mentioned you, when I first moved out here.'

'Moved where?'

'Here.'

'Where is here, exactly?'

'Didn't she say? Your mother is my landlord.'

'I'm pretty sure I'd know if you were living in my mother's house. That's the kind of thing she'd definitely have mentioned.'

'Not the house, I'm in the cabin.'

'Which cabin? *Our* cabin?'

'Yes.'

'The cabin that's eighty yards from our house… *that* cabin?'

'It's more like a hundred and twenty yards, but yes.'

'I can't believe she rented you the cabin. When?'

'About seven months ago.'

'I don't believe you.'

'Ask her, then.'

'I can't; she's gone on a cruise.'

'I take it that's why you're here.'

'Yes, that's why I'm here. Someone has to look after the old man and unfortunately I drew the short straw.'

'And you're angry about that? Because you sound kind of angry.'

'I'm not angry, I'm pissed off.'

I processed this. 'Isn't that the same thing?'

'I just can't believe she never mentioned you. We talk on the phone at *least* once a week. She's told me all about Ray's disgusting earwax and her hairdresser's scandalous affair with a married man, but did she ever mention the fact that she's rented out the family cabin to some random stranger?'

'Uh,' I started to answer, but she continued on without waiting.

'I mean, who even are you? And how did this all come about? Surely, she didn't advertise the cabin for rent? Why would she? She doesn't exactly need the money. And how did you even find out about it? Has everything been done properly, through the proper channels, with an actual tenancy agreement? Did she bother doing any reference checks before letting a complete stranger move in?'

I waited.

'Well?' she demanded.

'Oh, you're asking me this time. That was a lot of questions, but let me see if I can ease some of your concerns. My name is Jack. No, she didn't advertise. Someone mentioned the cabin one day at work, a friend of your mother's, so I drove out and asked her if she would consider leasing it to me. There isn't a formal agreement, but we shook hands on it. As far as I'm concerned, that's as good as any legal document. Your mother seemed happy with that too. She said that she's good at reading people, and could tell I am a good person. I haven't missed a payment yet and I won't. I also help your mom out by doing the lawns and other odd jobs around the place. This arrangement suits us both and is working well. You have nothing to worry about, I promise.'

'That's easy for you to say. But my mother is, how do I say

this? She's kind and caring, but she's also easily taken advantage of. I'm not sure I'm comfortable with your arrangement.'

'I've been living here for seven months already. Don't you think that if I was trying to scam your mother in some way, I'd have done it already?'

A long pause. 'Good point. I'm still not happy about it though, and you better believe I'll be doing some background checks. What's your last name, Jack?'

'Garrity.'

'And where do you hail from, Jack Garrity?'

'L.A.'

'L.A.?' She whistled. 'You're a long way from home.'

'I am.' I didn't want to go down that track and have to answer questions about why I'd left *there*, or why I'd moved *here*, so I changed the subject. 'Do you think that now we've got the introductions out of the way and established that neither of us are actually here illegally, I could get into the water? It's muggy as hell and all I can think about is getting in that water.'

There was a long pause.

'I suppose *technically* that's within your rights as a tenant.'

'Is that a yes?'

'It's an "I can't stop you".'

'So... a yes?'

'Oh my God. Yes. It's a yes.'

'Because if you don't want me to get in while you're in there, I won't. I can go back to the cabin, and come back later, when you've finished. If you'd prefer.'

'It's fine.'

'You're sure?'

'Just stop talking and get in the water.'

'OK.' My eyes had adjusted to the dark, and I could make out more details about her now. She had long hair piled in a messy bun on the top of her head with flyaway bits hanging down, exposing a long, slender neck. Lean, athletic shoulders above the waterline. When she turned her head, the moon highlighted the lines of her face. Her cheekbones and jaw, the tip of her nose.

Stepping forward, I curled my toes over the edge of the rocks on the side of the pool. 'I'm going to dive into the water now.'

'Do you always announce everything before you do it?'

'Not always,' I replied, then tucked my head between my arms and dove into the end where I knew the water was deepest, disturbing the black mirror surface that reflected the stars. The water was cold and refreshing. Coming back up for air, I shook my head, wiping the water from my eyes, smiling because I couldn't help it. These night swims had a way of calming my mind. Resetting the day. As I did a lazy breaststroke to the opposite side of the pool from her, a playful breeze swirled around me, carrying the salty scent of the sea and, briefly, something not quite as pleasant. A dead fish washed up on the beach, maybe, rotting under the heat of the sun. Then the breeze changed direction and the smell was gone. 'I just wanted to warn you.'

5

TAYLOR

I frowned as I processed his last words. 'Did you just say *warn* me?'

'No, sorry... warn wasn't the right word. What I meant was, I just wanted to make you aware that I was getting into the water, so you weren't frightened.'

I weighed up my options, which were few and far between. If this guy wanted to harm me there wouldn't be a hell of a lot I could do about it, apart from fight back. Down here on the beach no one would hear a call for help, and although I was pretty fast on my feet, I'd still have to get out of the pool and past him before I could try and get up the path to the house. But my instincts weren't screaming at me like they had in past situations where there had been even a hint of danger. The vibes Jack was giving off were more like golden retriever vibes. Harmless and potentially adorable.

'Do I need to be frightened?' I asked.

'No,' he said, sounding offended by the very thought. 'God no. Never. I would never hurt you. In any shape or form.'

'That's a pretty big promise to make. What if we kept

meeting in the pool every night and fell in love and then you decided that you couldn't be with a mermaid after all so broke it off and I spent the rest of my life here, pining under the stars.'

'Uh...'

I swam slowly to the other side of the pool and he did the same, as if we were sharks, circling each other. Somewhere down the bay, a seal barked. Just the once, as if that's all he could be bothered with in the heat. 'Just kidding. It'd be more likely to be me who did the dumping.'

'How do you figure that?'

'We mermaids are transient folk. Don't like to be tied down to any one place in particular.'

'I suppose you prefer to keep a sailor in every port.'

'God no. Imagine the effort involved. Trying to remember the right name every time. The potential to muck it up would be huge.'

He laughed. 'So, why weren't you?'

'Scared?'

'Yeah. I mean, we're far enough from town that I'd say we're pretty much on our own out here, and the closest house is what... four or five hundred yards away? I'm pretty sure it's a summer vacation home too, currently uninhabited. The grass by the gate hasn't been cut for a month or so, and there've been no new tire tracks on the drive. Even after we had all that rain a couple weeks back.'

I was taken aback. 'Who even notices things like that?'

'I do. I like to keep aware of my surroundings. Anyway, I've only met your uncle a couple of times, but I can't imagine he'd be able to get here very fast if you screamed, or offer you much assistance if I attacked you.'

I snorted. 'Great-uncle. And even if he *could* help me, he

wouldn't. He'd probably help you though. Help you dig a hole to bury me in.'

'I take it you guys don't get along.'

I pushed off the warm rocks and flipped over onto my back, staring up at the stars dotted across the sky and the moon that was only half full but was bright enough that I'd picked my way down the track to the beach without using a torch. The water buoyed me up, supporting me like an old friend. 'You could say that.'

'Why not?'

'Long story.'

'OK. So to get back to my question, a stranger, who happens to be of the masculine persuasion—'

'What's that got to do with anything?' I rolled back over onto my stomach and stared at him. I could see his broad shoulders above the water, his tousled hair silhouetted against the sky behind him. Before he'd got in, before he'd realized I was here, I'd had the chance to study him, purely from a defensive view-point of course. The way a boxer studies his opponent before a fight. Looks for weaknesses. All I could think while studying Jack was, *damn he's big*. He was all in proportion, wide shoulders, muscular arms and legs and a trunk that was broad at the chest but narrower at the waist, but all of it together was just... big. I should have felt afraid. I didn't.

'Well, you know. The whole, man versus bear thing,' he clarified. 'Hashtag-not-all-men.'

I smiled, knowing he couldn't see it in the dark. 'Right, of course.'

'So this male stranger starts to get in the water with you in the middle of nowhere, and you're telling me you weren't scared?'

'How do you know I wasn't?'

'You didn't *seem* scared.'

'Pure bravado. Never show fear. Also, I live in New York,' I said, as if that explained everything.

He was understandably not satisfied with this explanation. 'So?'

'So I know how to take care of myself. My friends and I have done self-defense classes at the gym. The instructor said he'd never seen anyone with natural self-preservation instincts like mine.'

'Congratulations.'

'Thanks. Although,' I added thoughtfully, 'given the size of you, I might not have been able to fight you off. But I would have one-hundred-percent gone down trying.'

'The size of me?' I could hear a smirk in his voice.

'You're not exactly small, are you.'

'Thanks. I guess the moonlight exposed more of me than I thought.'

It took me a few moments to realize what he was referring to. 'I wasn't talking about *that*,' I blurted, grateful for the dark so he couldn't see me blush.

He laughed. 'I know. I'm teasing.'

'Well, *anyway*,' I said, keen to change the subject. It felt like he was flirting with me, and even though I wasn't technically doing anything wrong, it was difficult to shake the muscle memory of being married. It was hard enough remembering to say my maiden name again. 'To answer your question—'

'Finally.'

I ignored that. 'I figured that you were here to swim in the pool, not specifically to attack me. Like you said, we're in the middle of nowhere, so how would you have known I was here? Besides, I gave *you* more of a fright than you did me. That was quite some scream.'

'I didn't scream,' he protested. 'Maybe I yelped a little. But that's understandable. I wasn't expecting anyone to be down here.'

'Neither was I, but I still didn't scream.'

'You had the advantage of watching me approach.'

'Don't flatter yourself, I wasn't watching you.'

He was quiet for a while, swimming lazy strokes across the pool. I watched him unobtrusively, trying to get more of a sense of what he looked like, but the moon had dipped behind a cloud and only his profile was visible. Still, it was a strong profile. Chiseled jawline, sharp cheekbones.

'Why New York?' he asked.

'What?'

'Why would you choose to live in New York when you could live here?'

'Because I want to live there.'

'Don't you like Pine Harbor?'

'It's not that I don't like it.'

'Then what is it?'

'I had to grow up here, remember.'

'You poor thing. Surrounded by all this beauty and nature right on your doorstep. Not to mention the tight-knit community of great people who, from what I've seen, look out for one another. I can see how that would be horrible.'

His sarcasm irked me. He sounded just like one of the thousands of tourists who poured into the place every year. Enchanted by the national park on our doorstep. The lighthouse that perched on the cliff overlooking the entrance to the harbor. The wharf covered in colorful fishing buoys. The picturesque town with its treelined streets and quaint buildings that looked like they were part of a rom-com movie set. The manicured park in its center with its colorful flower beds, water fountains, town clock and wrought-iron bench seats for resting. Blossom trees in spring, colorful oak leaves in autumn. Even the street lamps were the old-fashioned kind that looked like lanterns.

'You've got no idea.'

'Tell me.'

I resented the fact that he had so easily written me off as ungrateful for growing up here, but he knew nothing about it. 'Why should I? I don't even *know* you.'

'Isn't that what we're doing? Getting to know each other? I plan on staying here in your mother's cabin for a while, so we're bound to run into each other from time to time.'

I shook my head. 'As soon as my mother comes back, I'll be gone again.'

'Yeah, but you'll be back to visit your mom.'

I was instantly suspicious. Why did it matter to him if I visited my mother or not? 'Are you asking me or telling me?'

'Mm?' His tone was faux innocent.

'Let me guess. My mother complained that I don't visit enough and made you feel sorry for her.'

'She didn't complain, *exactly*,' he replied sheepishly. 'But she did mention it when we first met. Only in passing. She seemed sad.'

Familiar guilt flooded through me, followed swiftly by anger that my mother had confided in a stranger who was now the one making me feel guilty.

'I come home when I can,' I snapped. 'At least once a year, sometimes twice. But my life is in New York, and she knows that. I have my business there, a great apartment. Friends.'

'And your husband,' he added, when it was obvious that I had finished talking.

'What exactly has my mother told you?'

'Not much. Your mom just said you were married. Child-hood sweetheart, or something like that.'

'He was *not* my childhood sweetheart. And you and my mom seemed to have talked about an awful lot of personal stuff.'

'I didn't pry, if that's what you're insinuating. Your mother is just very forthcoming.'

He had a good point. My mother liked to talk, and not only talk, but overshare.

'Well whatever, I don't have a husband any more,' I said shortly. 'Not really.'

'Not really?'

'It's complicated.'

'Where is he?'

'At this time of the night? Probably in bed with his girlfriend.'

'Ah. *That* kind of complicated.'

'Yes.'

'I'm sorry.'

'Don't be. I should never have married him in the first place.'

'I'm sure a lot of people say that when a marriage breaks up. Hindsight is a wonderful thing.'

'It's not hindsight at all. I knew on our wedding day that I shouldn't be marrying him.'

If he was surprised that I was opening up to him almost immediately after telling him to mind his own business, he didn't show it. 'So why did you?'

I stared up the stars. 'Have you ever felt like you were caught up in something that you couldn't get out of? Like you were on a train heading somewhere that you knew was wrong, somewhere you had no business going, but with no way of stopping the train?'

To his credit, he thought about it. Didn't just dismiss the

question as absurd. As if he sensed that I was sharing something incredibly vulnerable. 'No. I don't think so.'

'Trust me, you'd know if you had. It's the worst feeling in the world.'

I moved my arms through the water, enjoying the feeling of my skin being cleansed, and the day being washed away. My sudden openness had shocked even me. Maybe it was because we had the cover of darkness, or my mother's tendency to over-share was rubbing off on me. Maybe it was because we were complete strangers. Or maybe it was because I'd had a few drinks and needed someone to vent to. I wasn't sure, but what-ever it was, I felt comfortable sharing things with him that I hadn't shared with anyone.

'I don't understand,' he said. 'If you knew that you didn't want to marry him, why didn't you just call it off?'

'The weight of other people's expectations, I suppose,' I admitted. 'And guilt.'

'Guilt?'

I realized I'd said too much. This was heading into dangerous territory. 'Ignore me. I've had a couple of wines and I'm wallowing.'

'Are you sure? I'm happy to listen if you need someone to vent to. I've been told I'm a good listener.'

'Does your wife say that?'

'I don't have a wife.'

'Divorced?'

'I've never been married.'

'Girlfriend?'

'Why don't you just come out with it and ask if I'm single?'

'What?' I blustered. 'That's not what... I wasn't... I don't care if you're single or not.'

He laughed.

'Let me guess, you're teasing again,' I said drily.

'Not my fault you make it so easy.'

'Your turn in the hot seat, Mr. L.A. Are you enjoying slumming it here in Pine Harbor?'

'I'd hardly call it slumming. This place has its appeal. It's very picturesque.'

'I'm sure L.A. has scenic highlights too.'

'Of course, but nothing like the small-town charm of this place.'

'You wouldn't think it was so adorable if you'd had to grow up here.'

'I never said it was adorable. I don't think I've ever called anything adorable in my life.'

'You said it was charming. Charming is a synonym for adorable.'

He sighed. 'You're one of those people.'

'What people?'

'People who use words like *synonym* in everyday conversation.'

'I suppose you think people from small towns have limited vocabularies. Stereotyping much?'

'I didn't say that.'

'Good, because it's my turn to warn *you*; we don't really like judgmental people around here.'

'I'm not judging anyone or anything.'

'Good.'

'I mean it.'

'Good,' I reiterated. 'Keep it that way and you'll be just fine.'

'You know, for a place you seemingly couldn't wait to get away from,' he said after a long silence, 'you're pretty defensive of it. And that's not judgment, merely an observation.'

'You know nothing about me.'

'That's true,' he conceded.

'All I wanted was a nice, peaceful swim to cool off,' I muttered.

'I'm sorry I ruined that for you.'

I sighed. 'You haven't ruined it. Not completely.'

'It's actually my favorite part of the day,' he admitted. 'Coming down here.'

'Do you come down every night?'

'The past few weeks, yeah. L.A. summers are hot, but this is a different kind of heat. It's been so hot that the tar on the roads has been melting. But it's the humidity that really gets to me. Even the air is sticky. A cold shower after work is good, but finding this swimming hole was a godsend. It cools me down long enough to get some sleep, at any rate.'

'Yeah, it's pretty special,' I agreed.

'There's something about being here that puts life into perspective.'

I groaned. 'You've been listening to my mother.'

'Why?'

'That's exactly the sort of cheesy thing that she's always saying.'

'Is it?'

'Yes, it is. And I don't buy into it when she says it, either.'

'You really don't like this place, do you?'

I couldn't answer that. Didn't know how.

6

JACK

Café on Main was busy when I entered the next morning, but that was nothing new. Painted a dark burgundy color inside that gave it a warm, cozy vibe, it was the most popular café in town with both the locals and the tourists, thanks largely to its online reviews for having the best drip coffee. Dark and full-roasted, it was the closest I'd found to the coffee back home and most mornings I needed the buzz it gave me to kick-start the day. I really needed it this morning especially. I'd been surprised, the night before, when I got back to the cabin and realized it was gone midnight. We'd been chatting in the tidal pool for a couple of hours, but the time had skipped by so fast I hadn't even noticed its passage. It had ended abruptly. One minute we were chatting and the next, Taylor swam to the end of the pool and climbed out, bidding me goodnight and disappearing into the darkness, leaving nothing but wet footprints on the rocks behind her.

I joined the line to the counter and scanned the menu board while I waited, even though I knew full well what I was going to order. I ordered the same thing every day, even though I kept telling myself I was going to try something new.

'Morning, Eve,' I said when it was my turn at the counter.

She looked up, harried, but smiled when she saw me. 'Morning, Jack. Let me guess, a Carpe Diem and a bagel sandwich to go?'

I smiled back. 'You got it.'

The Carpe Diem coffee was a blend of Sumatran, French, Colombian, Kenyan and French-roasted Costa Rica beans. It tasted as delicious and strong as it sounded. And the bagel sandwich was my go-to breakfast on the run. Smoked salmon, fried egg, cucumbers, dill cream cheese and capers on a whole grain bagel.

She rolled her eyes. 'When are you going to try something new? I got a whole selection up there.' She pointed to the board above her head without lifting her eyes. 'My blueberry pancakes are world famous, Jack. I'm not kidding. I had a guy last week from Australia who came here ten years ago on his honeymoon and has been dreaming of coming back just for my pancakes ever since. He finally made that dream happen, Jack. Came back here for his ten-year anniversary and first thing he did was come in and order my pancakes.'

'He came all the way back here and that's the first thing he did?'

'Well, he booked himself into the inn first,' she admitted. 'But the second thing he did was come here and order my pancakes.'

'Impressive.'

'It is. He said they were every bit as good as he remembered. Almost cried a little.'

'Wow.' Someone cleared their throat loudly behind me. 'As

amazing as that sounds, I don't feel like crying today, so I'll just take the coffee and bagel please, Eve. To go.'

She sighed. 'You're missing out, Jack.'

'I promise you that one day I'll sit down and try the pancakes.'

'You promise?'

'I promise.'

She scribbled my order down, ripped the piece of paper off the pad and passed it over to another staff member while I scanned my card to pay. 'I mean it doesn't make any difference to me if you eat something else or not,' she said. 'I'm just trying to expand your culinary experience. A man shouldn't eat the same thing every day. He should kiss the same woman, but he shouldn't eat the same food.'

'Thanks for looking out for me.'

'You're welcome. Now get lost, will you, you're holding up the line.'

'Amazing service as always, Eve. Same time tomorrow?'

'Yeah, yeah.' She waved a hand and looked over my shoulder to the next person. I was dismissed.

I perched myself on a barstool at a slim bench table against the side wall while I waited for my order. From there, I could see most of the people in the café. It was set up eclectically, with tables and couches and booths by the window. There were a few familiar faces – locals, mostly retired ones. Some I knew by name, others just by sight. The lady who walked her Labrador every single morning at dawn in the park opposite the restaurant. I used to watch her while I drank my coffee from the upstairs apartment. The dog would tug her towards the water to chase after seagulls.

I knew why I was studying faces. Trying to figure out if any of them were her.

When my order was ready, I took the coffee and bagel out to the park to eat, sitting on a bench seat and watching the ferry chug over from the mainland with a fresh batch of tourists ready to descend upon the island. I watched them disperse while I ate, some headed for the shops, others to eat, the rest of them choosing to take the scenic walk around the harbor first. The air smelled like coconut-scented sunscreen. Food finished, I threw my rubbish into the bin and drove my truck to the recently renamed hardware store, The Coastal Craftsman. It had previously been known simply as Fred's Store, until Fred died, shortly before I moved here. His son Jasper had taken over the business and decided it needed a catchier, more modern name. Hence, The Coastal Craftsman had been born. He'd had a new sign made for the storefront and held a grand reopening party, even though he never actually closed.

'Morning, Jack,' he said, when the little bell above the door announced my entrance. 'Hot enough for you?'

'Another day in paradise.'

'What can I do for you today?'

'I need a new showerhead.'

'I can help with that.' He put down the little handheld fan he had been holding up to his face and came out from behind the counter and headed off down one of the aisles. I followed him carefully. There was a reason people in town said you could get everything you need from The Coastal Craftsman, and that was because the store stocked anything and everything that any tradesman or self-respecting do-it-yourselfer could ever possibly need. It was dangerously overstocked, with boxes piled high in the aisles and shelves loaded to the max. Even though it went against a man's natural instincts to ask for directions in finding something, you asked in Jasper's store, because you might just get lost if you went looking yourself.

'Here we are,' he announced. 'What sort of showerhead are you after?'

'A normal one?'

'Normal.' He moved a couple of boxes to one side. 'We've got fixed, handheld, dual, and rain, to name a few. I'm afraid you'll have to be a bit more specific than just *normal*.'

My curiosity was piqued. 'Rain?'

He picked up a large square showerhead. 'It mimics gentle rainfall, so you feel like you're standing out in the rain.'

'And people like that?'

'Apparently. It's one of my bestsellers.'

'I've never heard of it before.'

'Then you clearly don't stay in many five-star hotels. They're quite common in those establishments, I believe.'

'Clearly not.'

'We've also got high-flow, low-flow, filtered showerheads, rail showerheads, outdoor showerheads.'

'I think I just want a plain, normal showerhead if they still make such a thing.'

He picked up the box that said *fixed head*. 'You *think* that's what you want?'

'Well, it's not actually for me.'

Jasper straightened up, immediately sensing gossip. 'I see. For a lady friend, perhaps?'

'Well, she is a lady, and she is a friend, so yes.'

'Someone I know?'

'Yeah, I reckon you do.'

His eyes lit up, and I knew exactly what he was thinking. The town seemed convinced that there was something going on between Hannah and me. After all, she was the whole reason I had come here in the first place.

'She's about... this high.' I demonstrated with one hand. 'And about… ooh, if I had to hazard a guess, I'd say around eighty, give or take.'

He looked confused. 'Pounds?'

'Years.'

'I don't think we're talking about the same person.'

'No.' I took the box from him. 'I don't think we are.'

I was still chuckling to myself about it when Irene opened her front door. She was petite and silver-haired and the epitome of a sweet, little old lady.

'Jack.' She beamed. 'How lovely.' She turned to look inside the house. 'Richard, Jack's here.'

'Who?'

'Jack,' she repeated, louder. 'You know, Jack from the restaurant.'

'Oh, that Jack. What's he want?'

She turned back to me. 'How can we help you, Jack?'

I held up the box and she looked at it.

'How lovely,' she said. 'What is it?'

'You mentioned the other night that your showerhead had calcified and your water flow was almost non-existent.'

'Oh, yes.' She frowned. 'I tried giving it a good scrub with an old toothbrush, but it didn't help.'

'I thought I could replace it for you. Picked up a new one from the store. I've got time to spare before I need to be at work, so, here I am.'

'You don't need to do that, Jack.'

'I want to. Is now a good time?'

'Close the door,' Richard called. 'I can feel a breeze.'

'Oh, shush you,' Irene scolded him. 'We need all the breeze we can get in this heat.' She stepped to one side. 'Come in, Jack. I'll put the kettle on. Would you like a tea? Coffee?'

I kicked off my shoes and stepped inside. 'A coffee would be great, thanks, Irene. I'll get to work changing this while you make it.'

'Aren't you lovely to think of us. Isn't he lovely, Richard?'

'What?'

'I said isn't he lovely?'

'Did you close the door?'

She rolled her eyes at him affectionately. 'Yes, I closed the door. If you're cold, put a blanket over your knees.' She turned to me again. 'He feels the cold dreadfully, even now in summer. I think it has to do with his circulation. He... *we*, both appreciate you doing this for us.'

I smiled. 'You're welcome. I couldn't have my favorite customers going without a decent shower now, could I?'

A mug of coffee was waiting on the kitchen table for me when I emerged. I washed my hands over the kitchen sink and then joined her at the table. Richard was in his La-Z-Boy in the lounge, watching a game show on TV.

'Van Gogh,' he said, answering a question I hadn't heard.

'All done?' Irene asked, pushing a packet of biscuits across the table towards me. 'I hope it wasn't too much trouble.'

'It was fine,' I assured her, helping myself to a biscuit and dunking it in my coffee. 'I tested the new one and it works well. You should get quite a few years out of it, but let me know if you have any issues. And not just with the shower. I'm happy to help with anything else you might need.'

'That's very kind of you, Jack. Richard used to do all the house repairs but he's not really up to it any more.' She picked up her purse. 'How much do we owe you?'

'Nothing.'

'Jack.'

'I mean it. You don't owe me anything.'

'At least let me pay for the part.'

'No. And if you keep pushing it we're going to fall out.' I said it with a smile though, so she knew I was only kidding.

'You're a lovely man, Jack. Pine Harbor is lucky to have you. You are planning on staying here with us, right?'

'For now, sure. I haven't really made any long-term plans. Kind of winging it as I go.'

'What you need is to find yourself a nice local lady.'

'I met one last night, actually. I mean, not in a romantic way. She's married. Sort of.'

Her eyebrows puckered. 'Sort of?'

'Long story. And not my story to tell, not that I know much about it anyway.'

'What's her name? I know most of the families in the area. Some better than others.'

'Taylor. She's actually the daughter of the lady I rent the cabin from.'

'Taylor Calderwood?'

'That's the one.'

'Oh, she's a lovely girl. From a lovely family. Well, her mother is a decent sort. The father wasn't on the scene a lot. From what I understand he left when the kids were young. I don't think they had all that much to do with him after that. Died a few years later in an accident. They brought him back here and buried him in the town cemetery but I don't think they visit him often. I go once a month to tidy up my sister's grave, put fresh flowers on, that sort of thing, and I never see so much as a single flower on his grave.'

'That's sad.'

'There's a lot of graves like that. Neglected. Forgotten. Then of course there was all that other business. Just horrible, it was.' She shook her head mournfully. 'That poor family is no stranger to tragedy. How is Taylor? Didn't she marry that Wilson lad? Adam?'

'She seemed fine. She's in town to look after her uncle while her mother is on a cruise.'

'Ray? Her mother has the patience of a saint, taking him in. He worked on the lobster boats with my brother for a while. He's one of those people who always has to be right.' She chuckled. 'My brother said there were many times the crew were tempted to throw him overboard.'

'Taylor didn't seem too happy about being stuck with him.'

'No, I bet she isn't. I bet he's none too thrilled either.'

I swirled the last of the coffee in my cup and then drained it. I was curious about what Irene had said relating to Taylor's family being no stranger to tragedy, but I couldn't ask what she'd meant by that. Or rather, I wouldn't. It would be prying, and I figured if Taylor wanted me to know she would tell me herself. If I ever saw her again.

7

TAYLOR

I don't know exactly what it was that alerted me to his presence. A noise, probably. Or the prickly sensation of being watched. Whatever it was, when I became aware of it I opened my eyes and saw the dark, unmistakable outline of someone looming over me. I couldn't make out features, but I could feel the strength of the glare.

'Fuck off,' I shouted. 'I know karate!'

'Calm down,' he said. 'It's me, Ray.'

'Jesus Christ,' I said. 'What do you want?'

'It's about time you woke up. Day's half gone already.'

I rolled my head, squinted. There was a little bit of light seeping through from around the curtains, but not enough to indicate the sun was properly up yet. 'What time is it?'

'Late.'

'That doesn't answer my question.'

He grumbled, waved a hand irritably. 'Noduiaguifsush.'

'Sorry?'

He glared, enunciating this time. 'Not... quite... six.'

'Are you in pain?'

'No.'

'Is the house on fire?'

'No.'

'Are either of us in danger of imminent death?'

'You mean more than usual?'

'Yes.'

'No.'

I rolled over, turning my back on him. 'Then go away. It's too early.'

I waited a few minutes. There was a distinct lack of sound behind me.

'You haven't moved, have you,' I mumbled into my pillow.

'I've been up for an hour,' he said. 'I'm hungry.'

'So get yourself something to eat.'

'Like what?'

'I don't know, toast.'

'I don't want toast.'

'Cereal then.'

'I don't want cereal.'

I stifled a scream. 'Then what *do* you want?'

'Porridge.'

'You really want porridge in this heat?'

'Yes.'

'Fine. Then have porridge.'

'I will. When you get up and make it for me.'

'Make it yourself.'

'I can't. My hip hurts if I stand on it for too long.'

'You're standing on it right now.'

'And it's hurting.'

'I can't believe you expect me to make porridge for you.'

'Your mother does.'

'My mother is more of a sucker than I am.'

'She's not a sucker. She's generous, kind and caring. Whereas you...'

The light in the room had got a bit brighter. I could see him studying me and felt the childish urge to pull a face. 'Why are you still in my room?'

'Which one are you again?'

'You know which one I am.'

'No, I don't.'

'I'm Taylor.'

'And where do you fit in?'

'You know where I fit in, Ray. Stop trying to make me think you're senile. I know you're not.'

'I'm an old man.'

'Ancient,' I agreed.

'I don't know how to work the oven.'

'Because it's complicated or because you've never bothered to learn?'

He shrugged. 'A little bit of both.'

'Fine.' I tried not to feel too resentful, aware that as far as he was concerned, I'd had a full night's sleep. 'I'll get up soon and make you porridge. Will that make you happy?'

'I'll be happy when you actually get up. You need to take me into town after breakfast too.'

'Why?'

'I have a doctor's appointment. And I want to go to the grocery store.'

I sighed. 'Fine.'

'When are you going to get up?'

'Soon. Now get out of my room.'

He shuffled off, banging his walker frame against the wall, then paused by the door. 'Do you really?'

'Do I really what?'

'Know karate.'

'Wake me up like that again and you'll find out.'

He left, mumbles trailing behind him as he slowly shuffled his way down the hallway. I lay on my back and stared at the ceiling, unable to shake the feeling that my life had taken a wrong turn somewhere. Even though I knew this was only temporary, and that in a few weeks' time I'd be back in my own sleek little house, for now, under this roof, in *this* bedroom, I felt... wrong. I didn't belong here. Not any more.

My room was exactly as I'd left it. Actually, that wasn't true. I left it in the state in which I lived in it. Messy and cluttered and disorganized. My mother worked her magic and turned it into the room she had always dreamed of it being. It still had my furniture and some of my belongings, but it was clean and tidy and like it was one of those staged photos you see when a real estate company is trying to sell a house. The walls and roof were painted white, just like through the rest of the house, and the carpet was a kind of pale peach color that I'd always hated. A large mirror hung on one wall, with a small, standing wardrobe in the space behind the door. There was a black wing-back chair in the opposite corner where I used to dump all my dirty clothes, and the bed took up pretty much the rest of the room. Except for my favorite part. A long window, almost the width of the room, looked out over the ocean, and in front of that, from wall to wall, was an inbuilt desk. It had a painted white top, with beautiful brown wooden drawers below on each side, with a space for a chair so someone could sit in the middle. My mother had added her own touches, a basket of dried hydrangea flowers in one corner, some seashells she'd no doubt collected from the shore. Bleached white from sitting in the sun. There was a little wooden house, for no apparent reason, and one of the kitschy lobster ornaments she found so endearing and that I hated.

I used to spend hours at that desk, staring out at the ocean for inspiration for my art. It all began in here. My sketches that, at first, were very much for my eyes only. Rough and clumsily drawn, but every single one helped me hone my skills. Sketching had broadened into painting, and now my large, ocean-inspired paintings were slowly becoming more sought after. My Instagram page even had over two hundred thousand followers. Unfortunately, art sales alone weren't enough to pay the bills, so to help with that, I'd become a tattoo artist as well. Now I was booked out months in advance. I specialized in colorful ocean themes. Waves, sunsets, sea creatures.

'You took your time,' Ray grumbled when I emerged into the kitchen twenty minutes later.

I paused, my hand on the fridge door, and stared at him. He was just as cantankerous as I remembered. Maybe even worse. He was an ex-fisherman, although according to him there was no such thing. Once a fisherman, always a fisherman. It didn't matter if he hadn't stepped foot on the deck of a boat in over a decade, he said. Salt water ran through his veins and he'd be longing for the thrill of the hunt, the smell of the nets and the feel of the bucking ocean beneath him until the day we planted him in the ground. As far as I was concerned, my mother was a veritable saint for taking him in when it became obvious he couldn't live on his own any more. If it'd been left up to me, he'd be living in the Acadia Retirement Village. But it wasn't, and now here I was, tasked with babysitting a man whose dislike for me was matched only by my dislike for him. 'If you're going to complain,' I informed him, 'I'll go and take a shower first. A nice long, leisurely shower. My legs need a shave. So do my armpits.'

That shut him up.

I made porridge, something I hadn't done since high school camp, with Ray supervising and offering suggestions.

'You need to stir it more,' he said. 'Otherwise it'll clump.'

'It's fine.'

'I don't like clumpy porridge.'

'It's not clumpy.'

'How do you know it's not when you're not stirring it?'

'I just do.'

He added a large knob of butter and four heaped teaspoons of sugar to his bowl of porridge and ate it with the gusto of someone who seemed to think it might be his last breakfast here on earth. Considering he also added three teaspoons of sugar to his cup of tea, he might not have been too far wrong.

'You know sugar is bad for you, right?' I said, leaning against the bench with my fingers wrapped around a lifesaving mug of coffee.

'Meh,' he mumbled. 'Lots of things are bad for you.'

'Yes, but sugar is right up near the top of the list.'

'The scientists used to say that about eggs, and animal fats. Now they tell you they're healthy for you again. They can't make up their minds.'

'I don't think they're going to change their minds about sugar.'

'Not in my lifetime, maybe. But eventually. Anyway, I don't care. I like it.'

I watched him push his empty bowl across the bench top in my general direction. 'Let me guess, you don't know how to work the dishwasher.'

'Technology and me,' he said. 'We don't mix.'

'You captained a lobster boat, Ray.'

'That's different.'

'Different how?'

'You start the boat, you turn the wheel to steer it. Easy. You learn how to drive a boat by feel. By touch. By instinct. *Those* contraptions have too many settings.' He pointed a wobbly finger at the dishwasher, frowning as if it might suddenly come to life and launch at him.

'It's hardly rocket science. You stack the dishes inside and put the powder in this little space here.' I rinsed the bowl, stacked it on the bottom shelf and demonstrated. 'Then you push a button and ta-da. It cleans the dishes for you.'

He refused to watch, scratching at an age spot on the back of his hand instead. 'I need you to get my newspaper.'

'From where?'

'Where do you think? The moon?' His watery, bloodshot eyes glared up at me through the gray wiry strands of his bushy eyebrows. They were impressive, but also alarming, and hadn't always been like that. Did eyebrows just start growing all out of control like that when you hit a certain age?

I drank my coffee and waited.

'It'll be in the letterbox,' he said, caving. 'Obviously.'

'Do you always use sarcasm to get what you want instead of manners?'

He grunted. 'Normally I'd get it myself, but...' He trailed off.

'But you're supposed to be resting. I know.'

'And you're supposed to be helping.'

'I just made you breakfast, didn't I?'

'It wasn't as good as your mother's.'

'You should prepare yourself for the fact that nothing I make or do will be.' I rinsed my mug and put it upside down on the top of the dishwasher, then closed the door and turned it on. 'Fine. I'll get your paper.'

'Don't rip it when you pull it out of the slot. The stupid boy jams it in too hard. No one takes any pride in their work any more.'

'He's probably twelve years old and paid a dollar an hour. If I was him, I'd throw it in a puddle.'

'I remember when you and your brother put my cigarettes in a bucket of water once,' he said darkly. 'You still owe me five dollars.'

'Ah, so you *do* remember who I am.'

He shrugged. 'Eh. It comes and goes.'

8

JACK

The lunch rush was just dying down when they walked in. I didn't pay them any attention at first, busy as I was behind the bar, wiping up spills, stacking empty glasses in a tray ready to be washed. They were just a couple of people in my peripheral vision, entering and taking a seat in a booth near the far wall.

'You can take your break now if you like,' I called to Fiona, one of the waitresses. A single mom to a seven-year-old boy named Oscar, she was struggling to make ends meet, so I tried to help out by giving her as many shifts as possible, but even that was a balancing act because of childcare. Most nights, she'd bring Oscar to the restaurant with her and he'd sit at a corner table or in the staffroom and do his homework. We had a deal. Homework first, then I'd let him watch shows on my tablet. Under my instructions, the chefs slipped him meals, and Fiona pretended not to notice. 'Lucy and I will be fine for a while.'

'OK, thanks,' she replied wearily, passing the iPad we used for ordering over the bar to me before heading out the back. The summer heat made everyone tired, but add the heat of the kitchen we had to go in and out of throughout a shift, and it was ten times worse.

'You want me to get that new table, Jack?' Lucy asked, gesturing towards the couple who had just sat down. I flicked a glance at them. The woman had her back to me, but the man was facing in my direction and looked vaguely familiar. We had a lot of repeat local customers though, so that meant nothing.

'Nah it's OK, I'll get them,' I told her. 'If you don't mind clearing those last couple of tables.'

'Sure.'

Tucking some menus underneath my arm and grabbing the iPad, I headed to the table.

'Good afternoon, folks.' I smiled. 'Welcome to The Cozy Catch.'

'What's so good about it?' the old man grumbled.

The woman looked up at me. 'Ignore him,' she said. 'He's sulking because the doctor refused to indulge his latest hypochondriac symptom.'

'That man wouldn't recognize if someone was dying right in front of him,' the man said. 'Probably got his degree online.'

She rolled her eyes. '"That man" has been a doctor since before I was born. I'm pretty sure he knows what he's talking about.'

'Exactly,' Ray said, as if she'd just proven his point. 'He's out of touch.'

As I stood there watching them bicker back and forth, the penny dropped.

'You're Ray,' I said. 'I met you in the driveway once.'

He looked at me suspiciously. 'What driveway? What are you on about?'

But my attention was already off him and onto the woman sitting opposite him. 'Taylor?'

She had been beautiful enough in the moonlight, but she was breath-taking in the light of day. It wasn't like me to get tongue-tied around anyone, but I felt tongue-tied in front of her. Her long, dark hair was loose, falling in waves that hung halfway down her back. She was wearing a black tank top, and her shoulders and arms were tanned and toned. One shoulder was covered with an intricate half-sleeve tattoo. Without staring too hard, I could see waves and stars and other intertwined designs. It suited her.

Her piercing brown eyes narrowed slightly. 'Maybe,' she said. 'Depends who's asking?'

I pointed at my chest. 'I'm Jack. We met last night.'

'Jack.' Her frown cleared as she looked me up and down. 'I didn't recognize you with your clothes on.'

'Well that didn't take you long,' Ray commented. 'You'd only been in town for, what, two hours?'

'Get your mind out of the gutter,' she told him. 'Jack is our neighbor. He's staying in the cabin. Something you and my mother neglected to mention. We met down on the beach last night when we both went for a swim.'

'Oh, you're that guy,' Ray replied. 'You cut the lawn too short last time. Almost killed it.'

'Sorry,' I said, even though I knew full well the lawn was perfectly fine. There was clearly no point in arguing with him. 'I'll make sure I lift the lawnmower a notch next time.'

'Good.' Then, clearly bored with that conversation, he changed the subject. 'I don't need a menu. Just bring me the chowder and some cheesy garlic bread. And don't be stingy with the cheese either. Last time I could barely see it, let alone taste it.'

I tapped at the iPad. 'Extra cheese. I'll make a note for the chef. And for you, Taylor?'

She reached out and plucked one of the menus out from underneath my arm. 'Give me a minute. It's been a while since I've been here; the menu might have changed.'

Ray sighed. 'Make our orders separate so I don't have to wait for her.'

'That's not very gentlemanly,' she commented idly, scanning the menu.

'You're no lady.'

She tilted her head up at me. 'I'll have the tuna poke bowl. And a Coke, please.'

Ray snorted. 'And you lectured me about sugar.'

'So I'm a hypocrite. If you've got a problem with it, you can walk home.'

Ray jabbed me in the hip with a finger to get my attention. 'Are you listening to this? Do you see what I have to put up with? It's elder abuse. Help me, please.'

Taylor snorted. 'It's not even close. I can try harder though, if you like.'

'Don't just stand there,' Ray said to me, his voice raised and agitated. 'You heard her, she threatened me. Call the authorities. I want her arrested.'

'Oh, uh.' I froze, unsure what to do, looking back and forth between them. They both stared at me expectantly. 'I... maybe we should all just, take a moment, to—'

'Relax. He's having you on,' Taylor said calmly. 'If he had me arrested, he'd have no one to boss around any more.'

Ray chuckled. 'Worth it. Look at his face; he's like a moose in headlights.'

I sagged with relief. 'You two are quite the comedy act.'

'He's been trying to get me arrested since I was eleven years old,' she said. 'No luck so far.'

His face darkened. 'I know it was you who stole my letterbox and tied it to the flagpole in town.'

'You couldn't prove it then, and you still can't,' she retorted.

'Why are you still standing there?' he said to me. 'The food isn't going to order itself.'

'It's already ordered,' I assured him. 'As soon as I enter it on here,' I tapped the screen of the iPad. 'The kitchen receives the order and gets to work on it.'

'It's called technology, Ray,' Taylor said loudly. Nearby tables turned to look. 'TECHNOLOGY.'

'I'm not deaf. Just hungry.'

'I'm sure your food won't take too long,' I promised him. 'You've come in at a good time. The lunch rush is over.'

'Don't hurry on our behalf,' Taylor said, passing the menu back to me. 'The food will take as long as it takes, Ray. You're the one who wanted to eat out.'

'We were already in town,' he replied. 'I couldn't pass up the opportunity. Who knows when I'll have a decent meal again.'

Taylor tilted her head towards me. 'He doesn't like my cooking. It's not as good as my mother's, apparently.'

'Not even close,' Ray said morosely. 'I'm probably going to starve to death.'

'Considering the amount of food we just bought that *you* chose, I highly doubt that.' She looked at me again. 'Have you eaten yet, Jack?'

'Sorry?'

'Food. Have you partaken in your own midday meal yet?'

'No, not yet.' I checked my watch. 'I usually grab something about now from the kitchen and eat it in my office.'

'Why don't you join us?' she suggested.

'Really?'

'Sure. Save me having to listen to this one complain the whole time.'

'This one has a name,' Ray said.

'See what I mean?'

I hovered. 'I guess I could. If you're sure?'

'I'm having serious déjà vu,' Taylor said. 'It's like last night all over again. Remember when you asked if you could get in the water about five hundred times and I kept saying yes but you still kept asking? Fun times.'

I stared at her.

'Snarky little thing, isn't she?' Ray commented.

She glared at him. 'I'm just saying, I wouldn't have invited him if I didn't want him to join us.'

'In that case,' I told her. 'I'll just let Fiona know and then I'll be right back.'

She shrugged. 'Fine. Only if you want to.'

'I do want to.'

'Fine.'

'Fine.'

'Good.'

'It is good.'

Ray sighed. 'This is going to be a long lunch, isn't it.'

9

TAYLOR

'What did you go and do that for?' Ray complained, as I watched Jack move through the tables back towards the bar.

'He's our neighbor,' I replied. 'I was being polite.'

'No, being polite is saying thanks when he takes our order, or complimenting him on the décor. What *you* did is borderline weird. Inviting a stranger to join us.'

'Again, he's not a stranger, he's our neighbor, and I want to find out more about the guy who's living next door to my mother, if that's OK with you.'

'Now we'll have to talk to him.'

'What's wrong with talking?'

'I can't be bothered with it. People natter on and on about the stupidest things.'

'You mean like porridge?'

He glared at me.

I wasn't about to admit it to Ray, but the invitation had slipped out of my mouth before I'd even thought about it, and Ray wasn't the only one questioning my motives. Yes, I *did* want to find out more about the guy my mother had invited to live in the family cabin, but was that all it was? I couldn't deny the fact that Jack was ridiculously good-looking, and our banter the night before had been fun. The most fun I'd had in a while, in fact. I couldn't blame my subconscious for wanting a repeat performance.

'I'm officially on a break and all yours,' Jack said, sliding into the booth beside Ray. 'Thanks again for inviting me. It makes a nice change from mindlessly shoveling in food while I go over the accounts in the office.'

'Did you hear that, Ray?' I said. 'He thanked me. You could learn from him.'

Ray ignored me. 'Are you sure our order went through?'

'Of course,' Jack reassured him. 'And I've added mine to it. It's all gone through to the kitchen and they'll be preparing it as we speak.'

I leaned back against the vinyl, padded red bench seat, which was warm from the heat of the day, and studied him through narrowed eyes. 'Let me guess, you ordered the sirloin steak.'

He shook his head. 'No. Why?'

'You just look like the kind of man who eats a pound of meat a day.'

He snorted, almost spitting out the mouthful of beer he'd just drunk. 'What do you mean, I look like I eat a pound of meat a day?'

'You know, you just have a healthy, outdoor, rugged woodsman look about you.'

'Woodsman?' he replied, amused. 'Are they even a thing any more?'

'One hundred percent,' I assured him. 'If the romance books I read are anything to go by. OK, so if you didn't order the sirloin,' I studied him. 'It has to be the lobster.' I flicked a sympathetic glance over at the live tank in the corner, from where people could choose their own live lobster to be cooked for their dinner. 'Poor bastards.'

'Wrong again.'

'Burger?'

'No. You're really bad at this, aren't you?'

'Not normally.' I protested. 'This is like my superpower, guessing what food people are going to order. I'm stupidly good at it.'

'That's a weird superpower.'

'Obviously. But still, I'm never wrong.'

He shrugged. 'I guess I'm the exception.'

'Like I said,' Ray muttered, as he unrolled cutlery from inside a napkin and placed them in front of him in preparation for his meal. 'People like to talk about stupid stuff.'

'How long have you been working here?' I asked Jack.

'About eight months. I'm managing the place for a friend.'

I cast my memory back to who had owned the place when I'd lived here. 'Cole Sullivan?'

Ray grunted. 'You're out of touch. Cole Sullivan died a few years ago.'

'You're joking.'

'Why would I joke about that?'

'He can't have been that old,' I said, shocked. 'Maybe what, late fifties? I went to school with his kids. Gracie was one of my closest friends.'

'Can't be that close if you didn't know her father had died,' Ray said pointedly.

'Well no, not any more. We lost touch after I left.'

'You mean when you cut contact with everyone.'

I flashed him a warning look. 'That's not what happened.'

He made a sound that indicated he disagreed. I wasn't about

to argue with him about it in front of Jack, so I let it drop. 'What happened to Cole?'

'Heart attack,' Ray replied. 'Wasn't that much of a surprise, the size he was.'

'That's an awful thing to say.'

'It's the truth. What, just because he's dead we're supposed to pretend he wasn't fat?'

I turned my attention back to Jack. 'So *anyway*, who owns this place now?'

'A friend of mine, from back in L.A. Her name is Hannah.'

'I do hope you're only saying good things about me.'

Jack stiffened slightly when he heard her voice, but only for a fraction of a second before he relaxed again, smiling up at the woman who was standing beside our booth. Her expression as she regarded us all, lingering on me in particular, was a mixture of curiosity and something else, something that instantly made me feel defensive. She dropped her hand onto Jack's shoulder and I realized what it was. She was marking her territory.

'Hannah,' Jack exclaimed, getting up and embracing her. 'I thought you'd gone back to L.A.'

'I had planned on it, but decided to stop off and visit an old college friend in Washington instead.' She lowered her voice, intending her next words to be for Jack's ears only, but I could still inadvertently hear everything she said. 'I told her about our last interaction,' she told him. 'She made me see how ungrateful I've been. I had to come back to say sorry in person and make sure you weren't upset with me.'

'It's fine,' he told her. 'Already forgotten.'

'You're so good to me.'

'Are you hungry?' he asked. 'We've just ordered, you're welcome to join us.'

'No,' she replied. 'Just tired. I think I'll head upstairs and make up the bed.'

'Of course.' He smiled. 'Do you need any help?'

'No, I can manage. Don't let me interrupt your lunch.' Her eyes dropped to mine. 'He's so protective of me, even though I'm perfectly capable of taking care of myself.' She held out her hand. 'I'm Hannah. Proprietor of this place.'

I shook her hand. 'Taylor. And this is Ray.'

'How do you all know each other?' Her question was delivered casually, but the underlying sharpness was there.

'Jack and I met for the first time last night,' I told her. 'Although I didn't recognize him with his clothes on.'

Her eyebrows shot up. 'Excuse me?'

'Taylor's family own the cabin I rent,' Jack explained. 'I came across her down in the swimming hole on the beach last night.'

'I see.' She stared at me. 'And now here you are.'

'Yes, here we are,' I confirmed cheerfully, ignoring her clear insinuation that I had engineered this meeting. 'But I didn't know Jack worked here until Ray dragged me in off the street to eat.'

'A decision I have come to regret,' Ray said.

The waitress chose that moment to arrive with our food, forcing Hannah to step to one side so she could put Ray's bowl of chowder and plate of cheesy garlic bread down on the table.

'Hannah,' she said warmly. 'Welcome back.'

'Lucy.' Hannah hugged the waitress. 'How is everything?'

'Great. Jack's doing an amazing job of running this place.'

Hannah smiled up at Jack. 'Of course he is. I never doubted he would.'

'Are you sure you won't join us?' Jack asked Hannah again as Fiona headed back to the kitchen for the rest of our order. 'There's nothing to eat upstairs.'

She shook her head. 'It's fine, Jack. I'm not hungry. I'll go and unpack, freshen up, then do a shop later.'

'Do you need a hand with your bags?'

She looked briefly tempted, but shook her head. 'No, you eat. I'm fine. Can we catch up later?'

'Of course.'

'Enjoy your lunch,' Hannah said, as the waitress arrived with our food.

'She seems nice,' I said, as Jack took a seat again.

He nodded. 'Yeah, she is.'

'How do you two know each other?'

'Her husband Alex and I were old friends.'

My ears pricked up, sensing a scandal. An illicit affair, perhaps. Enough to destroy a friendship. 'Were?'

'Yeah, he uh, he died.'

'Oh.' I hadn't been expecting *that*. 'So she's...?'

He nodded softly. 'Widowed.'

'Damn.' Immediately I felt bad for prying. 'I'm sorry.'

'No, it's fine. But I'd rather not talk about it. Hannah is still grieving. I don't want to risk her or one of the staff hearing us, if that's OK.'

'Of course. Totally understand. Let's just eat.'

Ray slurped his chowder. 'Ahead of you there.'

There was an awkward silence while we ate. The food was insanely good. My tuna was fresh and perfectly marinated, served with rice, cucumber and avocado and a sesame dressing.

'So,' I said finally, trying to break the silence and remind him of the fun banter we'd been having before Hannah had arrived. 'You got the fish tacos. That was going to be my next guess.'

Jack laughed, and I was relieved to hear it. 'You really expect me to believe that?'

'It's true,' I protested, laughing with him, glad to have lightened the mood.

'Don't believe her,' Ray advised him. 'She lies a lot.'

I didn't answer him, my attention caught instead by the sight of the woman who had just entered the restaurant and was now looking around the room.

'Oh shit,' I muttered, looking around for an escape or cover of some kind. There was nowhere to go and nothing to hide behind. There was only the floor underneath the table, and it was sticky with spilled food and drinks and God knows what else. Still, desperate times called for desperate measures.

Jack gave me a puzzled look. 'What's wrong?'

'If I disappear underneath the table, just go with it,' I hissed, starting to slide slowly down the seat.

'What?'

'Play along. Pretend you never saw me.'

'Why would I—?'

But it was too late. I locked eyes with her, watching her frown as she tried to reconcile what she was seeing with what she hadn't been expecting to see. Realization dawned, then she was on her way over. I had about five seconds to brace myself before she was standing in front of me. I stood out of habit and we hugged stiffly.

'Taylor,' she said, looking me up and down after I pulled away. 'What are you doing here?'

'I'm having lunch with Ray and um... uh...' I blinked. My mouth opened and closed a few times, but my mind had gone completely blank.

'Jack,' Jack supplied, watching me curiously.

I clicked my fingers at him. 'Yes, *Jack*. I knew that.'

'I'm well aware of who Jack is,' Celia said, her eyebrows arched. 'I meant, what are you doing here in Pine Harbor?'

'Oh, right. That.'

'Yes, that.'

'She's here to stay with me while Moira's away,' Ray said gruffly. 'And if you've got a problem with that, Celia Hamilton, then you can take it up with me.'

She shot him a glare and checked to see if anyone in earshot was listening. 'I don't have a problem with it, *Raymond*,' she said sharply. 'But it would have been nice to have a bit of warning that she was coming home so I didn't have to find out like this. But then I suppose I shouldn't expect that level of consideration from your family.'

'You can get off your high horse,' he shot back. 'Talking about families, as if your lot are the bloody Kennedys. Don't forget, your son is the one who had an affair and ran off with someone else.'

'I'm well aware of that, and while I'm not proud of how he went about it, it was a little more nuanced than that, as I'm sure Taylor is aware,' she sniffed. 'At the end of the day, Adam found someone who treats him right and makes him happy. We all know that life is unpredictable, and opportunities for happiness should be seized.'

'What about Taylor's happiness?'

'Oh, I'm fine,' I said. 'Honestly. Never better.'

'There, see?' Celia said, waving a hand in my direction. 'She's fine.'

'It's obvious to anyone with half a brain that she's putting on a brave act,' Ray said.

'It's not an act,' I argued feebly.

'Good,' Celia said. 'Because you should know that Adam and his fiancée are already discussing a spring wedding, here in Pine Harbor.'

'I'm sorry, did you just say *fiancée*?' The news that Adam was engaged hit me in the guts like a sucker punch. 'We haven't even discussed divorce yet.'

She shrugged. 'Merely paperwork, and shouldn't take too long to sort out I imagine. Especially if you really have moved on, as you say.'

I nodded, refusing to let her see she had rattled me. Obviously, I'd known that Adam and I would have to go through the official separation channels at *some* point, but I'd expected to have that discussion with him. Not his bloody mother.

'I'll sign whatever you need me to sign.'

'Excellent.' She looked me up and down again. 'You've lost weight.'

'I know.'

'It doesn't suit you. And didn't I send you a link to that article about the best hairstyles for women in their thirties to attract success?'

I nodded. 'You did.' I'd deleted it without evening opening it.

'Well, it was good to see you again.' She smiled, but it was a smile without warmth. 'Enjoy your lunch. Jack, you haven't forgotten the meeting about the festival, have you? It's just to go over a few final things.'

'Of course not,' Jack said. 'It's highlighted in my calendar.'

'Good.'

'I've already gone over the info you sent, and I'm happy to help out however I can.'

'This town needs more people like you,' she said pointedly. She was staring at him, but the volume and delivery of her words was clearly directed at me. 'Community-minded people who are keen to stay and help make this town a success.'

'Remind me where your son lives again?' Ray enquired. 'New York, isn't it? And didn't your daughter move to Boston?'

She ignored him. 'We'll be in touch regarding the divorce,

Taylor. Now I must go, so much to do, but I'll see you at the meeting, Jack.'

I watched her leave, feeling slightly shell-shocked, as I always did after any length of time in her presence. Somehow, one withering look from her and I regressed to my seventeen-year-old petulant and self-absorbed self. She brought out the worst in me, always had, and for as long as I'd known her she'd made it quite clear that I wasn't good enough for her son, or her family for that matter.

'So,' Jake said, his tone conversational but his expression shrewd, as if he could see how rattled I was. 'Your mother-in-law is the town chair.'

'*Ex* mother-in-law,' I corrected him. 'And soon to be absolutely nothing to me at all, once the divorce is done and dusted.'

'She's a horrible woman,' Ray said, using a finger to run around the rim on the bowl to wipe up the last traces of his chowder. Normally I'd have told him to stop being so disgusting in public, but right at the moment I was just grateful that he'd stood up for me. 'And that son of hers is a coward. Always has been. Imagine getting your mother to do your dirty work for you.'

'I don't think that was planned,' I reminded him. 'She had no idea I was even in town.'

'Maybe not. But she has no business getting involved. What you do in your private life is nobody's business. I've half a mind to go to that meeting too, just to annoy her.'

'Thanks for sticking up for me.'

'You and I might not be best friends,' Ray replied. 'But that woman is insufferable. Always has been. If your mother was here she'd have told her where to go.'

'Yeah she would have. But I didn't expect *you* to.'

'Don't make a big deal out of it.'

'I'm not.'

'Good. I'm tired. Let's go home.' He glared at Jack. 'Shift, will you?'

I gave Jack an apologetic smile. 'Sorry about him.'

'Don't be. He's entertaining.'

I slid out of the booth, shaking my head. 'I guess that's one word for it.'

10

JACK

I knocked on the door at the top of the stairs with my knuckles, aiming for not too loud in case she was still asleep, but loud enough that she'd hear me if she wasn't. 'Hannah?'

'One second,' she called.

There was the shuffling sound of footsteps and then the door opened and she smiled at me, stepping to one side to let me pass. She'd changed into a pair of old faded jeans and a white T-shirt. Her long blonde hair was loose.

'You know you don't have to knock, Jack,' she said. 'This is your home too. Well it was, until you abandoned me.' Her tone was light, jovial. But her face told the real story. I knew it had hurt her when I'd moved out to the cabin. But I'd had good reasons. And I hoped that one day she'd see that. She looked at the bags I was carrying. 'What have you got there?'

'Just the staples.' I turned sideways to pass her and headed for the kitchen. 'Enough to get you through a couple of days. I ducked out and got them before closing up the restaurant.'

'You didn't have to do that.' She closed the door and followed me, perching herself up onto one of the black metal barstools and watching as I started pulling items out of the bags and putting them away. 'I told you I'd go to the shop later.'

'I know. But you also said you were tired,' I reminded her. 'This way you don't have to go.'

'You're too good to me, Jack.'

'I'd do the same for anyone.'

'Oh, well that makes me feel less special.'

'You know what I mean.'

'Any wine in those bags?'

I lifted out a bottle of the New Zealand Sauvignon Blanc that I knew she loved and held it up. She sighed happily.

'Oh yes,' she said, reaching out and taking it from me. 'I need this. Join me?'

I reached up into a cupboard and got her a glass, holding it up against the light to check for cleanliness out of habit. 'Not tonight.'

'Why not?'

'I had a beer earlier, at lunch. And I have to drive home.'

Her face tightened ever so slightly at the word *home,* before she relaxed it again. 'You could just sleep here. Your room is right there, all made up still. Just like it was back in L.A.'

'Hannah.'

'God, is this still about that stupid kiss?'

'I'm doing what I think is right for both of us.'

'I was drunk and sad. You overreacted.'

'Maybe. But this way we don't have to worry about being in that situation again.'

She sighed, then poured herself a wine and walked over to the couch, curling herself up with her feet tucked underneath her. 'I can tell you're itching to get to the boring stuff. How is the business going?'

'It's not boring,' I chided her gently, taking a seat on an

armchair. 'And business is doing well. Really well. I can run through the books and figures with you tomorrow, but it's been a good start to summer. Profits are even up on the same time in the last few years.'

She took a sip of wine. 'I'll take your word for it.'

'Hannah.'

'I know.' She rolled her eyes. 'You want me to learn how all that stuff works. But I've never been a numbers girl, Jack. I just don't understand all that ingoing and outgoing stuff.'

'That's why I'm here. To help you. It's *your* business.'

She ran a finger around the rim of her glass and there was a quiet, high-pitched ringing noise. 'Is that the only reason you're here?'

I shook my head. 'Don't.'

'I'm sorry. I'm just... I hate this, Jack. When I'm back home in the city, I feel so alone. There are reminders of him, and you, and our life before...' She trailed off, her voice breaking. 'But I feel alone here too, especially with you moving out. It's like I don't belong anywhere any more.'

'That's not true.'

'Maybe not, but it's how I feel. I mean, how can my life have gone so horribly wrong? I had everything, and now?'

'You still have me. And you have this place.'

She chuckled bitterly. 'This place was Alex's dream, not mine. I bought it on a whim because I thought it would make me feel closer to him, but of course it doesn't. How could it? He was never here. And I have no idea what I'm doing. If it wasn't for you stepping in to save me, I would have lost it all.'

'It's not that hard; you're overthinking things. If I can figure it out, you sure as hell can.'

She stared up at me with her big, puppy-dog eyes. 'I don't know what I'd do without you.'

When she looked at me like that, lines got blurred. I stood up. 'You don't have to worry about that.'

'Where are you going?'

'Home.'

'That cabin is not your home,' she snapped, then composed herself again. 'Does that woman live there? On the property?'

'What woman? Taylor?'

'I don't remember her name. The one you were with today.'

'Yeah, that's Taylor. And yes, she is staying in her mother's house.'

'For how long?'

'I'm not sure. Her mother is away on a cruise, so she's back to look after the old man.'

'That's nice of her.'

'It is.'

'Will you be seeing her again?'

'Why are you asking?'

'I'm just making conversation.'

'I have no idea. But it's a small town, and we do live on the same property. Our paths are bound to cross. Right, I'll get going, but I'll see you tomorrow.'

'Do you really have to go? I can cook you dinner. That pasta dish you love. We can catch up.'

'I don't think that's a good idea.'

She looked desperate. 'I just got back. What am I supposed to do?'

'I don't know. Maybe watch a show, or read a book, or even go for a walk or swim?' I suggested, my voice softening. It broke my heart to see how sad she looked, but I knew I had to be firm to be kind. 'I'm here for you, Hannah. I always will be. But some of this stuff you've got to figure out for yourself.'

11

TAYLOR

'I wasn't sure if you were going to show up tonight,' I called out, watching him pick his way across the rocks towards the pool. The moon was bright, bathing everything in a beautiful silvery blue light.

'I told you, I come down here every night.' His voice carried easily in the still of the night, the silence broken only by the sound of the tide gently lapping against the rocks.

'I know, but with your friend arriving back in town today I thought you might be busy catching up.'

He stood at the edge of the pool and tilted his head up towards the sky. I heard him exhale slowly, as if releasing stress from his body. 'I've just left her actually.'

'Everything OK?'

'Why do you ask?'

'Your tone seemed... weary.'

'You've known me twenty-four hours and you can pick up on my mood just from my tone? Impressive.'

'I'm an empath. I pick up on the small clues people often don't realize they're dropping.'

'Hannah's fine.' He sighed. 'It's just hard for her. She's struggling, without Alex.'

'I bet. It must be awful, being widowed so young.'

'Yeah.'

'Want to talk about it?'

'Not really.' He dipped his toes into the water, then gently lowered himself in, exhaling again as the water embraced his body. 'I needed this.'

'Better than any expensive spa, right?'

'I wouldn't know. I'm not exactly a spa kind of guy.'

'You'll just have to take my word for it then.'

He smiled, his teeth bright in the moonlight. 'I guess I will.'

I swished my arms gently through the beautiful clear water. In the day, it was a gorgeous blue and you could see right through to the bottom. But at night the water was pitch-black, with only the reflection of the stars above. It had always been my secret place. An escape from reality. 'I used to think this pool had magical powers.'

'You did?'

'Yeah. When I was a kid, and my parents would argue, I'd sneak out of the house and come down here. My mom would have killed me if she'd known; I was only eight or nine at the time.'

'You swam down here by yourself in the dark when you were a kid?'

'Yeah.'

'I'm beginning to understand why you weren't scared of me last night.'

'I used to swim under the stars and wish that I was a mermaid so I could go anywhere I wanted. Failing that, I'd wish that my dad would leave us. Leave my mom alone. And then one day he did.'

'I take it he wasn't a nice guy.'

I shrugged. 'I used to think that, but now I realize he was just human. Had flaws like we all do. I think he was just miserable with his life, and so he took it out on us.'

'That's horrible.'

'I know. But plenty of people make the wrong choices, right? Choose a career because it pays well, but secretly hate it. Or marry someone just because they've been together for a few years and it's the logical, generally expected next step. They don't stop to think about whether spending the rest of their life with that person is actually going to make them happy.'

'Is that what happened with you and Adam?'

'No.' I pulled a face. '*That* was a disaster right from the get-go. Doomed in fact, from the very moment of its conception.'

'Wow.'

'Anyway, here I am spilling my deeply personal secrets with you and you're giving me nothing in return.'

'I'm not trying to be secretive, I just don't like rehashing the past. I find it counterproductive.'

'So you're just going to stick with the whole mysterious vibe thing you've got going on. Gotcha.'

'I have a mysterious vibe?'

'Don't act like you don't know it.'

'I didn't, until you pointed it out.'

'Yeah right. It's like the plot of a romance book. Hot, broody, single guy moves from the city to a small town to help out an old "friend".'

'Why did you say "friend" like that?'

'Like what?'

'You know what.'

'I don't know what you're talking about.'

'You had a tone.'

'No, I didn't. What's your problem?'

He sighed. 'It's just... people like to gossip. I don't want anyone to get the wrong idea about Hannah and I.'

'Number one, I'm not a gossip. And number two, what *is* the deal with you guys?'

'There's no deal. It's like I told you, she was married to my best friend. He died. Now I'm helping her out with her business. That's it.'

'That's it?'

'That's it.'

'OK. I believe you.'

There was a brief silence and then he swore. 'OK fine, that's not *all* of it.'

'I knew it.'

'About eight months ago, when I first came out here to help her out, she had a bit too much to drink and she kissed me.'

'Ah,' I said. The proprietary looks Hannah had given me at the restaurant suddenly made sense.

'That's it? I open up to you like you wanted and that's all you have to say? Ah?'

'What did you expect me to say?'

'I don't know. Something other than, ah, I guess.'

'It's none of my business what you two get up to.'

'That's the point. There is no "us two".'

'And are you sure *she* knows that?'

'Of course. That's why I moved out here to the cabin. To put a bit of space between us.'

'Sounds like you've got it all figured out.'

'I have.'

'Good.'

He swam closer to me, the moon contouring the lines of his face. 'How did you do that?'

'What?'

'Get me to tell you something I had no intention of telling you.'

I shrugged. 'Special talent, I guess?'

'I thought your special talent was guessing what food people have ordered.'

I snorted at the reminder. 'A girl can have more than one special talent.'

'Well, thank God you're better at getting people to open up than you are at guessing their food.'

I splashed him without thinking, and he splashed back. Bigger.

I wiped water from my eyes. 'You shouldn't have done that.'

'You started it.'

I swam towards him. 'I happen to be a bit of a champion at water fights.'

He grinned. 'Another special talent of yours?'

I shrugged. 'It's less of a talent and more of a survival skill.'

'I'm not scared of—'

His words were cut off as I leapt on him, my hands on his shoulders, pushing him underneath the water before releasing him. He re-emerged above the surface seconds later, spluttering.

'What was that for?' he gasped.

'Payback, obviously. You splashed me; I dunked you.'

He narrowed his eyes at me as he shook the water from his hair. 'Oh, it is *on*.'

'You wouldn't dare,' I called over my shoulder, already swimming away from him. The next thing I knew, I was underwater too, his hands clamped around my waist. I squealed, releasing bubbles, before he let go and I burst through the surface.

'I guess I do dare.' He laughed as I gaped at him. 'Weren't expecting that now, were yghusfh?'

The last word came out incoherent thanks to the mouthful of water I'd just splashed in his direction.

'Do you give up?' I asked, grinning.

He shook his head. 'Never.'

He lunged towards me and I squealed again, freestyling away from him but not getting far before I felt his fingers wrap around my ankle. I was yanked back through the water, only stopping when I came smack bang up against his chest, face to face with him, one of his hands curled behind my back, holding me against him. Our laughter trailed off as we stared at each other, before his eyes lowered to my lips. I could feel his heartbeat, strong and steady beneath my palm. See water drops beading on his sharp, angular jaw. Without thinking, I lifted my hand and touched them, tracing my fingers along the length of his jaw, stopping to rest my fingertips in that soft place beneath his ear. I heard him suck in a breath sharply, his eyes probing mine.

'I'm sorry,' he said suddenly, releasing me and almost pushing me away. 'I misjudged the distance. I didn't mean to...'

'It's fine,' I reassured him, hoping my face didn't reflect the emotions I was feeling.

'No, I shouldn't have...'

'Do you give up?' I interjected, cutting him off before he could overthink what had just happened, or rather *almost* happened.

He smiled. 'Never.'

12

JACK

'Surprise.'

The first thing I saw when I entered the restaurant just after eleven the next morning was Hannah beaming at me from behind the bar. She wasn't wrong. It *was* a surprise, seeing her standing there. Normally she avoided it and the kitchen, preferring to stay upstairs or at a table as if she were just another patron instead of the person who owned the place.

'Hey,' I greeted her, slinging my keys and phone onto a little shelf underneath the bar. 'Sleep OK?'

'Better than you, by the look of it. You have bags under your eyes bigger than the ones I flew in with.'

'Warm night,' I replied, by way of explanation. 'The wood in the cabin really holds the heat in.'

'I don't seem to have that problem upstairs,' she said smugly, then quickly added when she saw my expression. 'I'm just saying.'

'Yeah, well don't.'

'You're touchy this morning. Something wrong?'

A memory of Taylor's face in front of mine flashed through

my mind. The way her lips had parted under my gaze, as if she'd wanted me to kiss her. I'd been so close to doing it too, but in the end something had held me back.

'No. Just tired. Like I said, rough night.'

'OK.' She looked as if she didn't believe me, but knew better than to push it. 'Where do you want me?'

'Sorry?'

'To work. I've got my comfortable shoes on and I'm ready to learn the ropes.' She did a little pirouette and ended with a flourish of her hands. 'Keen to dive in and do my bit.'

I stared at her. 'Seriously?'

She nodded. 'You were right last night. This is my business. I have to figure this stuff out if I'm going to make it work. If *we're* going to make this work.'

'You're sure about this?'

She nodded. 'Of course.'

'It's not that I don't want to believe you,' I said cautiously. 'But it wouldn't be the first time you've said you'll stay and when things get hard you run back to the city.'

Annoyance flickered briefly across her face. 'I can't promise to stay here forever, but for now, I'm all in.'

'No one can promise forever; we both know that.'

She looked briefly stricken at the reminder.

'Sorry,' I said quickly. 'I didn't mean to upset you.'

'It's OK. After everything you've done for me, I suppose I can forgive you for the occasional thoughtless comment.' She clapped her hands together. 'But let's not dwell. I woke up this morning determined to be a good girl and listen to what you've said and take charge of my own future. I can't lose that determination in the first hour, can I? So, where do you want me?'

'I guess you could shadow me for a while, get a feel for how things work around here. The good news is that you have the best staff anyone could hope for. Hell, they could probably run this place by themselves if they had to.'

She put her hands on her hips. 'Then what am I paying you for?'

'Good question. I'm not complaining though. This place has been just what I needed.' I smiled ruefully. 'I didn't even know how much I needed it until I got here.'

'I guess I can see why Alex always talked about moving here and running a restaurant,' she agreed. 'All this nature, places to hike and fish. He would have loved it. Me? Not so much. I like the *idea* of this place, but actually living here? I'm just not sure the whole small-town vibe is really my thing. I prefer being surrounded by buildings and people and noise.' She saw my mouth open and quickly continued. '*But...* like I said. I'm prepared to give this a go. Who knows, maybe this place will make a small-town girl out of me yet.'

'Hey, bigger miracles have happened, right?'

'If they could just get some decent clothing boutiques.' She sighed. 'Seriously, there are three dress stores in this town and not one of them sells anything even remotely like you'd find on Fifth Avenue. They're all a decade behind, at *least*. I guess I'll just have to make do with online shopping. They *do* get mail here, right?'

'Sure, comes over the hill on horseback, but it gets here eventually.'

'Oh my God.' She laughed. 'That actually wouldn't surprise me.'

For the next couple of hours, she stuck with me, clearing tables, taking orders, preparing and delivering drinks. She even dealt with a customer complaint, calming an irate woman with a free cocktail and a ten percent discount off her bill.

'You're a natural,' I told her after the restaurant had mostly cleared out again. 'Honestly, I'm impressed.'

'I'm impressed with myself,' she admitted. 'That was kind of fun.'

'Water?'

'God no.' She pulled a face. 'After that shift I deserve a wine.'

'You handled that complaint well.'

'Of course I did.' She smiled. 'Have you forgotten how charming I can be?'

'Hannah.'

'What?'

I lowered my voice, checking to make sure none of the staff were within earshot. 'You know what. The flirting, it's not appropriate.'

'It's not flirting.' She pouted. 'It's banter. And it's always been like this between us. Even when Alex was alive. I don't see why that has to change.'

'It just does.' I rubbed a hand through my hair. 'Everything is different now.'

'You think I don't know that?' she retorted, her eyes flashing. 'I'm the one who had to bury my husband. The man that *you* promised me you'd look after.'

The words stung. 'You blame me.'

Instantly her anger deflated. 'No, of course not. I'm sorry, it's just been a long day. I don't blame you. I *need* you. You're the only constant I have left. I just... I miss him. I miss him so much it hurts.'

'I know. I miss him too.'

She rubbed her face with the back of her hand. 'I just want things to go back to the way they were.'

'If only the world worked like that.'

She looked up at me and the expression on her face broke my heart. 'Promise you won't leave me too?'

I swallowed hard, remembered the promise I'd made to Alex as he died in my arms.

'I promise.'

The chef, Kevin, poked his head out from the kitchen. 'Jack, phone call for you,' he said. 'It's Connie from the police department,' he said. 'A hiker's gone over the cliff at Sailor's Bluff.'

The harsh cliffs and rock faces at Sailor's Bluff flashed into my mind. 'They still alive?'

'Yeah, for now. Condition unknown at this stage, but apparently they're in danger of being swept off the rocks by the tide. Connie's rallying the troops.'

'Will you be OK on your own for a bit? Lucy will be back from her break soon and Fiona's shift starts at three.'

'Go,' she said. 'I'll be fine.'

I reached behind me to untie the apron I was wearing. 'Tell Connie I'm on my way.'

13

TAYLOR

I picked up my keys from the sideboard and tucked my phone into an inside pocket of my jacket. 'Will you be OK on your own if I go out for a few hours?'

'No. I'll pine to death from loneliness.'

I stared at Ray. He stared back at me. He caved first.

'Of course I'll bloody be OK,' he snapped. 'I've managed ninety-four years on this planet without you mollycoddling me, I'll be perfectly fine to manage by myself for a few hours.'

'You're going to feel really stupid if you die now while I'm out.'

'As long as I can come back and haunt you, it'll be worth it. Anyway, you're the one going out on that bike of yours.'

'So?'

'So if I had to put money on which one of us would be more likely to die today, it'd be you.'

I picked up my helmet and dusted a speck of dust off the top. 'Sorry to be the one to break it to you, but I am an excellent and very careful rider.'

We both realized we'd strayed into dangerous territory at the

same moment and exchanged a look of acknowledgment, signi-
fying a truce and an end to that conversation.

'Just... be careful,' he said. 'Your mother has been through
enough.'

'Agreed. You be careful too.'

'I don't plan on leaving my chair. It's not me you need to
worry about.'

It felt good to be on the bike again. I took the long way to
town, around the island in the opposite direction. It was a ride
that would normally take about an hour, but with the conversation with Ray fresh in mind, I took my time. Enjoyed the scenery.
I did love living in the city, but I'd forgotten how much being
surrounded by nature could do for the soul. Blow off the
cobwebs, oxygenate the blood, that sort of thing. The road took
me past the mountain lake and I stopped for ten minutes,
skimmed a few rocks across the mirror surface of the water.
Remembered countless swims here when I was a kid, nights
drinking around campfires as a teen.

It struck me that away from here I thought of this place as
constricting and small, somewhere I couldn't wait to get out of.
But when I was home, I was reminded of the beauty of this
place. That a small community wasn't necessarily a bad thing. I
peed behind a bush and got on the road again, feeling my mood
darken as I got closer to my destination. It wasn't nerves, but
something akin to that. Apprehension.

The cemetery parking lot was empty when I got there, which
I was relieved about. I didn't want anyone I knew seeing me
there. It would no doubt spark a conversation I didn't want to
have. A conversation I had, in fact, actively avoided for the past
fourteen years. It wasn't the only reason I'd left Pine Harbor, but
it had been a big part of it.

It wasn't the main cemetery in town. That honor went to

Whispering Pines Cemetery down on Main Street, behind the church. I had a few relatives buried there, great-grandparents, my grandparents on my mother's side, a great-aunt who I'd never met. Ray's sister. She had died young from pneumonia, but I knew very little else about her. Whispering Pines was a nice cemetery, as far as cemeteries go. Well maintained, with manicured lawns and hedges and a rose garden in the center with a little water fountain in the shape of an angel. Even the older graves, the hulking gray stones with the barely legible writing, were looked after by council staff. There was a group of women in town, including my mother, who unofficially placed flowers onto strangers' graves. Flowers they had grown in their own gardens. It was a nice gesture. The local paper had even run a front-page feature on them once. My mother had clipped out the article and sent it to me.

But the cemetery on the top of the hill overlooking the Atlantic Ocean was different. Most of the graves were older, dating back to when settlers first arrived here and built the town and the shipbuilding yards. There were exceptions though, the odd newer graves dotted here and there, obvious by their modern headstones. I headed for one in the back row, closest to the top of the cliff, the spot chosen by me all those years ago. I'd been adamant that it had to be that spot, even though my mother had been less keen. I was glad, now, as I made my way through the older graves up to it, that I had stuck to my guns.

He'd always loved the ocean, had been a proper water baby. Whether it was swimming, fishing, surfing or sailing, most of the time if you needed him, that's where you'd find him. Either in or on the water. That last summer he'd finally landed his dream job, out on one of the lobster boats. My mother had been less than thrilled; she wanted him to go to university, find a career less dangerous, less taxing. More profitable. But it was all he'd ever wanted to do. Unlike me, he never planned on leaving Pine Harbor. His dreams were simple: work his way up to owning his own boat, build himself a house on the water somewhere, marry a nice girl and have a few kids. I found his certainty in his future unnerving, but I was also jealous. Unlike him, I had no idea what I wanted to do or where I wanted to go. I loved my art, and I was good at it, but I had no idea how to turn that into an actual career. It was actually his death that had pointed me in the right direction. A few months after he died, Adam and I got matching tattoos in his honor, and watching the man use the needle to create art on my skin had been one of those defining moments in life.

My mother had been here fairly recently. The glass vase on his grave was stuffed with flowers – daylilies and lavender. I could hear bees humming as they took advantage. The day was warm and I was wearing my bike leathers, but I wasn't uncomfortable because of that. Most of the time I could ignore the guilt that had been a permanent part of my psyche since the moment I found out he had died. The years had made it easier to live with. It was just another part of me, absorbed and acclimatized. But here in this town, and especially right here in front of his grave, it bubbled through the apathy to the surface again, making itself known, weighing me down with its unbearable weight.

'Hey Cal,' I said softly, my eyes tracing the white lettering of his name.

Calvin Calderwood

12/06/1993 – 12/06/2011

Loved and cherished son of Moira and John Calderwood

Adored twin brother of Taylor Calderwood

Gone but never forgotten, he rests now amongst the stars.

Because my mother had conceded to my insistence that he be buried here, in this spot, I had let her take the lead with the design of his headstone. Nothing had seemed right anyway. No words were good enough to express how I felt at his loss. No trite poem or pithy epitaph could ever convey how much I'd loved him. As far as I was concerned, it both didn't matter what she chose to have engraved, as much as it mattered immensely. It could never be enough, but I desperately needed it to be. I needed anyone who stood in front of his grave to know how much my brother, my twin brother, had meant to me. How much I'd loved the irritating bones of him. How he'd been a part of me since always, for as long as I could remember, and even before that. I needed them to understand that a part of me lay buried here with him. That when he'd died, a piece of me had died too.

But there wasn't a headstone big enough to fit everything I needed to say, and not enough adjectives in the world to say it. There was just this, and because anything would be inadequate, this would have to do.

I saw down beside the headstone, and ran my fingers over the ceramic photo of him. They came away salty from the sea spray that made its way even up here to the top of the cliff. I loved this photo of him. Felt that it summed him up pretty effectively in one image. It was taken only a few weeks before he died, out on the lobster boat, by one of his crewmates. He'd emailed it to me after Cal died, and when I clicked on the attachment and this photo had opened, my brother's face filling the screen, it had completely stolen the breath from me.

He was wearing a plain white T-shirt and a pair of shorts, sunglasses high on his head keeping his sandy blond mop out of his piercing blue eyes. His skin tanned and freckled, his teeth white and his smile beaming as he held out a large lobster for the cameraman to see. He was beautifully, achingly perfect. Animated and so, so alive.

I still couldn't understand how all that could just stop in an instant. I couldn't wrap my brain around or reconcile the Cal in this photo with the Cal lying six feet underneath me in a box in the ground. How could someone so young and vivid and alive just... cease to exist any more? It didn't seem possible, and it sure as hell wasn't fair.

'I know it's been awhile,' I told him. 'I'm sorry I didn't bring you any flowers. Kind of hard to carry on the bike.'

I jumped as a gull screeched loudly as it flew overhead. It headed out to sea as I watched, its gray-and-white wings stretched wide, tail feathers spread. They looked majestic in flight. Nothing like they did on shore, noisy and begging for food. The number of times I'd fallen for one standing with a leg tucked out of sight to garner sympathy. They'd conned quite a few fries out of me over the years.

'I'm guessing Mom told you what happened with Adam,' I said. 'It's probably karma.'

There was no sound apart from the rustling of the breeze in the trees surrounding the cemetery and the sound of the waves breaking onto rocks at the bottom of the cliff. I unzipped my jacket and took it off, laying it on the grass beside Cal's grave. Underneath I was wearing a black tank top. The sun was deliciously warm on my skin, and I realized it had been a long time since I'd sat like this, skin exposed, and soaked up some vitamin D.

'Do you remember how we used to live in our bathing suits all summer long?' I said, leaning my back against the side of Cal's headstone. 'We'd put them on in the morning instead of clothes. Eat breakfast then head for the beach.' I shook my head sadly at the memory. 'God, I miss those days. When summer seemed to last forever and the only thing we had to worry about was sneaking in past Mom before she could see how much sand we were tracking into the house. Everything was so... trivial then. So easy. I wish I had enjoyed it more before it was over, you know? If I'd known our childhood, and my time with you was limited, I would have...' I trailed off.

I would have *what*? Enjoyed it more? No. I would have done things differently. But regret was a road that led to madness. I knew that. At the very least it led to impulsive decisions and borderline alcoholism. I couldn't understand people who said they had no regrets. Surely there had to be *something* about their past they would change if they could? Some teeny tiny thing, maybe harsh words spoken or a small action taken that rippled with far-reaching consequences. The kind of ripples that change lives, send them coursing in another direction. Sometimes nothing more than a look, a missed appointment, a kiss.

There was another screech of a gull. I turned my face skywards to search for it, but the sky was empty. The sound came again, this time louder. Intrigued, I got to my feet and took a few steps. It sounded in pain, and not in the sky as I'd first thought. Somewhere lower. I scanned the tree line, the grass at the top of the cliff, but there was no sign of an injured bird anywhere. Then I heard it again, and this time I recognized it for what it was.

'Help!'

My stomach dropped when I realized that it was coming from over the edge of the cliff.

'Hello?' I shouted, gingerly making my way over to the edge carefully. I lay on my stomach and wriggled as far as I could, peering down. There was a woman sprawled on her back on the rocks below. Her leg was at a weird angle, and she had blood on her face. When she saw me, she started sobbing with relief.

'Oh, thank God,' she called out between sobs. 'I didn't think anyone was going to come along. Please help me.'

'What happened?'

'I don't know,' she wailed. 'I was just walking along the trail, enjoying the view and then the next thing I knew I was down here. I think maybe I stood on some loose rock or something. I fell and now my ankle is broken. There was a snapping sound, and now there's a piece of bone poking...' Her voice broke and she started sobbing. 'There's so much blood. I don't know what to do. I'm so scared.'

'It's OK,' I called back to her. 'Just...' I'd been about to say *wait there,* but where was she going to go? 'I'm going to get you some help,' I promised, starting to wriggle back away from the edge.

'Don't leave me,' she shouted. 'I think the tide is coming in.'

'I'm not going anywhere,' I reassured her. 'I just need to get my phone from my jacket so I can get you some help, OK? Then I'll be right back.'

'You promise?'

'I promise. What's your name?'

She sobbed. 'Casey.'

'I'm not leaving you, Casey. I'm going to get you some help, and you're going to be just fine.'

'I'm so scared.'

'I know.'

14

JACK

'I hear Hannah's back already,' Dion said to me as we drove in his truck out towards Sailor's Bluff. He was a plumber by trade. Had his own business, imaginatively called 'The Plumber'. He had been working a job at the school in town when the emergency call had come in and had got to search and rescue headquarters at the same time as I did, so we loaded the gear into his truck and headed out together. He was one of the first guys I met when I'd moved here and I'd liked him instantly. I fancied myself as being a pretty good judge of character, and Dion was an easygoing, good-natured guy. Anyone who volunteered to be part of search and rescue had to be a good person.

'Mm,' I muttered back, turning my head to stare out of the window at the scenery flashing past. His two-way radio crackled with the voice of one of the other men updating us with their ETA, thankfully distracting him.

The rest of the team were also volunteers who held down other day jobs like Dion and me, and would make their own way out shortly as they could get away from work. They were good people, and I'd trust any one of them with my back in an emergency, but my private life was my business and nobody else's.

Years of training and experience from my old job kicked in and I ran all the possible scenarios we could face when we got there, mentally preparing myself for any action we'd need to take. The one thing I didn't anticipate, could never have anticipated, was the sight of Taylor Calderwood lying stretched out on the ground at the top of the cliff, her head hanging down over the edge, her long hair cascading down. She was wearing black jeans, boots and a tight black tank top, and must have been absolutely cooking in the heat.

'Taylor?'

Her hair was blown and pushed to one side so that she could look up at me. Her eyes moved up and down my body, taking in my high-vis vest and the gear I was carrying. 'Jack?'

I dropped the gear gently to the ground. 'What are you doing here?'

'Oh, you know, just hanging out.' She smiled but it was a tight smile. She turned her face away again. 'The cavalry's arrived, Casey,' she called. 'I told you we'd have you back up here in no time.'

'You know the patient?'

'No. I just happened to be in the right place at the right time. For her, anyway.'

'You were visiting the cemetery?'

'Does that have anything to do with rescuing Casey?'

'No, of course not.'

'Then can we maybe just concentrate on that?' she said tersely. 'She's nineteen, and pretty scared right now, which is understandable.'

I recognized when someone was trying to shut a conversation down. It was the same thing I'd done to Dion in the truck ten minutes ago.

'Got it. Sorry.' I braced myself, leaned out over the edge and took in the sight below. 'Hi, Casey,' I called out. 'I'm Jack, from the Pine Harbor search and rescue team. We're going to get you up from there, OK? Are you hurt?'

'Of course she's hurt,' Taylor muttered. 'She fell off a forty-foot cliff.'

'Yes, thank you, I'm aware of that.' I suppressed a smile. 'But if you could just let her answer for herself I'd appreciate it. It helps me to judge the severity of her injuries and her level of consciousness et cetera.'

'Oh right,' she said. 'Go ahead.'

'Thanks. Casey, can you tell me if you're hurt?'

'Yes,' she called up, her voice wobbly. 'My ankle is in a really bad way.'

'OK. Anything else?'

'Uh, I banged my head.'

'Do you know if you lost consciousness at all?'

'I don't know. I don't think so.'

'OK, that's good. Is there anything else you need to tell me before we work out a plan? And other injuries, pre-existing medical conditions or disabilities?'

'No, I mean I have some cuts and bruises, but my ankle is the worst.' She sobbed, and the sound was heart-wrenching, but I knew better than to react impulsively. 'Please hurry,' she continued. 'It hurts and the water is getting closer.'

'We're going to do this as fast as we can,' I assured her. 'But we have to make sure your safety, and the safety of the team, is our priority, OK?'

'I want my mom.'

'I've tried calling her on the number you gave me, Casey,'

Taylor told her. 'I've left a message asking her to call me back. As soon as she does, I'll let you know.'

'What do you reckon?' Dion asked. 'Do we attempt this one ourselves?'

I shook my head. 'Negative. I think we need to call in air support. She's clearly in a lot of pain, so pulling her back up the cliff is only going to cause her more distress, as is a trip to the hospital by road ambulance. I'm concerned with the height of the drop and the fact she's not sure whether she lost consciousness or not. I think the sooner she gets pain relief and medical attention the better.'

'Agreed,' Taylor said, and Dion looked at her. I saw him take in her disheveled beauty and stand up a little straighter. It irked me that he noticed in a moment like this.

'And you are...?' he said.

She got to her feet and rubbed dirt off the front of her jeans with her hands. 'I'm the person who called this in.'

'Right.' He flashed her a smile. 'Thanks for that; you've probably saved her life. We can take it from here though.'

'She's already been down there for a couple of hours,' Taylor said, ignoring him and focusing on me. 'It's a hell of a drop, and I can see even from here that her ankle is at an angle that is completely unnatural. It's bent kind of upwards and facing completely the wrong way.'

Dion sucked air in between his teeth. 'Ouch.'

'Yeah, ouch. BIG ouch. That's why I don't think we should muck around. Jack, call in the chopper, *please*.'

There was something about her expression that told me this was personal for her. I'd already made my decision, but I nodded anyway, picking up my two-way radio. 'On it.'

'Thank you,' Taylor said, her eyes drilling into mine, her

expression a mixture of gratitude and vulnerability. I felt a jolt in my chest.

'Can you start setting up the gear while I make the call?' I barked at Dion, a little harsher than intended. I told myself it wasn't because of the way he'd looked at Taylor. 'Use that big spruce as an anchor point. One of us will need to go down and stay with her until they get here.'

'Sure,' he said. If he was bothered with me taking the lead he didn't show it. As first on the scene, either of us could have assumed that role.

The rest of the team arrived while I was making the call and I saw Dion fill them in on our plan. They agreed with what I'd decided, and even though I knew it really was the best course of action, it was still a relief to have it confirmed. It bugged the hell out of me that I even needed that validation. Once upon a time I wouldn't have. Second-guessing myself had only become a thing after Alex died.

'Belay system is all set up, Jack,' Dion called over. 'Who do you want to go down?'

'I'll go,' I replied, conscious of Taylor's eyes on me, but deliberately not looking at her. Right now, I needed to focus on Casey and her predicament, not that feeling I'd got when Taylor had looked at me the way she did. I strapped myself in and grabbed a helmet. One of my teammates, Wendy, double-checked to make sure I'd secured everything properly, before I headed for the edge of the cliff.

'Let me come with you,' Taylor said, falling into step beside me.

'What?'

'I'm the one who's been talking to her for the last forty minutes, keeping her calm until you guys arrived.'

'No. I'm sorry, but that's out of the question.'

'Jack, she's terrified. I think she could do with a feminine presence to reassure her down there.'

'It's too dangerous.'

'Oh, but it's not dangerous for you?' she retorted.

'I've had training, Taylor.'

'And I've been to camp. So what?'

'What's camp got to do with anything?'

'I've rappelled before, plenty of times.'

I stopped. 'Down a natural cliff face? This high?'

'Not quite,' she admitted.

'That's what I thought. I'm sorry Taylor, this is just the way it works. I can't let you put yourself in danger and risk having another patient on our hands.' I lowered my voice. 'I don't want to see you to get hurt.'

'I won't. But fine, I guess your stupid rules are there for a reason. Just, tell her I hope she's OK. Please?'

'Of course.'

15

TAYLOR

I watched as he lowered himself over the edge slowly and methodically. Randomly, I noticed how big and strong his hands were as they threaded the rope between them. It didn't seem to take him long at all to get down, maybe ten minutes or so. Once at the bottom, he unclipped himself and picked his way across the rocks to where Casey was lying. I could see him chatting to her as he assessed her injuries, and watching him, I was struck by the thought that he looked pretty damn expert at it, more than the usual volunteer training. Jack reached for his radio clipped to his chest, and a few seconds later Dion's radio crackled beside me.

'Do we have an ETA on that helicopter yet?' Jack asked.

'I'll call and check,' Wendy said, heading for her truck.

'How's the patient's condition?' Dion asked.

'Casey,' I muttered. 'Her name is Casey.'

'Casey is alert,' Jack answered. 'Responsive to pain and my voice. She has a compound fracture to her left ankle, a large laceration to her knee, and minor lacerations and bruises to the rest of her body.' His tone suddenly lowered. 'She also has some bleeding from her left ear.'

'Damn.' Dion closed his eyes for a brief moment and winced. 'OK, I'll get on to the chopper crew and update them on her injuries.'

'What does that mean?' I asked him.

'What, the bleeding from the ear?'

I nodded.

He pulled a face. 'Could be a number of things, none of them good.'

'Like what?'

'She could have a brain injury, or a skull fracture. They won't know until they give her a CT scan at the hospital, so the sooner we get her there, the better.'

We both heard it then, a distant *whop whop whop* sound. I turned my head skywards, to the west where the sound was coming from, but couldn't see it at first. Then I noticed it, a tiny black dot against the blue of the sky, moving, slowly getting bigger.

'Chopper's almost here,' Dion radioed to Jack.

A thought occurred to me. 'Where are they going to land?'

'They won't,' he replied. 'Nearest flat ground is a good mile or two from here. They'll have to winch her up.'

'Won't that hurt her even more?'

'Not if they do it right.' He saw my worried face and gave me a reassuring smile. 'Don't worry, these guys are the real deal. They'll give her pain relief first. She'll be in good hands, I promise.'

'I just felt so helpless,' I admitted. 'Seeing her down there and being unable to do anything to help.'

'Hey,' he soothed. 'You *did* help. If it wasn't for you, we wouldn't have got here when we did. Who knows how long she might have been down there before someone else came along and heard her. It could have been days.'

'Yeah, I guess.'

The chopper was close now, hovering fifty meters offshore. Dion directed everyone who wasn't necessary, including myself, to stand well back, away from the powerful downwash of wind created by the rotor blades. I watched from the tree line as a man was winched down from the chopper to where Jack and Casey were, out of sight. Not long after that, a stretcher was also winched down, and about twenty minutes later Casey was lifted up by the winch, in the stretcher, to the waiting helicopter. I felt a swell of emotion as I watched her disappear inside the aircraft.

Relief, mostly, that she was now safe and would soon be in a hospital where she would have a team of medical professionals fussing over her and giving her the tests and treatment that she needed. But I wasn't naïve enough to think she was completely out of the woods. The possibility that she had a brain injury was scary stuff, and potentially life-changing for her. All I could do was watch and hope that she would come through it all OK.

The helicopter departed, *whop whop whopping* off towards a hospital in one of the big cities on the mainland. The search and rescue team, relaxed now, started packing up the gear. I waited at the top of the cliff while Jack climbed back up, not relaxing myself until he was safely back on solid ground again. I don't think I imagined how his eyes searched the crowd and softened when they found me, his shoulders relaxing.

'Hey,' he said, unclipping himself from the harnesses and taking them off. 'You OK?'

I nodded. 'Yeah. I'm fine.'

'You sure? Don't be surprised if you get a little shaky when the adrenaline wears off.'

Now that he mentioned it, my legs *did* feel a little wobbly. My face must have gone a bit pale, or something else gave the game away because the next thing I knew he was beside me, his strong arms around my shoulders, steadying me.

'Easy,' he said softly. 'I've got you.'

I breathed in the smell of him. It was woody and salty and masculine, and it felt somehow like I was right where I supposed to be. It was the weirdest feeling but I relaxed into it, mostly because I wasn't sure in that moment that I could stand without him.

'I'm fine,' I babbled. 'Sorry. God, how embarrassing.'

'Don't be embarrassed,' he said. 'It can happen to the best of us. *Has* happened, many times. We're all human. Nobody judges anybody around here.'

I buried my face in his jersey, feeling his warmth, enjoying how his arms felt around me. I couldn't remember the last time I'd been held like this by a man. Adam and I, we'd drifted apart long before he started seeking comfort elsewhere. Towards the end, we'd been more like roommates than anything else, although occasionally the guilt would strike, the realization that something was very wrong, and one of us would make a move, but if I was honest with myself I hadn't enjoyed it. Hadn't leaned into him the way I was leaning into Jack.

'Feeling any better?' he asked after a few minutes, and reluctantly I nodded and pulled away from him.

'Yeah, I am. My heart feels like it's beating normally again at least. Thanks.'

He smiled, his eyes intensely boring into mine, and something inside me went *flop*. My heart, assumedly.

'Any time,' he said, and I wasn't sure what to make of that.

Someone cleared their throat pointedly nearby, and I took

another quick step away from Jack. It was Dion, looking apologetic, as if he was interrupting something.

'You OK, Taylor?' he asked.

'Yeah I'm all good,' I replied brightly. 'Just felt a bit lightheaded for a second. I think I was lying out in the sun at the top of the cliff for too long. Bit overdressed for this heat.'

His eyes dropped to my black jeans, his look appreciative. 'That would certainly do it.'

Jack moved so that he was standing slightly in front of me, but I couldn't tell whether it was intentional or not.

'Gear all packed up?' he asked gruffly. 'Sorry I wasn't any help.'

'It's fine,' Dion replied, a smirk in his voice. 'I could see you had your hands full. Plus, you kind of pulled off all the heroics today. It was the least the rest of us could do.'

'It was a team effort, like always.'

'Well, I need to get back to work, so...' Dion made a thumbing gesture over his shoulder.

'Oh right,' Jack said. 'I came with you, didn't I?'

'You did.'

Jack turned back to me. 'Can we give you a lift back to town?'

'No, I'm OK, thanks. I have my bike.'

He frowned. 'You *biked* all the way here?'

'My motorbike,' I clarified.

The expression that came over his face was very different to the one that came over Jack's.

'Cool,' Dion said, nodding appreciatively. 'You're a biker chick.'

I gave him a withering look that made him immediately shut up and start backing away. 'I'll wait over by the truck while you guys figure this out.'

Jack scowled. 'You have a motorbike?'

I crossed my arms over my chest and stared at him. 'Sure do.'

'I don't think you should be riding it.'

I tilted my head. 'That's funny, I don't remember needing, or asking, for your permission.'

'You've been through a lot today,' he said. 'You're most likely still processing it.'

'I haven't been through anything. It's Casey you should be worried about.'

'I *meant* that you might still have some residual shock. Coming across a situation like you did today and handling it the way you did.'

'I didn't handle anything,' I pointed out. 'I just called 911. *You're* the one who scaled a cliff like some...' I fumbled for the words '...some ridiculously buff... *Spider-Man*.'

His frown morphed into an amused grin. 'You think I'm buff?'

'What? Maybe, I don't know,' I stammered, feeling my cheeks flush under his gaze. It was that damn hug that had brought this on. The stupid bloody delicious smell of him. '*The point is,* I'm fine, and you don't get to tell me when I can or can't ride my bike. Got it?'

He held his hands up, palms facing outwards in a concilia-tory gesture. 'Got it.'

'Good.'

'But for the record, I wasn't trying to say you shouldn't ride the bike in general, although I do have a view on that. I was merely worried that you might be more affected by today than you realize.'

My eyes narrowed as I considered his words. They had struck home in a way he could never have anticipated. 'You're worried I might be impaired?'

He shrugged. 'Shock affects people differently. And some-times those effects can be delayed.'

'What about you?'

'I've had a lot of training. And experience. This isn't even in the top ten of worst injuries I've seen.'

I mulled over his words, then fished my keys out of my pocket and held them out towards him. 'Fine. You can ride it then.'

His eyebrows shot up. 'That's not what I meant.'

'Well I'm not leaving it here, if that's what you're suggesting.'

'Sorry to interrupt, guys,' Dion said, approaching. 'But I really do need to get back to work. My apprentice called in sick again today and I'm really under the pump to finish the job.'

I lifted my chin, my eyes challenging Jack. 'Your call,' I said.

'Fine.' He took the keys from me. 'You go with Dion, and I'll take your bike back to town.'

I shook my head. 'That's not going to work for me either. You can take control; I'll ride pillion.'

'But we only have one helmet,' he pointed out, his tone triumphant as if he believed he had won one over me.

'I've got my dirt bike gear in the back of the truck,' Dion said helpfully. 'You can borrow my helmet, Jack.'

Jack glared at him. 'Aren't you helpful.'

Dion shrugged, his grin suggesting he knew full well what he was doing. 'I try to be.'

'That's settled then.' I zipped my jacket up while he fetched the helmet. 'Unless you're scared.'

'Scared?' Jack scoffed, taking the helmet from Dion. 'I'm not scared.'

'Good. Let's go then.' I gave Dion a little wave. 'Thanks for the pep talk earlier,' I told him. 'It really helped.'

'You're welcome.' He doffed an imaginary hat. 'It was nice to meet you. Maybe you'd like to catch up for a drink sometime?'

'I thought you were in a hurry,' Jack said brusquely.

'Maybe, but I'm only here for a few weeks,' I told Dion.

He sighed. 'That's a shame.'

16

JACK

'I was hoping you'd show up,' she said, and my ego inflated like a helium balloon, drifting towards the stars overhead.

I dropped my towel onto the rocks and stretched. It had been a long day. 'You were?'

'Yes.' She swam across the pool, and rested her hands on a rock, her chin on her hands. 'I've been desperate to know how Casey is. Have you heard anything?'

The ego balloon sustained a puncture, deflating and sinking back down towards earth.

'We had an update about an hour ago. She's OK. Will have surgery tomorrow on her ankle, and it might need pinning, which will mean she'll need some rehab from a physio. But she's going to be OK. All thanks to you.'

'Hardly. You're the one who did all the heroic stuff.'

'But I wouldn't have been able to do that if you hadn't called it in.'

'I wish I could have done more.'

'Would you really have gone down the cliff with me, if I'd let you?'

'Of course.'

'Really?'

'Yes.'

'Huh.'

'What?'

'Nothing.'

'And FYI, the only reason I didn't keep pushing you to let me go was so you didn't look bad in front of the other guys. You're welcome.'

'Wow,' I said. 'That's so kind of you to protect my reputation like that.'

'I know, right? I'm such a considerate person.'

I climbed carefully down the rocks and eased myself into the water, exhaling as my body relaxed. It really was like a magic tonic for weary bodies. I dipped my head under then came back up, shaking my head, flicking water everywhere.

'How are you feeling?' I asked, paddling over next to her. 'Besides virtuous, even though that's wildly misplaced.'

'Rude. But I'm OK. Just relived, really, that it all worked out.'

'Me too. That was quite a fall she had. Could easily have killed her. I told her she needs to buy a lottery ticket with luck like that.'

'What made you join the search and rescue volunteers?'

I leaned my back against the rocks that were still warm from the sun and shrugged. 'I like helping people.'

'I like helping people too. Just the other week I yelled at an impatient taxi driver for honking his horn at a mom with a pram, made him wait until she was safely across the road. But there's a difference between being helpful, and helping people by scaling cliff faces or being winched out of a helicopter.'

'I don't get winched out of helicopters. That's a whole different level of skill and training.'

'You know what I mean.'

'What can I say? I wanted to give something back to the community that has been so welcoming to me. Gerry and another guy were talking about it at the bar one night, how they needed more volunteers, so I signed up.'

'Just like that.'

'Just like that,' I confirmed. 'Worship me if you must, but I'm no hero. I'm just an ordinary man, doing extraordinary things.'

She burst out laughing. Her teeth were bright in the silver light of the moon. 'Oh my God, could you be any more full of yourself?'

I grinned at her. 'I was clearly joking.'

'If you say so.'

I laughed. Watched her kick off the side and float on her back, her face pale in the moonlight. Somewhere out on the water, a loon called mournfully, the sound haunting across the water.

'You never answered my question, by the way,' I said.

'What question?'

'About why you were at the cemetery.'

She was silent for so long I thought I'd upset her. So quiet that all I could hear was the soothing sigh of the waves and the quiet hum of crickets from up in the pine trees.

'I was doing what everyone does at a cemetery,' she said eventually.

'Visiting a grave.'

'Yes, Captain Obvious.'

I waited to see if she would be more forthcoming, but she stayed quiet.

'Family?' I asked.

'Yes.'

'I'm getting the strangest feeling that you don't want to talk about it.'

'You should trust that feeling.'

'Fine.' I pushed off the rocks and swam across to the other side of the pool, the side closest to the ocean. 'Keep your secrets.'

'It's not a secret,' she said. 'I'd just rather not talk about it, if you don't mind.'

Something in her tone was fragile, warning me that I'd almost gone too far.

'I don't mind. Sorry for being pushy.'

She sighed. 'You weren't. Not really. It's just... being back here again. It's hard.'

'It's really that bad?'

'It's not bad, just hard. A lot of memories. Some good, some not so good.'

'Tell me a good one.'

She didn't have to think for too long. 'This pool,' she said. 'This beach. We had it all to ourselves, growing up. I'd spend whole days down here. Swimming, climbing all over the rocks, looking for bits of sea glass or cool shells, exploring the little pockets of water left behind by the tide for sea creatures. We found an octopus once. It was just a small, common one. But we thought it was so cool. It kept trying to change color and camouflage itself, blend into the rocks. I stayed there all day, watching it, until the tide came back in and filled the pool again and then it was gone.'

'The joys of a childhood by the sea,' I said. 'L.A. beaches are very different to this one. More sand, for a start.'

'More toned, tanned and taut bodies too, I imagine.'

I snorted. 'You got that right. Back home, a lot of people spend a hell of a lot of time and money obsessing about their bodies. You don't seem to get that here.'

'Iona Connolly ran women's fitness classes in the community hall when I was a teen,' she said. 'My mother signed up and used to drag me along. They'd jump up and down for an hour and then afterwards all go to the café to drink coffee and eat muffins and I'd sit there and think, *what was the point*? Now that I'm older, I understand. It was more of a social thing, for most of them. Making connections. It's easy to feel isolated here, especially in the winter.'

'The winter we just had was brutal,' I agreed, shuddering at the memory. 'Obviously I knew that winters here on the East Coast would be a lot colder than I was used to, but I was still woefully ill-prepared.'

'I used to love winters as a child. We'd sit on the porch with blankets wrapped around us and our fingers wrapped around mugs of delicious hot chocolate, and we'd watch storms rage out at sea. Count the lightning strikes and thunderclaps to figure out how far away the storms were.'

'That sounds like a nice memory,' I said softly.

She shrugged. 'Like I said, it wasn't all bad.'

'Maybe, one day, you'll have the chance to make more happy memories here,' I said. 'Drown out some of the bad.'

'Maybe.'

I remembered how her arms had felt around my waist, her chest pressed against my back as she leaned into me. I didn't think I'd imagined the look of regret on her own face when we got back to town and the ride was over. I suspected that it mirrored my own.

17

TAYLOR

I almost hadn't gone down to the pool. When I held on to Jack on the back of the bike, I had felt a mix of confused feelings that I put down to residual adrenaline from the rescue. A high-pressure, life-or-death kind of situation like that *had* to have some effect on you, so it was understandable that I had felt drawn to him when he showed up and saved the day. At least, that's how I justified it to myself. But hanging on to him, watching over his shoulder as he'd effortlessly ridden my motorbike back into town had been as sexy as hell. He was as sexy as hell, and I had felt far, *far* too comfortable touching a man I'd known for only a few days.

I'd been eighteen, literally, the day Adam and I first got together. He kissed me the night of my eighteenth birthday, and from that moment on, despite the avalanche it triggered, we were a couple. Before that, before *him*, there had been nothing but teenage crushes, stolen kisses and tentative hands fumbled underneath clothing at parties. He hadn't even been on my radar before that night, then suddenly he was my boyfriend. My fiancé. My husband. All within the space of a year. I thought I loved him, the way a teenager thinks first love will last forever, that no one has ever felt that way ever before, could ever feel that way again.

But it was a weird version of love that we had. One born out of guilt and regret. Because if we weren't together, then it had all been for nothing. He was the only person in the world who understood that. It was a silent understanding between us. We never spoke about it. Maybe we should have, I'd thought so many times since he'd left. Maybe we wouldn't have spent a decade hating ourselves, and resenting each other.

18

JACK

The community center was already bustling with people by the time I arrived, but I found a vacant aisle seat in a row near the back and settled in, checking my phone to make sure Hannah hadn't sent any messages of SOS out yet, and to switch the sound off. I had no idea what Celia Hamilton did to people whose phones went off during one of her meetings, and I had no desire to find out either. The woman had a reputation around town as a no-nonsense ball buster, and judging by the way she was with Taylor the other day, the reputation was warranted.

The hall was old and in dire need of renovation. Concrete walls, with small, high windows, one of which was missing a pane of glass. The curtains were navy and ripped in places. The whole place smelled like instant coffee and sweat, thanks to its daytime use as a dance class venue. Sunlight streamed inside and dappled the floor with warm, yellow light, and the breeze that wafted through the open doors was gentle and caressing, though not particularly refreshing. I felt beads of sweat already start to form in the center of my back.

At the far end of the room, a long table had been set up. Several of the town's art council members were already seated at the table, talking among themselves while they waited for their esteemed leader to arrive. Another table was set up along the side wall, with jugs of ice-cold water, a coffee urn, mugs and teabags and small jugs of milk.

'Is this seat taken?'

I smiled at the sound of her voice, relieved that she was still in town. She hadn't come down for a swim at all the last three nights, and if it wasn't for the fact her motorbike was still parked in the garage – I knew because I kept taking the long way off the property, just so I could check – I would have been sure she'd upped and left and gone back to the city without even saying goodbye.

'So, you *are* still here,' I said, moving my leg so she could scoot past to the empty seat.

She picked up the printed agenda that someone had laid out onto every seat and sat down. 'Were you worried I'd left?'

'A little,' I admitted. 'It's been really quiet at the pool at night.'

'Aw, you missed me,' she said.

'Weird, I know, considering how annoying you are.'

Her mouth dropped open, and I laughed at her outraged expression. 'I am *not* annoying,' she said.

'Where am I supposed to sit?' a voice demanded.

Taylor rolled her eyes. '*He*, on the other hand.'

'Hi, Ray,' I greeted him smoothly. 'You can take my seat if you like.'

'Good, thank you. I'm better off by the aisle in case I need to dash to the bathroom,' he said. 'Taylor, move along, will you.'

Taylor shifted along a seat, and I followed. Ray sank down

into the folding chair with an *oof*. He was wearing slippers, I noticed.

'You've never "dashed" anywhere in your life,' Taylor said, leaning forward to speak over me to Ray. 'And you've just been to the bathroom. Surely you can last an hour before you need to go again.'

'It's a figure of speech, you dingbat.'

'Hey, this dingbat drove you here, remember. A little gratitude would be nice.'

'I told her to stay in the car,' Ray told me. 'But she never listens.'

'It's too muggy to sit in the car,' she protested. 'Besides, I thought there might be snacks on offer. Don't they usually have snacks at these kinds of meetings?'

'Just beverages today, I'm afraid,' I told her.

She leaned forward, stretching to see the table for herself. 'That's disappointing.'

'Budget cuts, probably,' Ray said. 'Damn council keep increasing property taxes, but where does the money go? Eh?'

'You don't even pay rent, let alone property tax,' Taylor retorted.

I took the opportunity to study her surreptitiously. She was wearing blue denim shorts and a cute white top with straps that showed off her toned arms. Her hair was up today in a ponytail that revealed her long, slender neck. I stared at it for a moment too long, wondering how it would feel to kiss her there.

'What?' she said, lifting a hand to touch her chin. 'Have I got something on my face?' she asked.

'No.' I felt my cheeks redden at being caught. 'Sorry. I got... distracted. Why are you here?'

'Ray dragged me along,' she said. 'Apparently the food options at last year's festival were not to his liking, so he wanted to voice his displeasure and request more "Ray-friendly" food this year.'

'Ray-friendly food?'

'Yeah. He's not a fan of anything he deems to be "fancy".'

'He's a complicated man, isn't he?'

She sighed. 'You don't know the half of it.'

There was a hive of activity near the door and a murmur swept through the crowd, before Celia Hamilton swept into the room and up the aisle towards her seat at the top table.

'She always has to make an entrance,' Taylor whispered.

'Yeah, I've kind of noticed,' I whispered back, trying not to focus on the fact that our knees were touching. Her denim shorts showed off her long, slender, smooth legs. 'When she comes into the restaurant, she stops at every table to say hi to people, as if they're guests at a dinner party she's hosting.'

'That doesn't surprise me.'

'Will you two stop whispering,' Ray growled. 'As much as I can't stand the woman, I'd still quite like to hear what she's saying.'

Taylor rolled her eyes again, and I had to stifle laughter.

'Welcome to the final meeting for the twenty-first annual Pine Harbor Summer Arts Festival,' Celia announced. She looked sideways to one of the men sitting at the end of the table. 'Don't we have a microphone, Doug? I'm worried the people in the back rows won't be able to hear me.'

Taylor scoffed quietly. 'No chance. The people in the next *town* can probably hear her.'

'Shush,' Ray hissed at her, frowning.

'This isn't a library,' she told him. 'You don't have to shush me every time I speak.'

Doug pushed back his chair, scurrying off into the small side room where the sound system gear was kept beside brooms, extra toilet paper and props for the kids' dance classes. People murmured amongst themselves while we waited.

'Sorry, everyone.' Celia smiled tightly. 'This was all supposed to have been set up before we started. It's hard to get good help these days.' She tittered with laughter to show she was joking, but the smile didn't quite reach her eyes.

19

TAYLOR

I knew how much she hated looking foolish and, even though it was petty, I drew a small amount of satisfaction from that. I took the opportunity while we waited for Doug to look around the crowd. Anything to help me ignore the fact that Jack's elbow kept bumping into mine. He was wearing a faded blue T-shirt, and his arms were tanned and muscled, with a light crop of fine blond hair on his forearms. Every time our arms bumped, and I looked at them, I remembered how it had felt to have them around me, and how much I'd like to feel it again.

There were a lot of familiar faces. Some of my old teachers, who somehow looked exactly the same as they had fourteen years ago. Business owners. Friends of my mother's. The gray-haired old ducks who liked to sit in the park and feed the actual ducks. A flash of familiar auburn-colored hair caught my attention, and I craned forward, peering over the head of the man in front of me to get a better look. She turned to say something to the person beside her, and I caught a glimpse of her face. Megan Clark. She'd grown up a hell of a lot since I'd last seen her and apparently started using hair straighteners to get rid of the unruly curls I'd known and loved since we were seven years old, but it was unmistakably her. Seeing her brought both a pang of familiar warmth and a twist of guilt. She'd tried to keep in touch with me after Adam and I had left town, but I'd never replied.

Doug, looking suitably chastened, finished setting up the gear, plugging the box in and turning it all on, giving Celia a double thumbs up to indicate that they were all systems go.

'Testing, testing,' Celia spoke into the microphone, her lips far too close, and it squealed with feedback that reverberated around the room.

Ray winced. 'I felt that right in my bones,' he muttered.

I shushed him. He glared at me.

'Right, let's get straight down to business, seeing as we've already lost some time,' Celia said. 'As you are all aware, the Pine Harbor Summer Arts Festival will be held next week, from July 25th to 27th. A three-day festival, celebrating the fantastic range of creativity we have here in our wonderful little town.'

A murmur of patriotic pride rippled around the room.

'Now, I know that choosing a theme for the festival every year is something the community likes to be involved in, but I'm happy to say that you didn't have to worry about that this year, because the arts committee and I came up with a theme that we believe represents our town perfectly. I've had a few messages from disgruntled townsfolk that the decision was made without public consultation, but I think once you hear it, you'll understand.' She paused for dramatic effect. 'Ladies and gentlemen, I present to you our festival for this year, *Harbor and Harvest, The Heart of the Sea.*'

She waited, clearly expecting wild applause or proclamations of her brilliance, or at the very least *some* kind of reaction. What she got instead was a sort of puzzled silence. People exchanged glances. Shoulders shrugged. Throats were cleared.

A chair loudly scraped across the wooden floor, followed by a swift muffled apology.

'What'd she say?' Ray asked. 'I missed it.'

Jack repeated it to him.

'That's the stupidest name for a festival that I've ever heard,' Ray declared, loudly. Heads swiveled in our direction. Megan saw me, and her face lit up.

'Oh my God,' she mouthed. 'You're back!'

I gave her a nod and a small wave, conscious that the eyes of half the room, including Celia's, were on us.

'Do you have a better suggestion, Raymond?' Celia asked in a clipped voice.

'Anything's got to be better than that,' he replied. 'It sounds like that annoying song from that horribly long movie, the one the radio stations played all day long for months on end. You know the one I mean.'

Eyes narrowed as people struggled to connect the dots. I got there first.

'You mean the *Celine Dion* one? From the *Titanic* movie? "My Heart Will Go On".'

'That's the one,' he said. 'Nobody sing it. Bloody song gets stuck in your head, and you can't get rid of it for days.'

'Well, you're entitled to your opinion, of course,' Celia said. 'But I'm sure others might have a more refined view.'

'Sorry,' I said. 'But I agree with Ray. It kind of bites.'

Beside me, Jack snorted with laughter, then quickly turned it into a cough in an effort to cover it up.

If looks could kill, Celia would have murdered me right then and there. But I was sick of kowtowing to the woman. Sick of fourteen years of keeping my mouth shut and listening, just to keep her happy. I had 'trapped' her son. Dragged him away from his hometown and the bosom of his family. Failed to provide her with grandchildren. Didn't look the way a daughter-in-law of Celia Hamilton should look. My list of failings was long and detailed. But none of that mattered any more. I feel suddenly lighter, as if a weight had been lifted off me. There might be perks to my marriage breakup after all.

'That's a very juvenile response, Taylor.'

I shrugged. 'You asked for our opinion. And I thought the festival theme was always decided by the community.'

'Normally, yes,' she admitted. 'But, as I've already explained, I didn't think that was necessary this time.'

'You mean you wanted to control the narrative and do it yourself.'

She sighed. 'Wearisome, Taylor. Have you come along to this meeting just to be difficult? I know that my son broke your heart when he fell in love with someone else, but I'm not to blame, and this isn't a place for you to get your revenge.'

I sagged back against my seat, feeling as if she'd knocked all the air out of me, broadcasting my marriage breakdown so publicly.

She gave me a hard stare, almost as if she was daring me to keep going. I knew how vicious she could be though. I looked down at my feet.

'I think the young lady has a point,' said Luis Morales, owner of a local art gallery. 'The community should have been consulted.'

'Fine,' Celia snapped. 'I mean, our graphic designer has already made up posters, and I've run some adverts in nearby towns, but I suppose the theme can still be changed, if anyone has a better idea?'

She looked around the room, and people shifted in their seats underneath her gaze.

'I have an idea,' an old man in the front row put his hand up.

'I was sitting on the wharf the other day, watching the boats come in and out of the harbor, and I was thinking, how about something that showcases our seafood industry, and our rich maritime heritage. Perhaps something like *Shells and Sails.*'

Henry Newsom, the postman, nodded. 'That's not bad. Or, what about, *From Trap to Table.*' He looked around the room. 'Because of the lobster traps?'

Megan stood up from her seat. 'I was thinking,' she said. '*Tides and Treasures.* I find all sorts of cool things washed up on the beach that have come from God only knows where in the world. Journeying across the waves to our shores.'

'*Harbor Lights,*' someone suggested.

'*Paint the Harbor,*' suggested someone else.

'How about, *Catch of the Day,*' Tom Hoyes, owner of the Lobster Shack located on the wharf, said loudly. He had a booming voice, which he'd used for years to attract tourists as they disembarked from the ferries. The room fell silent as his suggestion was given due consideration.

'I like that,' Ray announced. 'It's not stupid, like her-up-there's idea.'

Jack laughed/coughed again.

Celia narrowed her eyes. 'If you would like to remain at this meeting, Raymond, please refrain from calling anybody's ideas "stupid".'

'It was only yours,' he clarified. 'But I'll do my best.'

'I agree with Ray,' said Bill McIntyre, Pine Harbor's dentist for the past forty-odd years. 'It's simple and relevant.'

Celia squeezed her eyes shut for a few moments, as if summoning inner strength and then smiled. 'Can I get a show of hands please, for who would like our summer arts festival theme to be *Harbor and Harvest, The Heart of the Sea.*'

Doug's hand shot up, followed by a handful of others around the room. Celia forced a smile.

'And who would like Tom's suggestion, *Catch of the Day*?'

Almost every other hand in the room went up, including both of mine.

'I guess *Catch of the Day* it is, then,' she said, crossing something off a clipboard on the table in front of her and scribbling down the new name. 'Personally, I think it sounds like something you see on a fish shop menu, but if it's what the town wants, then who am I to object.'

'And yet she still is,' Ray said.

'Right,' Celia consulted the clipboard. 'Moving swiftly on, as we have a lot to cover tonight, I'm delighted to announce we've received enough funding this year, thanks to a generous donation from our very own Pine Harbor bank – thank you, Tony – as well as many other, wonderful benefactors. I have a list of all individuals and businesses who have contributed, and I will make sure your kindness and generosity are acknowledged.'

Jack started clapping. I arched my eyebrows at him.

'What?' he said, as the rest of the room started clapping with him. 'It felt like one of those moments where you're supposed to applaud.'

'Yes, yes,' Celia tutted. 'Now, I'm not going to run through the full list of events we have planned, as that would take far too long, but a draft program is available if anyone would like to see it.' She held up a pile of paper briefly. 'But to give you a brief idea, the opening ceremony will take place on Friday, July 19th at 10.00 a.m. at the waterfront. Stallholders and food vendors will already be set up on the boardwalk, in Northspire Park and the surrounding side street loop. Over the three days there will be live music on the boardwalk and dock area, as well as live theatre performances and residents sharing their stories of life at sea and in this town. Megan and some of the high school students have been granted permission by the council to paint a mural on the side of the old Johnson building, so they will be doing that over the course of the festival.'

'What's the mural going to be of, exactly?' an older lady asked. 'That wall is right next to the town square. We don't want to be looking at an eyesore every time we drive past, and you know what young people consider to be "art".'

Megan stood up to answer her. 'We're keeping the design confidential at this stage, Betty. But don't worry, it's nothing too out there.'

'The committee have already sighted and approved a draft mockup of the design,' Celia agreed. 'And I can promise you that it will enhance main street, not detract from it.'

'I hope you're right,' Betty grumbled.

'She's a cheerful sort,' Ray said, and the hypocrisy was so great I couldn't even rustle up the words to respond to him.

'Moving on.' Celia consulted her clipboard. 'There will be the children's section again, with activities and crafts. A sunset picnic on the first night, starlight dance on the second and a closing toast on the dock at 5.00 p.m., Sunday. We'll have sunrise yoga, parades, competitions, hands-on workshops and, of course, food and drink tastings. Copies of the full program are available here but just bear in mind it's not a finalized version yet, as we're still waiting to hear back from a few artists and performers.'

She put the clipboard down and ran her eyes over the room. 'To summarize, it's all come together nicely, thanks to a huge amount of work behind the scenes by the committee. I have a proposed set-up map available for those of you who will be setting up art or food stalls, so please collect one before you leave tonight and if you have any questions or issues with your placement, flick me a message. Bear in mind, please, that I can't put all of you around the square in the high-foot-traffic area. I have tried to be fair and alternate with those of you who were in the side street loop last year.'

'Where were you placed last year?' I whispered to Jack as Celia carried on talking.

'No idea,' he whispered back. 'That was before my time at the restaurant, so this is all new to me.'

'Oh right. Are you nervous?'

'No.' He shook his head. 'My staff have done this festival before, so I will bow to their superior wisdom and let them take the lead.'

'Wait, they don't actually need you at all. That's what you're saying?'

'I'd like to think I can be of *some* help and maybe even bring something new to the table,' he said defensively.

'Right, but they could do it without you if they had to.'

'They could.'

I smiled smugly. 'Which makes you one of *those* managers.'

'What managers?'

'The ones who look good on paper and on LinkedIn and are paid the big bucks, but really, when it comes down to it, they're pretty much surplus to requirements.'

'Hey,' he protested. 'First of all, *big bucks* is a wild overstate-ment and factually incorrect. I'm not in this for the salary; I'm here to help a friend. I take a basic living wage and that's it.'

I shrugged. 'OK, that's admirable I suppose.'

'Thank you. It is. And second of all, according to you I don't just look good on paper...' He paused to grin at me. 'I look good in real life too.'

'Excuse me?'

'You said I was buff, remember?'

'I was in shock, remember?'

His grin turned into a pout. 'Wait, so that's the only reason you said it?' He leaned his head down closer to mine and when he spoke again, I felt his breath warm on my shoulder. 'You have no idea how many times I've replayed that conversation in my head over the last few days.'

I swallowed hard, on edge by how close he was. I could smell the fresh, clean smell of his hair. It reminded me of green apples. If I turned my cheek, our faces would probably touch.

'Seriously?'

'Of course. And now you're telling me you didn't actually mean it. I'm crushed.'

I turned my head, risking contact. Our faces were merely inches apart. One small lunge and my lips could be on his. His green eyes sparkled with mischief, telling me he was thinking the same thing.

'If you're trying to get me to say it again,' I said softly, lowering my eyes to his mouth suggestively, 'it's not going to work.'

His lips parted and for a moment I thought he was actually going to kiss me this time. But then the next second, I almost got whiplash from how quickly he pulled away, sitting up straight in his chair and throwing up his hand.

'Celia,' he called out, waving his hand around.

She stopped talking about insurance and frowned at him. 'Yes, Jack?'

'Taylor and I have just had *the* most brilliant idea for a stall that will tie in perfectly with the art theme, make us stand out from the other towns and their festivals, and, I think, draw in quite a crowd.'

'What are you doing?' I hissed.

'Give me a call tomorrow,' she said dismissively. 'We can discuss it then.'

He stood up. 'Why can't we discuss it now?'

'I feel like we've held people up enough tonight already,' she said, looking around the room for support.

'I'd like to hear what their idea is,' Megan said, turning in her seat to smile at me. I saw her eyes flicker over Jack, and she gave me a pointed look that clearly translated to *Ooh, he's hot!*

'Yes, let's hear this big idea,' Ray said, and there was a chorus of agreement from a few others.

Celia visibly sighed, her emerald green, satin ruched-blouse catching the light. 'Fine,' she said tightly. 'Go ahead, Jack.'

'OK. I was thinking...' He looked down at me. 'Sorry, *we*, that is Taylor and I, were thinking, how about a tattoo stall?'

Celia's nose crinkled up in distaste. 'Oh, no I don't think that's a good idea.'

I'd been about to hiss at Jack to shut up, but as soon as I knew that Celia was against it, everything changed.

Suddenly, I wanted nothing more than to have a stall at the festival. I needed to do it. *Had* to do it. She'd never bothered to make it a secret that my choice of career was not to her liking. In her opinion, it wasn't a career, rather a hobby, as she'd once said condescendingly. And a disgusting one at that. No matter how many awards I won, she was still too ashamed to tell people what I really did for a living. When I'd opened my own studio five years ago, she couldn't even bring herself to congratulate me. Made some snide comment about how I was lucky Adam made enough money for me to indulge myself. Never mind the fact that in the last three years of our marriage, I'd made more money than him and now employed four people. In fact, when he'd first left me and the affair had come to light, she'd told me that it was probably because I made him feel emasculated. I *had* to do it, if for no other reason than to annoy her.

'Why not?' Jack said. 'Think about it. We have, in our midst, one of this year's one-hundred-most-influential tattoo artists, according to *Under the Needle* magazine. A woman with over two hundred thousand followers on Instagram, and who *Inkspire* magazine named as one of their top-ten female artists who are changing the industry. Not to mention she's also appeared on the TV show, *NY Ink*.'

'Whoa, that is seriously impressive,' said Megan, whistling. 'Nice one, Taylor.'

I stopped gaping at Jack long enough to flash her a smile. How did he even know all that stuff? 'Thanks.'

'Yes, very impressive,' Celia agreed reluctantly. 'But I still don't think it's suitable for our festival.'

I stood up beside Jack, crossed my arms over my chest and stared at her defiantly. 'And why not?'

'Because it's an art festival.'

'Tattoos *are* art.'

'I suppose so,' she conceded. 'But not the kind of art that we typically showcase here though.'

'Then maybe it's time for a change.'

We stared at each other, both aware that this was about more than the festival and tattooing. This was bigger than that. This was about control, specifically *me* reasserting mine.

'I agree,' Megan chimed in. 'Tattoos are hugely popular right now. This could be a big drawcard for the festival. Really set us apart from the other towns.'

'Exactly,' Jack said.

Celia stared at him. 'Fine. I'll think about it.'

'You could do that,' I told her. 'Or... excuse me, gentlemen, can I just squeeze... thank you. How about we put it to the committee and the community,' I suggested, edging past Jack and Ray's knees and striding up the aisle. 'Let them decide. Or are you the only one who has any say around here?'

Her eyes narrowed. 'Of course not.'

'Good.' I reached the top table and turned to face the room. Seeing all the faces staring at me, a lot of them familiar, I nearly lost my nerve. Public speaking had never been my thing, but I'd come this far, so I took a deep breath, slapped on a smile and went for it.

'Hi, some of you might remember me, although maybe not. It's been a while,' I admitted. 'Fourteen years, in fact. I'm Taylor Calderwood.'

'Hamilton,' Celia corrected, without thinking. 'For now, anyway.'

I grimaced. 'Yes, legally. But not for much longer. I'm Moira's daughter, Moira Calderwood. I grew up on Bayside Drive. Raymond Owens...' I pointed at him '...is my great-uncle. A lot of you probably know him, whether you want to or not.'

'Get to the point,' Ray said.

'Yes, thank you for that, Ray. Uh, I think Jack's right, and a tattoo pop-up studio would be a great addition to the festival. I specialize in ocean and marine tattoos, which is obviously quite fitting for the town *and* for the festival theme.'

'Can you do them outside though?' someone asked. 'Don't you have to be in a shop?'

'I can do them anywhere,' I answered. 'I can have all the gear I would need sent here from my studio back in New York. We have portable machines. I could also offer tattoos to the kids,' I added, warming up to the idea and spitballing on the spot.

'Absolutely not,' Celia snapped.

'*Fake* tattoos,' I clarified. 'Stick-on, temporary ones. Kids love that sort of stuff.'

'That's true,' a blonde woman in the front said, nodding. 'My kids would definitely be up for something like that.'

'Mine too,' another woman agreed.

I gestured towards her, grateful for her support. 'There you go then.'

'I'm still not convinced this is a good idea,' said Celia.

'No one's expecting you to get one,' I snapped back at her. 'So I don't really see how it affects you.'

She drew her five-foot-two body up straight. 'This is my festival.' Then she remembered where she was. 'Our festival, I mean. Pine Harbor's.'

'Then I think it's only fitting that the people of Pine Harbor should decide.' I faced the crowd. 'Show of hands. Who thinks we should have a tattoo stall at the festival?'

Almost every hand in the room went up, except for Celia's, of course. And Doug's. And another lady on the committee whose name was Mary, according to the sticker stuck to her chest, but she looked about ninety-eight years old, so I wasn't sure if she'd even heard the question.

'Looks like the people have spoken,' I announced, unable to keep the grin off my face. 'I'll get onto my studio straight away, get them to courier over everything I need.'

If looks could kill, I'd have been dead. 'Fine. I guess we're having a tattoo stall.'

I searched for Jack's face in the crowd, and when I found it, he gave me a thumbs up, his face grinning as broadly as my own.

'So, Mr. L.A.,' I said to him, a few minutes later after the meeting had ended and we were joining the queue to file out of the hall. 'You've been looking me up, huh?'

'I might have typed your name into a search engine,' he admitted. 'Purely for research purposes.'

'Researching what, exactly?'

'I just like to know who my neighbors are.'

'Find out anything interesting?'

'Plenty. You've made quite the name for yourself in the tattoo world. You even have your own Wikipedia page.'

'I do?'

'Yeah. If that's not making it, I don't know what is.'

'Well, if you put me on the spot like that again,' I told him, 'And they'll be needing to add a criminal record section to it.'

'Duly noted.' He bumped into me with his hip. 'You should be thanking me, though.'

I gaped at him. 'For what, embarrassing me in public?'

'What have you got to be embarrassed about? I thought you handled yourself well with Celia. No, you should be thanking me because now, thanks to me, we get to hang out at the festival.'

'Who says I want to hang out with you?'

Ray poked me in the ribs with his bony finger.

'Ouch.' I rubbed the spot. 'What was that for?'

'Do you think you could stop flirting long enough to take me home? My hip hurts. I don't want to stand around all night watching you drool over this guy.'

Mortified, I glared at him. 'I am not *flirting*, or drooling.'

'As good as,' he replied. 'If you like him, just say so. Stop playing silly games.'

Jack grinned. 'Yeah, Taylor. If you like me, just say so.'

Ray swiveled his body so he could scowl at Jack. 'You can wipe that smug look off your face, because you're no better than she is,' he informed him. 'Staring at her with that soppy look on your face all night when you think she isn't watching. I saw you.

In my day, if a man fancied a woman, he asked her out on a date.'

'I don't... we're not...' I stammered.

'Yeah, we only just... I mean we don't even...' Jack added.

Ray sighed. 'Pathetic.'

20

JACK

I couldn't sleep that night, and it wasn't just because the summer heat was stifling. It was my thoughts that kept me tossing and turning, mulling over and over Ray's words. Was he right? I mean, what wasn't there to like about Taylor? She was funny, caring and kind, judging by the way she'd worried about Casey after her fall. Not to mention of course, that she was gorgeous and every time I was around her, I felt ridiculously nervous and jittery. It seemed to get worse the more I got to know her, and that could only mean one thing.

Ray was right.

I liked Taylor.

As in, *liked*.

It was a startling thing to admit to myself. After everything that had happened with Alex and Hannah and moving here to Pine Harbor, I had closed that part of my life off. Ignored it. Tried not to let myself think about love or romance. I made sure to keep myself busy so that I could ignore the occasional sense of loneliness that crept in, and the little pangs inside that reminded me there was a part of life that I was missing out on.

Not just love, but friendship. Companionship. Having that someone special to come home to. To confide in. I missed being someone's reason to smile.

But Taylor... what was the point? She was only here for a few weeks and then she'd be gone, back to her life in New York again. It didn't matter if seeing her made me feel goofy inside, or that for some bizarre, unknown reason, since I'd met her, she was the first person I thought of when I woke up, and the last person I thought about as I drifted off to sleep. It made no difference that she'd started invading my thoughts at inopportune moments, like the other day when I was in a staff meeting and mid-sentence I'd remembered that first night I met her and she was nothing but a silhouette in the dark against a starry sky, and I'd mused how special it was that we'd got to know each other by voice only. And then someone had coughed and reminded me that I was supposed to be talking about rosters and overtime and I couldn't believe my thoughts had just drifted off like that. It just wasn't like me *at all*.

I went for a morning jog along the beach to try and sweat out the angst. I hadn't felt angsty about a girl since I was seventeen years old and madly in love with Deborah Martin, a gorgeous, blonde cheerleader at my school. Unfortunately for me, she only dated jocks and had no idea I even existed. Hence the angst. The jog certainly made me sweat, but it did nothing to banish Taylor from my mind. I showered, and afterwards I stood there, with my towel wrapped around my waist, and stared at myself in the mirror.

'Ray's right,' I told myself. 'You *are* pathetic. Since when did you let someone get inside your head like this?' I pulled the lid off my deodorant and rolled it onto my armpits. 'You like someone, you ask them out. That's how it works. You've *never* been afraid to ask a woman out before. So what if she's only sticking around for a few weeks? It's not like you're planning on marrying her. Go out for a meal, enjoy yourself for a change.' I put the deodorant down and ran a hand along the stubble on my jaw, deciding it wasn't too bad and would be fine for another day. 'She'll either say yes, or she'll say no,' I pointed out the obvious. 'And if she *does* say no, nothing lost. Life goes back to the way it was and you can stop thinking about her all the damn time.'

Which was a very good point.

'Also...' I pulled a face as I reached to flick off the light switch. 'Since when did you become the kind of guy who talks to himself in the bathroom mirror?'

At the fork in the driveway I took a left instead of a right, parked my truck behind the garage where her motorcycle was, and headed on foot towards the main house. She opened the door thirty seconds after I knocked, wearing tiny denim shorts and a white tank top. In her hand was a slice of watermelon. I could see the juices running down her arm.

'Oh,' she said, wiping her mouth with the back of her hand. 'It's you.'

Which wasn't exactly the warm welcome I'd been hoping for.

'Go out with me,' I blurted.

Her eyebrows shot up. 'Excuse me?'

'On a date, I mean. Well not a date. We don't have to label it. We can just call it two friends going out for a meal.'

'A meal.'

I nodded. 'Yeah, you know that thing people do? Eating?'

'Are you asking me or telling me?'

'Asking of course.'

'Because it sounded more like an order.'

I replayed the last thirty seconds in my mind. 'Oh. It did kind of, didn't it?'

'Yeah. It did.'

'It wasn't supposed to. I guess I'm more nervous than I thought.'

'What are you nervous about?'

'It's been a while since I've done this,' I admitted. 'I'm a little rusty.'

'This?'

'Yeah, asked someone out.'

'For a meal, not a date.'

'Yeah. Well?'

She shrugged. 'I suppose I have to eat. And you'd probably be slightly better company than Ray.'

'Wow. Don't sound too enthusiastic.'

'I'm still mad at you.'

'Come on, seriously? I might have thrown you under the bus with Celia, and for that I am sorry, but I really do think your tattoo stall will be a hit at the festival.'

'Of course it'll be a hit,' she said, rolling her eyes. 'That's not the point.'

'What is?'

'You said it yourself, you threw me under the bus with Celia.'

'And you emerged unscathed and triumphant,' I pointed out.

'Mm.' She leaned against the doorframe and regarded me through narrowed eyes.

'The whole town was on your side, not hers. That had to have stung her.'

'Oh, undoubtedly. She'll be furious, with me *and* with you for suggesting it.'

I shrugged. 'I'm not scared of her. People like that are enjoying life for the wrong reasons, in my experience.'

'Meaning?'

'They thrive on power, on control, on keeping up the appearance of being important. More important than everyone else. It's trivial and pointless. In my opinion. At the end of the day, people don't really respect them. They concede to them, to keep the peace. Sometimes they even fear them. But it doesn't make them any *more* of a person than anyone else.'

'Interesting take.'

'Thanks. I've always been interested in the human psyche. Figuring out what makes people tick.'

She lifted her chin, her eyes a challenge. 'Figured me out yet?'

'I'm working on it,' I said gently.

The earnestness in my voice made her smile slip, just for a second. I watched as she swallowed.

'Well good luck with that,' she said. 'I'm still trying to figure it out myself.'

'What is with you and Celia, anyway?' I asked. She looked sad and vulnerable, and it made me want to step forward and wrap my arms around her like I had at the top of the cliff, but I didn't have the adrenaline excuse this time, and I wasn't sure if she'd welcome it. 'I mean, I understand the whole mother-in-law cliché, but is that all it is?'

'Let's just say, as far as she was concerned, I was never good enough for her precious son, and she made damn sure I never forgot that.'

I pulled a face. 'That can't have been an easy family dynamic to be a part of.'

'I wouldn't exactly call Celia *family*. She's never felt like that to me, and I'm pretty sure she feels the same way.'

'Well, it's good that she'll be out of your life soon. In that regard.'

She smiled again, and it was like the sun had come through the clouds. 'That day can't come quick enough.'

'So...' I stared at her hopefully. 'Dinner?'

'Why not. I think I can handle being in your presence for an entire meal.'

'I'm flattered.'

'You should be.'

'I'll pick you at eight?'

'Or I could just meet you there.'

'I want to do this properly. Humor me.'

'I thought it wasn't a date.'

'It's not.'

'Where are we going?'

'I happen to know this great place, good atmosphere, *really* good food. The manager's a really cool guy, or so I've heard. Buff, is the word I think I've heard someone call him.'

'You're never going to let me forget about that, are you?'

I grinned at her. 'Nope.'

21

TAYLOR

My bed was littered with a thousand rejected outfits. OK, maybe not a thousand. I hadn't bought that many clothes with me from New York, and I certainly hadn't brought anything I would consider date-worthy. If this was a date. What had Jack called it?

Two friends going out for a meal.

Is that what we were? Friends? I barely knew the guy, and yet, that wasn't how I felt when I was around him. Jack made me feel safe. I hadn't known until I met him that I even needed to feel that. After all, I was a strong, independent, self-made woman who didn't need a man. And I didn't *need* Jack either. But I liked how he made me feel. I liked the way he looked at me, the way he smiled at me, the way he made me laugh. I liked how it had felt when he'd held me. I *really* liked that. He gave me goose bumps, in the best possible way.

'I see nothing's changed,' Ray commented from the hallway, through my ajar bedroom door.

I frowned at his intrusion, tempted to kick the door shut in his face. 'What?'

'You're still as messy as you always were.'

'I am *not* messy.'

He stared at the clothes scattered across the bed pointedly.

'That's not mess, and I'm going to tidy it up later. Go away.'

'What are you trying on all your clothes for?'

'None of your business.'

He waited.

'Fine.' I sighed. 'If you must know, I have a date. Sort of. Not really a date, more of a meal between friends kind of situation.'

'Which friend are we talking about?'

'Does it matter?'

'Humor me.'

'Jack.'

'Ah.'

'Ah what?'

'Nothing. I'm glad he took my advice and asked you out.'

'He didn't ask me out just because you told him to.'

'Eh, believe what you want.'

'He didn't.'

He pulled a face.

'Oh God.' I sank to the bed. 'He did, didn't he? This is all your fault.'

'It's not *all* on me,' he said. 'I just gave him a subtle little nudge.'

'You don't do anything subtly, Ray. It's not in your nature.' I surveyed my pile of options. 'I guess it'll just have to be jeans and a top.'

'You mean the same thing that you wear every day,' he said. 'Like you're off to a casual funeral. That's typical of you, make no effort at all.'

I threw the black top I had picked up back down onto the bed and scowled at him. 'That's it, I'm canceling.'

'Why?'

'Because I have nothing to wear, and because I refuse to go out on a date with a guy that *you* set me up with.'

'I didn't set you up. Like I said, I just gave him a nudge in the right direction.'

'Whatever. It was a stupid idea.'

He took pity on me. 'Look, maybe there's something in your mother's wardrobe that you could borrow?'

'You're joking, right?'

'Have you ever heard me joke?'

'I don't think I've ever even seen you smile.'

'Exactly.'

'Mom and I don't share the same taste in clothes.'

'Obviously. Your mother always makes an effort to look nice, whereas you...'

'I'd think carefully before finishing that sentence, if you want me to make your dinner before I go out.'

'I'm starting to think frozen TV dinners would be a better option anyway.'

'You're so ungrateful.'

'And you're so predictable. One little obstacle or problem, and you take the easy way out.'

'No, I don't.'

He stared straight at me. 'Oh really? Isn't that why you married that Hamilton boy?'

I felt like he'd slapped me, my lungs sucking in air sharply. The old man was more astute than I gave him credit for. 'Get out,' I snapped.

'Gladly,' he retorted, lifting his walker and turning it. 'There's just no helping some people.'

'I never asked for your help,' I yelled after him.

I waited until he was gone, poking my head around the door-frame to make sure, then quietly went into my mother's room, sliding open her floor-to-ceiling wardrobe doors. The racks were crammed tight, and first impressions weren't good and confirmed my earlier suspicions. There was a lot of color, and a lot of patterns. Spots, stripes, florals, geometric shapes that made my eyes hurt. I flicked through the coat hangers, discounting them all.

'Nope, nope, nope, *hell no,* not a chance, disgusting, nope.'

I was just about to give up when I saw something wedged between two floral dresses. It wasn't black, but then nothing in my mother's wardrobe was. It was close though, a kind of dark navy, and shiny. Intrigued, I pulled it out and laid it down on the bed to examine it.

It wasn't something I'd normally ever wear, but maybe that was the point. Ray's earlier words were stuck in my head like an annoying little ear worm.

'Where on earth would she have worn this?' I muttered to myself, lifting it up again and holding it up against me so I could see how it looked in the full-length mirror.

It was a beautiful shade of dark navy blue, and shiny, like satin, but made from polyester. It had a strapless sweetheart neckline, with boning for support, and an asymmetrical hem, shorter at the front and longer at the back, with a split up one thigh. The hem was ruffled for romantic effect. It was a gorgeous dress, there was no denying that, but was I brave enough to wear it? It was completely over the top for The Cozy Catch restaurant in little old Pine Harbor, but I was still stewing over Ray's comments. I'd give him 'make no effort' and 'off to a casual funeral'.

When I opened the door to Jack almost bang on eight o'clock though, I realized I'd made a horrible mistake.

'Holy crap,' he said as he looked me up and down.

'That's exactly the reaction a woman wants when she opens the door.'

'It was a good "holy crap",' he reassured me, his eyes wide and appreciative. 'A *really* good "holy crap".'

The dress was snug and revealing, but in the sanctuary of my own bedroom and with a wine under my belt, I'd felt brave enough to pull it off. In front of Jack, reality came crashing back in, and I felt ridiculous, as though I may as well have been naked.

'That's it, I'm changing,' I said.

He dragged his eyes up my revealed thigh, over my bodice and up to my eyes, blinking. 'What? Why?'

'It's too much.'

He shook his head emphatically. 'No, definitely not.'

I tugged the bodice up higher, worried my breasts were about to make a break for it.

'Give me five minutes,' I told him.

His hand shot out and lightly gripped my wrist.

'Please don't change,' he said softly. 'You look beautiful.'

Warmth flooded through me at his touch, his words. I'd never been looked at the way he was looking at me. Never. It gave me confidence, like I was invincible. It didn't matter what anyone else thought; I only cared what *he* thought. And he was looking at me like I was everything. He looked pretty damn hot himself, in a light-blue shirt and black pants. His hair was styled and he smelled like cologne. A sexy, intriguing cologne that made me want to nibble his neck.

'OK,' I said, taking a step to the side. 'Come in. I'll just grab my jacket.'

Ray's eyebrows shot up when I walked into the lounge to where my jacket was draped over the back of the couch and picked it up.

'Shut up,' I said.

'I didn't say anything.'

'Good. Don't. Your dinner is on a plate in the oven keeping warm. Make sure you turn the oven off when you take it out. You can manage that, can't you?'

'I guess we'll find out.'

'Evening, Ray,' Jack said, hovering in the doorway.

'Jack.'

Jack nodded towards the TV. 'Watching the game?'

'No.'

'Oh.'

'Of course I'm watching the game. It's on, isn't it? That was a stupid question.'

'Ignore him,' I instructed Jack as I shrugged my black leather jacket on. 'I do.'

'Wait.' Ray shuffled his butt cheeks towards the front of his armchair and looked at us earnestly. 'What exactly are your intentions, Jack?'

'Sorry?'

'With Taylor. As her elderly male relative, it's my duty to look out for her, so what are your intentions?'

'Oh?' Jack looked at me. I stared back at him, knowing I *could* put him out of his misery, but enjoying the look of panic that had come over his face. It was my turn to see *him* put on the spot and find out how much *he* liked it.

'Ah. OK.' He shifted on the spot nervously. 'Um, I haven't really...' he said. 'I mean, I'm not sure what...'

Ray cackled with laughter. 'Your face,' he said.

Jack's eyes narrowed. 'You mean?'

'He's having you on,' I said. 'I'm surprised you fell for that, honestly.'

'Yes, I'm having you on,' Ray agreed, still barking out the

occasional wheeze of laughter, like an aging, emphysemic Labrador. 'I couldn't care less what your intentions are. Take her off our hands, please.'

'Love you too, Ray,' I called out over my shoulder sarcastically, as I pushed Jack towards the door. 'Don't wait up.'

'I wasn't going to.'

22

JACK

She looked incredible. Seriously. The dress clung to her in all
the right places, revealing her long, toned legs, arms and shoulders. Her hair was loose and side parted, old-Hollywood style. I
couldn't believe I was lucky enough to be the guy taking her out.
She seemed way out of my league. It was hard to keep my eyes
off her, and I couldn't help sneaking little sideways glances as we
drove in my truck to town. I didn't think she'd noticed.

'Can you please keep your eyes on the road,' she said, with a
smile tugging at her lips.

'Sorry. It's just, you look incredible.'

'You already said that.'

'No, I said you looked beautiful.'

'Same thing.'

'Oh, here we go with the synonym conversation again.'

'Eyes on the road.'

'I'm just saying, you look incredible. *Incredibly* incredible.
Magnificent. In fact, all the adjectives, all the good ones. That's
how you look.'

'You're very kind.'

'I'm not being kind, I'm just stating the truth. That dress is...'

'My mother's.'

I stared at her. 'You're kidding. It is?'

'Eyes on the road, please, and yes, it is. I found it in her wardrobe.'

'Whoa,' I mused. 'Go, Moira.'

She pulled a face. 'Can we not? I really don't want to imagine her wearing this.'

'I *can't* imagine her wearing it. It fits you like it was made for you.'

'You don't look so bad yourself,' she said.

'Thanks.' I was wearing a long-sleeved light-blue shirt. Top buttons undone, sleeves slightly rolled up, and a pair of black dress pants. I was glad I'd gone with the pants instead of jeans, considering how much effort she had gone to.

I parked outside the restaurant. She moved to open her door.

'Wait,' I said loudly. 'I want to do this properly.'

I hurried around to her side of my truck and opened her door with a flourish.

'I thought this wasn't a date,' she said, carefully dismounting, swinging her long legs around together and placing her heeled feet on the pavement.

'It's not,' I said. 'Just two people who happen to be dressed up nice, going out for a meal.'

Inside, I guided her towards the back corner of the restaurant with my hand in the small of her back, towards the table I'd called ahead and had Fiona set up just for us. She'd outdone herself, with flowers in a vase and fairy lights stuffed inside a jar to create a romantic ambience. Taylor's eyebrows arched when she saw it.

'Still not a date?' she asked.

'Still not a date,' I confirmed, pulling out her chair.

Fiona appeared beside the table. 'Good evening,' she said, grinning in an entirely unsubtle way. She was always on at me about my lack of a social life, so I knew she'd be loving this. 'I'm Fiona, and I'll be your waitress tonight. Can I get you both some drinks while you look over the menus?'

'Fiona,' I said, willing her with my eyes to calm the hell down. 'This is Taylor.'

Fiona's hand shot out in greeting. 'It's so nice to meet you. I've never met a friend of Jack's before. Well, apart from Hannah, but she doesn't count because she's a *friend* friend, you know, not a... whatever this is...' She trailed off when saw me cringe. 'I've just gone and put my foot in it, haven't I?'

'It's nice to meet you too.' Taylor smiled.

'I know I've said too much already,' Fiona continued. 'But can I just add, that dress is gorgeous on you. I've never seen anyone in this town look so glamorous.'

In one of those moments that the universe likes to create just for fun, right at that second a woman ventured past our table on her way to the bathroom. She was a wearing a tiny, butt-skimming denim skirt, a tight T-shirt that said MINNESOTA ROCKS and Ugg boots.

'Thanks,' Taylor said. 'But I think I might be a tad over-dressed.'

'Not at all,' Fiona protested. 'If anything, everyone else in this place is underdressed. At least you guys have made an effort for your date. That's more than most people in this town bother with.'

'It's not a date,' Taylor and I said at exactly the same time.

'Sure it's not.' Fiona smiled smugly.

I changed the subject. 'What do you feel like?' I asked Taylor. 'Wine or cocktails?'

'Oh definitely cocktails,' she replied emphatically.

'In that case, I'll have a Nor'easter, please,' I informed Fiona, passing her the menu.

'What's in that?' Taylor asked.

'Bourbon, maple syrup and ginger beer.'

She looked skeptical. 'Maple syrup?'

I nodded. 'The good stuff. Direct from Quebec.'

'Sounds sweet, but interesting. What the hell, I'll have the same, thanks, Fiona.'

'Coming right up.'

Taylor rested her elbows on the table and leaned forward. I tried really hard not to notice how her breasts swelled out of the top of her dress when she did so. 'Is this the point of the evening when we make small talk and get to know each other better?'

'You tell me. I'm a little rusty at this.'

Her eyebrows arched. 'Really? Someone like you? I would have thought you'd have dates lined up every Friday and Saturday night.'

I smirked. 'Someone like me?'

'Yeah.'

'Meaning?'

'You're not too horrible to look at, I suppose.'

I laughed. 'And also ridiculously buff, don't forget.'

She rolled her eyes. 'How could I forget when you remind me every three seconds?'

'Well excuse me for not wanting to let go of the best compliment anyone has paid me in years.'

'I find that hard to believe.'

'Why?'

'Don't make me say it.'

I focused on the little dimple on her cheek, beside her mouth. It curled into a cute little comma shape when she smiled. 'Don't make you say what?'

Her head tilted. 'Jack.'

'What?' I asked innocently, well aware that I was fishing for compliments. Usually, I couldn't care less what people thought of me. I was who I was, and you either liked me or you didn't. But with her, I cared. I cared a hell of a lot.

'You know you're good-looking, Jack. You don't need me to say it.'

'Maybe I *want* to hear you say it.'

'You're very needy.'

'Not normally,' I protested. 'It's all your fault.'

She looked outraged. 'How do you figure that?'

'I was doing just fine until you came along, now I'm...' I trailed off, unsure how to explain what I was feeling. That since I'd met her, I'd started thinking about things that I hadn't thought for quite a while. Things like the future, and sharing that with someone. Over the last few years, I hadn't thought more beyond taking each day at a time. It had been a self-preservation thing, I realized now.

Her eyes softened, as if she sensed my inner turmoil. She reached out a hand and touched my arm lightly. 'It's OK. You don't have to explain.'

'It's not that I don't want to.' I smiled ruefully. 'I just don't know how. It sounds crazy, but meeting you has been like an ice-cold bucket of water thrown over my life.'

She looked understandably confused. 'OK. That's not an effect I usually have on people. Well, not one that anyone has ever mentioned before anyway.'

'Told you I couldn't explain it very well.'

'Just tell me whether it's a good thing or a bad thing?'

'Good. Definitely good.'

'That's OK then.'

She smiled, so beautiful in the glow of the fairy lights that I couldn't stop staring at her. I knew then what I wanted to say. I wanted to tell her that I hadn't met anyone like her before. That ever since that first night in the tidal pool, she'd fascinated the hell out of me, with her motorbike and career choice and the way she was so smart-ass in her interactions with her uncle, but so incredibly kind and caring towards Casey. I loved the banter we had going on, the way she'd been so insecure when I'd picked her up for our non-date date, and yet so confident when she'd stood up at the meeting in front of half the town.

'I—'

'Jack?'

I turned my head to see Hannah hovering, her eyes uncertain as they flicked between Taylor, the flowers and fairy lights.

'Hey.' I smiled. 'Going for a walk?'

She held up a brown paper bag. 'Just picked up some takeout.' She stared at Taylor. 'It's Taylor, right?'

Taylor nodded. 'It is. Nice to see you again.'

'Are you two... is this a date?' Hannah asked.

'It's dinner,' I replied briskly.

'Just dinner?' She looked Taylor up and down. 'Dressed up like that, you look like you should be heading out to the opera, or a gala,' she said, smiling sweetly. 'Definitely somewhere a hell of a lot more glamorous than this place.'

'What, this old thing?' Taylor replied, smoothing down the fabric of her dress over her stomach. 'It's just something I threw on.'

'Was there something you wanted?' I asked curtly.

Hannah pouted. 'You wouldn't mind if I joined you, would you? It gets a bit lonely eating by myself upstairs.'

'I think Taylor and—'

She cut me off. 'I mean you said it wasn't a date, right? And I get so bored of my own conversation. Plus there's nothing new on Netflix.'

'Actually,' I said. 'We're—'

'Great!' Without waiting for me to finish again, she reached for an empty chair from a nearby table and placed it next to mine. 'Have you guys ordered yet?'

'Just drinks,' I replied, as Fiona arrived. She looked understandably confused when she realized that Hannah had joined us. She wasn't the only one. I tried to convey my apologies to Taylor with my eyes.

'They look good,' Hannah said, as Fiona placed the drinks down in front of us. 'I'll have one of those too, thanks, Fiona. Oh...' She picked up the brown paper bag and held it out. 'And can you give this to the chef and ask him to keep it warm until Jack and Taylor's food is ready too?'

'Oh. Uh...' Fiona gave me a questioning look.

'Hannah,' I said smoothly. 'If you don't mind, Taylor and I were actually just getting to know each other better.'

She frowned. 'I thought you said this wasn't a date.'

I nodded. 'I did say that, yes. But still, labels aside, we'd prefer to be alone.'

'Oh.' She blinked. 'Oh my God. I am *so* sorry. I've completely misread the situation, haven't I? I'm so stupid. *Of course* you guys don't want me gatecrashing this, whatever *this* is.' She pushed back her chair with a loud scrape. 'I'm normally much better at reading social cues, Taylor, I promise. I think it's just the loneliness, since Alex died. It's made me clingy, and I don't really have many friends left, apart from Jack. But still, I shouldn't be trying to latch on to you guys when you clearly don't want me here. I'm absolutely mortified.'

'Please don't be,' Taylor reassured her. 'You're not stupid at all.'

'That's nice of you to say, but I should have realized that I wasn't welcome.'

'That's not what I said, or meant,' I told her.

She blinked again and I could see that her eyes were glassy, as if she was trying to hold back tears.

'Forget you ever saw me,' she said, pushing in her chair, then forced a little laugh. 'Hell, forget I even exist. Enjoy your evening, and I'm sorry again.' She bumped into the table as she turned to go. 'I can't even *walk* like a normal person.'

Taylor and I exchanged a look, and I knew immediately what she was thinking. The problem was, she didn't know Hannah the way I did. How adept she was at manipulating feelings. Case in point, she was making us feel guilty when neither of us had done anything wrong. But I knew Hannah wasn't doing it to be malicious. She genuinely was lonely.

'Wait,' Taylor called out. 'You can join us.'

Hannah froze, turning slowly, wiping a non-existent tear from her cheek as she did. 'I don't want to intrude.'

Taylor smiled. 'You won't be.'

Hannah looked at me. 'Jack?'

Clearly, Taylor was kind to waifs and strays, even manipulative ones. I liked that. 'Of course you can join us.'

It was like the sun came out from behind the clouds, how quickly and drastically Hannah's expression changed once she had what she wanted. 'Well if you both insist.'

'So, what do you do, Taylor?' Hannah asked, once Fiona had bought her drink over to the table and taken her food to the kitchen to be kept warm.

'I'm an artist,' Taylor told her, and the way she leaned back in her chair told me she was anticipating a reaction from Hannah that she'd clearly come up against before.

'Really. And what sort of art do you do?'

'That's a bit like asking a chef if he only ever cooks one sort of dish. I dabble in a lot of different art forms, but my passion is painting. I do a lot of canvases. Paintings of the ocean and the creatures who dwell within.'

'How fun,' Hannah drawled. 'And you manage to make a living from it?'

I frowned at her intrusiveness. 'That's not really our business, Hannah.'

'It's fine,' Taylor said. 'I own an art gallery/studio back in New York. My paintings, while popular, do not solely pay the bills, no. So I also do tattooing. And that does.'

Hannah took a moment to process this. 'Wait, you mean you tattoo people? Like, as an actual job?'

'Yes.'

Hannah stared at her. 'How extraordinary.'

She said it as if Taylor had just told her she trained leprechauns for a living. I opened my mouth to change the subject but she wasn't finished with the interrogation yet.

'What does your husband do?'

'My *ex*-husband is a financial operations analyst.'

Hannah took a large mouthful of her drink and I felt myself stiffen. 'I'm guessing he makes a pretty good living.'

'He does. So do I.'

'I think that's enough of the questions,' I interjected.

Hannah shrugged, took another drink. 'I thought you said you and Taylor were getting to know each other. I'm just hastening it along.'

'I wasn't planning on asking Taylor about her finances,' I pointed out. 'That's nobody's business but hers.'

Hannah rolled her eyes. 'Relax, Jack. Taylor doesn't mind me asking questions, do you, Taylor?'

'Not at all. I have nothing to hide.'

'See?' She drained the last of her drink. I couldn't help but notice that Taylor's glass was still almost full, as was mine. 'It's how people get to know each other, Jack. Which you'd know if you ever actually went anywhere.' She rolled her eyes at Taylor as if they were co-conspirators. 'The number of times we tried to get this man to come to events with us but he much preferred to stay at home.'

'There's nothing wrong with being a homebody,' Taylor replied.

'Well of course, we *all* like curling up at home sometimes,' Hannah said, 'but there has to be a balance.' She rested her head against my shoulder and I stiffened. 'Remember how almost every Sunday you'd come over? You and Alex would watch a game, then fire up the grill and drink a few beers while you put the world to rights. And then after dinner the three of us would watch a movie, and most of the time you'd end up sleeping in our spare room instead of going home. Well, I say spare room. But really it was your room, Jack. It was only ever yours.'

'I remember.'

'I'm sorry about your husband,' Taylor said, and her sympathy was genuine.

Hannah picked up my drink and took a sip. Taylor's eyebrows arched.

'Thanks,' Hannah said. 'How much has Jack told you about it, exactly?'

'Nothing really. Just that he passed away.'

'He didn't tell you what happened?'

'No.'

'Good.'

'Hannah,' I admonished her gently.

'I'm sorry if that sounded harsh,' Hannah apologized, sounding unapologetic. 'It's just… it's our business, Jack. No one else's.'

'It's fine,' Taylor assured her. 'I completely understand.'

Hannah frowned at her. 'No, you don't. You haven't got a clue.'

'*Hannah*,' I growled, louder this time. 'That's enough.'

'I'm sorry,' she exclaimed. 'But you know how it is, Jack. All the empty platitudes that people say when you lose someone. They ask you how you are, and when you say, "Well actually, I'm not doing so great, because my whole world has just been ripped out from underneath me," and they look at you with that annoying, sympathetic head tilt, and they say something completely inane, like, "Oh, I can imagine how you must be feeling."' She looked up at me with eyes that reflected her grief. 'But they *can't* imagine it. No one can imagine how it feels until it happens to you.'

'I know,' I said patiently. 'But they mean well. *Taylor* meant well.'

'You're right. You always are.' There was an undercurrent of bitterness to her voice. Draining my glass and plonking it back on the table, she faced Taylor and took a deep breath, exhaling softly. 'I'm sorry, Taylor. It's just been a really hard time. Can you possibly forgive me?'

'Of course. No need to apologize.'

'I'm just grateful that I still have my Jack,' Hannah said, wrapping a hand around my bicep. 'I don't know where I'd be without him. Honestly, I shudder to think.'

'Lucky for you he's right here then,' Taylor agreed, her eyes meeting mine.

'Dependable old Jack,' Hannah gushed, still holding on to my arm. I couldn't shake her off without being rude, but I knew it was giving Taylor the wrong impression. 'And not just for the small things, either. I mean, he moved all the way across the country to help me run this place, and I didn't even ask him to. He could see I was completely out of my depth and he just swooped right in. My own knight in shining armor.'

'I just did what any friend would do.'

'Don't be modest.' Hannah smiled, her eyes soft but ever so slightly unfocused. I could see it because I knew to look for it. 'You've gone above and beyond for me, Jack. And I'll never forget it.'

Taylor's chair scraped loudly on the floor as she pushed it back. 'Excuse me, guys, but I need to visit the bathroom. And the bar. Time for another drink.'

'I can get Fiona to get one for you,' I told her.

'It's fine,' she replied lightly. 'I'm perfectly capable of taking care of myself.'

I watched her walk away, feeling frustrated at the turn the evening had taken. This wasn't how I had planned it to go at all.

'Was that a dig at me?' Hannah asked, her nose crinkling.

'What the hell are you doing?' I asked her tightly.

'What? You said it wasn't a date.'

'I know what I said, but that's complicated, and sort of an inside joke between me and Taylor. It was blindingly obvious to everyone here that this was a date.'

Hannah shrugged, her expression petulant. 'Then you shouldn't have invited me to join you.'

'You invited yourself.'

'And *she* said it was fine. What does that tell you?'

'That she's kind?'

'Or she's not interested.'

'We didn't have enough time together alone for her to form any opinion at all, because you gatecrashed our date.'

'Once again, you said it wasn't a date. You can't blame me for being confused, Jack, when you say one thing and mean another.'

'We both know it's not just my words that are confusing you, Hannah.'

Her eyes narrowed. 'What's that supposed to mean?'

I slid my empty glass across the table, next to hers. 'Two drinks in less than fifteen minutes.'

'I was thirsty.'

'Did you have any wines before you came downstairs?'

'I don't like what you're insinuating, Jack.'

I sighed. 'I'm not insinuating anything. I'm worried, OK? Look.' I took a deep breath and summoned the courage to say what I knew I needed to say. 'I've noticed more empty bottles in the recycling lately. I think you might be using alcohol to cope with your grief, Hannah. I think you might need some help.'

She glared at me, outraged. 'You've been *spying* on me? Going through my rubbish?'

'I'm not going through your rubbish. Your bins are right there next to the bar's. I've just noticed, that's all.'

She pushed to her feet. 'I can't believe this.'

'I'm trying to be your friend.'

'No,' she spat, her eyes angry. 'You're trying to get rid of me. Now that *she's* here.'

'Who, Taylor? This has nothing to do with her.'

'Don't be naïve. I know how this works. Three's a crowd. She's moving in and now suddenly you don't want me around any more.'

I stood up. 'That's not true. I'm always going to be here for you, and you know that.'

'I know why,' she agreed. 'We both do. Out of loyalty. That's the only reason you're still here. Well, guess what. I don't need you, Jack, if you're going to accuse me of drinking too much. I release you from your promise, OK? You're free to forget all about me and move on with Taylor or whoever you damn want.'

I watched her stalk away, heading for the stairs, and I let her go.

23

TAYLOR

I wasn't mad at *him*, I realized as I looked at my reflection in the bathroom mirror while I washed my hands. How could I be? All the evening had proven was how much of a great guy Jack was. And I couldn't really be mad at Hannah either, even though it was obvious that she felt as though she had some kind of claim over Jack. She couldn't be more obvious with her effusive gushing about how wonderful he was, how much she relied on him, and how he dropped everything and changed his whole life just to be there for her. But the woman was a widow, for crying out loud. I'd have to be a pretty crappy person to be mad at her after everything she'd been through.

So I wasn't mad at him, or her, exactly, but I sure as hell was mad at *something*. Myself, probably, for getting my hopes up. For making such an effort and looking so ridiculously overdressed for an evening that, it turned out, was a total bust. I'd thought Jack and I had a joke going about whether this was a date or not, but now I wasn't so sure. And for a woman fresh out of marriage who'd never really done the whole dating thing, it was all a bit too confusing.

Back at the bar, I joined the queue, humming along to the music while I waited.

'Can I get another Nor'easter, please?' I asked Fiona when it was my turn. The place was pretty busy, the restaurant side nearly packed out, and a fair number of people standing around the bar as well. There was music playing somewhere, and the hum of different conversations. Laughter. The night was warm and the atmosphere pleasant, but I couldn't shake the feeling of being alone and out of my depth.

She smiled. 'Sure thing. How's the non-date date going? It's nice to see Jack looking so happy.'

'We're just friends.'

Her eyebrows shot up. 'I've never dressed like *that* for a dinner with a friend before.'

'I'm from New York. This is basically the city equivalent of wearing sweatpants.'

'Mm, sure.' She smiled knowingly.

'Taylor?'

I swiveled my head. Dion was standing just behind me, eyes wide, his expression as he looked me up and down comically over the top, and very flattering. He didn't look too bad himself, in a pair of blue jeans and with a black shirt, his beard freshly groomed and hair damp. Clearly, he'd not long ago showered.

'Hey, Dion.'

'Damn,' he growled, his tone appreciative. 'You look *incredible.*'

'Thanks.'

His eyes searched over my shoulder. 'Are you here on your own?'

'No, I came with Jack.'

He didn't even bother to hide his disappointment, rubbing the back of his neck with one hand. 'Ah. Right.'

'Not like that,' I added, even though I wasn't sure any more what *that* was.

He brightened. 'Really? So I can buy you a drink without stepping on anyone's toes?'

'I can buy my own drink,' I informed him. 'And you shouldn't talk about women like that. We don't belong to anyone, so the whole stepping on someone's toes by moving in on their turf thing, is just distasteful.'

He looked thoughtful as he processed my words, then nodded. 'Noted. And I apologize. I didn't mean to offend you.'

I smiled. 'I know. That's why I haven't walked away yet.'

He grinned, back to his cocksureness. 'Well, can I sit beside you while you drink the drink that you bought yourself? Is that allowed?'

I flicked a look back at the table. Hannah was still there; she and Jack had their heads together and looked deep in earnest conversation.

'You know what?' I said, facing Dion again. 'Sure. You can join us.'

'Us?'

'Yeah, Me, Jack and Hannah.' I gestured with a nod of my head. 'We've already ordered, but if you're hungry I'm sure the kitchen can add to the order, right, Fiona?'

'I think we can manage that.' Her expression was unreadable. I knew what she was thinking. But as far as I was concerned, if it was OK for Hannah join us, surely Jack wouldn't have a problem if Dion joined us too? It would at least give me someone to talk to while Hannah tripped down memory lane with Jack. But as we made our way back to the table, we heard raised voices, before Hannah suddenly stormed off. It was too late to take back the invitation then though.

'Dion,' Jack said, his tone clipped. 'What are you doing here?'

'He's joining us,' I said, answering for him as I took my seat again, and Dion dragged an extra chair over, slotting it beside mine. 'Is that OK?'

Jack's eyes scrutinized mine, as if trying to figure out what game I was playing. But I wasn't playing a game, I just wasn't happy to sit there and be the third wheel while he and Hannah reminisced about the past.

'Of course,' he said. 'Although, we've already ordered, so...'

'Not a problem,' Dion said cheerfully. 'Fiona added my order onto yours at the bar. It might be a little delayed, but I'm all good with that. It'll give Taylor more time to school me on my toxic, masculine ways.'

I laughed, as Jack looked understandably confused. 'Are you here on your own, Dion?' he asked abruptly. 'You're not meeting someone?'

'Nah. I was planning on heading out to my sister's for dinner, but decided to pop in here first for a drink.'

'Shouldn't you get going then, if Kate's expecting you?'

Dion smiled at me. 'I already messaged her and told her I got a better offer.'

'You didn't tell me you had plans already with your sister,' I scolded him. 'You should have said you were busy. I feel bad for stealing you away now.'

He shrugged. 'Well don't. She invites me to dinner at least three times a week.' He held up his hands. 'I have magic hands, see. My niece, River, and nephew, Bodhi, are a handful. My brother-in-law is in real estate and works nights a lot. She likes it when I'm there because the kids don't argue as much when I put them to bed, like they do with her.'

He leaned closer, his lips near my ear. 'My secret is to tickle them. The giggling wears them out and then they crash asleep quicker. Are you ticklish, Taylor?'

'You'll never know.'

His eyes sparkled with mischief. 'I like a challenge.'

I felt the weight of Jack's glare as Fiona approached our table with plates of food balanced delicately on her arms.

'Scallops with angel hair pasta for you, Taylor,' she said placing it down in front of me. It looked, and smelled, incredible.

She looked quizzically at Jack. 'Where's Hannah? I have her warm lamb salad.'

'Upstairs.'

'Is she coming back?'

'Your guess is as good as mine.'

Dion dipped a fry into his aioli, oblivious to the tension. 'If she doesn't want her meal, I'll have it.'

Jack sat back down, his eyes boring into mine.

24

JACK

I kept trying to catch her eye, to express how sorry I was at the direction the evening had taken, but she barely looked at me. Instead she focused most of her attention on Dion. How could she not, when he seemed determined to monopolize her. I couldn't blame him. Hannah's meal sat untouched.

'Dessert?' he asked, as Fiona cleared the empty dinner plates from the table. 'I'm not sure about you guys, but I always feel like a meal isn't complete without a little sweet to finish it off.'

'Actually, you know what,' Taylor replied, 'I think I'm just going to call it a night.'

'OK. Let me just sort out the bill and I'll run you home,' I told her, pushing my chair away from the table.

'No need,' she replied. 'I already paid for my meal when I was at the bar, and Dion has offered to take me.'

I frowned. 'He has?'

'I have,' Dion confirmed, answering for her. 'I'll be heading out that way anyway. Better check in on Kate and the kids, make sure they haven't driven her completely around the bend.'

I ignored him and stared at her, confused. 'I don't understand.'

She shrugged. 'You should probably check on Hannah. Take her meal up to her.'

I stared at Dion. 'Would you mind if I had a quick word with Taylor? A private one?'

'Sure.' He wiped his mouth on his napkin and stood up, smiling down at her. 'I'll wait for you over by the bar. No rush.'

'Thanks.' She smiled at him.

'I'm sorry,' I said softly, when he was out of earshot. 'I really am. I had no idea she would be here.'

'She *lives* here, Jack. The odds were pretty high.'

'You're right.' I rubbed my free hand through my hair, feeling sheepish. 'I should have taken you somewhere else. I guess I just wanted to show this place off to you.'

She smiled. 'I can understand why. The food is great, your staff are friendly and welcoming, and there's an amazing vibe, seriously.' She looked around the room. Every table was full, every seat at the bar taken. 'The place is packed out, so you're obviously doing something right.'

I felt my chest swell with pride at her praise. 'Can I take you home, please? I brought you here, I'd like to see the evening through. It's important to me.'

She lifted her chin, her eyes vulnerable. 'Jack, I like you, I do, but I'm not interested in complications.'

'What complications?'

She gave me a look. 'I think you know.'

'If you're referring to Hannah, there's nothing going on there.'

'It's none of my business if there is.'

'But there's not.'

'Jack, you don't owe me an explanation. Whatever is or isn't going on, it's clearly complicated, and I've just come out of something complicated. I'm not looking to jump right back in.'

'I don't understand where all this is coming from.'

She stared up at me, exasperated. 'I have eyes, Jack.'

'I know you do. Very pretty eyes.'

'You might think there's nothing going on,' she told me. 'But Hannah clearly wants more. Trust me, a woman knows these things.'

It was my turn to sound exasperated. 'Don't I get a say?'

'Of course. But that's for you guys to work out. I like you, but I'm only here for another couple of weeks anyway. We should quit while we're ahead.'

I stared down at her, disheartened at the turn the evening had taken. I hadn't picked her up earlier that evening with any expectations, but still, subconsciously I'd expected more than this.

'I like you too,' I told her. 'More than I should, for someone I really haven't known all that long. I can't say I understand it, but I don't have any reason to question it either. I'm a big believer in trusting my gut, and my gut is telling me you're someone special. I can't seem to stop thinking about you.'

She was torn. I could see it on her face, in the way her eyes flickered with uncertainty, and her lips trembled, almost imperceptible unless you were watching her as intently as I was.

'Jack?' Fiona interrupted. 'Sorry to interrupt, but what do you want me to do with Hannah's meal?'

'You should take it up to her,' Taylor encouraged. 'Check in on your friend.' She put a hand on my chest before withdrawing it quickly, as if it had been burned. 'It's fine, honestly.'

Then she turned and walked away from me. I watched her

weave her way through the crowd to where Dion was waiting for her. He grinned as she approached, looking like a man whose Christmases had all come at once, and pushed off the bar, holding his arm out for her to crook her hand through. She did, and I felt jealousy swell in my stomach.

25

TAYLOR

From my vantage point on the cabin porch, I watched him climb the steps, trying to judge his mood by his demeanor. Was he angry? Upset? Relieved? It was hard to tell.

'How was Hannah?' I asked when he reached the top.

He clutched a hand to his chest. 'Jesus, Taylor. What is it with you and waiting for me in the dark?'

'The first time, I wasn't waiting for you. I was having a swim and minding my own business.'

'And tonight?'

'Tonight, I was waiting for you,' I conceded.

'Why?'

'I'm not sure,' I admitted.

He walked over and sat down on the other dark green cape cod chair next to mine, stretched his long legs out in front of him.

'Where's Dion?' he asked, fighting, and failing, to keep the tinge of jealousy out of his voice.

'At his sister's, I'm assuming. That's where he was heading after he dropped me off.'

He cleared his throat. 'That's all he did? Drop you off?'

'If you're asking whether he tried to kiss me, the answer is no. He did not. He was a perfect gentleman.'

'Oh.' His relief was evident.

'But for the record, if he *had* tried, I'd have said no.'

'I wouldn't blame you if you fancied him. Half the single women in Pine Harbor seem to.'

'I can see why. He's pretty hot. Got that sexy lumberjack look going on.'

'Is this you trying to make me feel better?'

'Plus, he seems like a really decent guy.'

'He is.'

'How's Hannah?'

'Remorseful. She said to tell you she's sorry for hijacking our night. Admitted she was jealous. I've set her straight, again, about my feelings.'

'Which are?'

'Purely platonic.'

'Are you sure?'

'One hundred percent.'

'You guys have a lot of history.'

'We do.'

'You told me she kissed you.'

'She did. Once. But she knows it can't happen again.'

'That's not how it comes across when she's around you. She's very... territorial.'

'I know.'

'And you're very protective of her.'

He took a deep breath in and exhaled slowly. 'I am.'

I stood up. 'I'm going to head home. I just wanted to check in on you.'

He reached out a hand and lightly clasped my wrist. 'Do you have to go?'

My breath caught in my throat when he touched me. 'I think it's for the best. You guys need to figure out whatever's going on between you two, before you start dragging other people into it.'

'I don't remember dragging you anywhere.'

'You know what I mean.'

'Don't go.'

'Goodnight, Jack.'

'Alex was my partner,' he blurted. 'In the police force.'

I froze, letting the words sink in. 'You're a cop?'

He nodded. His face was pained, as if even uttering the words dredged up horrible memories for him. 'I was. Feels like a lifetime ago now.'

'You don't have to tell me if you don't want to.'

'I want to.' He patted the seat beside him. 'Please? I always knew I wanted to be a cop,' he said, when I was seated beside him again. 'I joined the police academy as soon as I turned twenty, and that's where I met Alex. We hit it off straight away. I never had a brother, but he felt like one. Same world views, same sense of humor. We very rarely argued, and if we did it was over stupid stuff, like what we were going to eat for lunch while on shift. We met Hannah and some of her friends at a bar one night. Her friend's drink had been spiked; we were sent to make inquiries.' He sighed heavily. 'We both liked Hannah at first, but Alex was the one who caught her attention. I didn't blame her. He was larger than life, like a blond Viking. Muscles for Africa. The kind of smile that made woman fall all over him. Seriously, he was stupidly good-looking.'

'Have you looked in a mirror lately?'

He flashed me a smile. 'Thanks. But next to him, I may as well have been Gomez Addams.'

I snorted. 'I doubt that.'

'It's true. But I couldn't even resent him for it because he was just as nice a guy on the inside. Kind, funny, empathetic. He cared about people, I mean *really* cared. That's why he made such a good cop. He saw the person behind the crime. Didn't just automatically write people off. He tried to help them.'

'Sounds like a nice guy. I can understand why you two were such close friends.'

'He fell for Hannah, big time, and of course, she fell madly in love with him. They were perfect for each other, and I was genuinely happy for them. They had a whirlwind romance, moved in together after only a few months. Bought their first house a year later. They were happy. *Really* happy. I thought maybe it would change our friendship, but it didn't. They never once treated me like I was a third wheel, even though I felt like I was, and I was grateful for that. I mean, I ate dinner at their place more than I did at my own, and that's not an exaggeration. They were like family to me.'

'What happened to him?' I asked gently, after he'd been silently lost in his memories for a minute or two.

'He was killed on duty. We were on a night shift together and dispatch sent us to check out reports of a burglar breaking into a commercial building. When we got there, he went one way around the building, and I went the other way. I never even heard him scream, just came around a corner and saw him on the ground being stabbed, over and over and over. I can still hear the sound.'

He buried his face in his hands, his voice breaking. Seeing and hearing him in so much pain, my heart broke for him.

'The perp must have surprised him,' he continued. 'Because he didn't even have time to draw his gun. He never had the chance to defend himself.'

'I'm so sorry,' I said, even though it sounded incredibly inadequate.

'I yelled out, ran towards them, but, the guy, he didn't turn and bolt like I expected him to. Instead he started running towards me, holding the knife above his head. I had seconds, if that, to react, although it felt like an eternity. Like everything was moving in slow motion. I've replayed it, so many times in my head. And the only thing I really see is the knife blade glinting in the light, Alex's blood all over it, and his eyes. They were… vacant, that's the only word I can think of to explain it. It was like he wasn't even home in his own body. He wasn't looking at us like we were people. I don't what he was seeing, but there was no emotion in his eyes. Nothing. Just a blank stare.'

'What did you do?'

'The only thing I could. I shot him.'

My hands flew to my mouth. 'Oh my God. Jack. I can't even… That must have…' I had no words.

'His name was Kane Brown and we found out later he was heavily under the influence of drugs. Extensive criminal record, mainly for burglary. Nothing violent, until that night.'

'Did he…?'

'Die? No. I got him in the shoulder and the calf. It was enough to incapacitate him so that I could get to Alex and call for help.'

I tentatively reached out and put a hand on his shoulder, giving it a gentle squeeze. I wanted to let him know that I was there for him. He had my support.

'He died in my arms,' he said. 'My best friend died in my arms, and there was nothing I could do about it. I tried to stem the bleeding but he was too badly injured. His wounds were…' He shook his head, unable to finish the sentence. 'I can't unsee them. I wish I could.'

'Oh, Jack.'

'His dying words were about Hannah. How much he loved her. He told me to tell her he was sorry, and then he asked me to promise I would look after her. It was the least I could do. I owed it to him.'

Suddenly, it all made sense. Their connection. His protectiveness over her. Her need to keep him close. There was only one thing I couldn't understand.

'What do you mean, you owed it to him?'

He looked up at me with eyes swimming with pain. 'Because it should have been me.'

'What?'

'*I* should have gone that way around the building. I had less to lose. He had Hannah, a whole future ahead of him. It should have been me who died.'

'How can you say that?'

'Because it's how I felt, for a long time.'

I stared at him. 'Do you think Alex would agree with you?'

He shook his head. 'No.'

'Exactly,' I reassured him. 'There's only one person to blame, and that's the guy with the knife.'

'I know. I blamed myself at first, but that wasn't fair. I've accepted what happened. That nothing I could have done would have changed the outcome.'

'Thank you, for telling me. I'm sorry if I pushed you into it.'

He shook his head again. 'You didn't. I wanted to tell you. I need you to understand that I look out for Hannah as a way to honor my friend. To do this last favor for him.'

'I do understand.'

'And I really am sorry.'

'For what?'

'Stuffing tonight up so spectacularly.'

'It was a bit of a disaster,' I agreed. 'As far as non-date dates go.'

'For the record, I wanted it to be a date.'

'Then why didn't you just say so?'

'I didn't want to scare you off.'

'Do I seem like the kind of woman who scares easily?'

'No,' he admitted. 'You don't.'

I took pity on him. 'I'm not completely blameless either.'

'You're not?'

I shook my head. 'I wanted it to be a date too, although I told myself I didn't.'

'Why would you do that?'

I sighed loudly. 'Good question. And one I was trying to figure out the answer for the whole time I was sitting here waiting for you.'

'And? Did you figure out the answer?'

'No, not yet.'

'We're as hopeless as each other, then.'

'Seems that way.'

'Where to from here?'

'I don't know,' I admitted. 'You're a complication that I didn't plan for.'

'I've been called worse.'

I laughed, because if I didn't, it felt like I might cry instead. 'I'm only here for a few weeks.'

'You keep saying that.'

'Because it's true,' I insisted. 'Pine Harbor is not my future.'

'Why do you hate it here so much?'

'I don't hate it. It's more of a love-hate relationship. This place holds a lot of bittersweet memories for me.'

'Are you talking about your dad?'

'Amongst other things.'

'I can understand that,' he nods. 'L.A. was like that for me, after Alex died.'

'Exactly. So, what's the point in even liking you when there's no future in it?'

'You like me?'

'You know I do.'

'For the record, I like you too. Although *like* seems inadequate.'

My eyebrows arched. 'You're not going to tell me you believe in love at first sight, are you?'

'I take it you don't?'

'I don't.'

'Seems cynical.'

'It's not cynicism, it's realism,' I argued. 'Do I believe in attraction at first sight? Sure.'

'Lust.'

'No, not necessarily. I mean, are there people you meet that you immediately fantasize about jumping into bed with? Sure. But it's not always about sex. Sometimes it's more of an innate feeling. A sense of, "Oh, there you are." Like you've been waiting for them without knowing. But you can't love someone when you don't know the first thing about them.'

He stared at me, and when he stared at me like that, I felt like I could melt into a puddle at his feet. 'What?'

'Nothing. It's just… I've never met anyone like you.'

I couldn't help it, I groaned quietly. 'You're not going to say I'm different to any woman you've ever met, are you?'

'No.' He shook his head. 'I'm not going to say that you're unlike any woman I've ever met, or that you're different. Because that's obvious. Every person on this planet is different. Unique. Special. I've met many amazing women. Beautiful women. Intelligent. All equally special. The quiet, bookworm, introverted women; the soft, girly and feminine women; the tomboys; the athletes; the extroverts; the party women; the career women; and the domestic goddesses... I mean, I could go on and on because every single woman is unique and it's all beautiful. *They're* all beautiful.' He leaned forward earnestly, and I wanted him to touch me. Ached for it. 'So, no, you're not different to anyone I've ever met before, Taylor. I've met gorgeous, rebellious, witty women before. But I've never met *you*.'

I swallowed hard. 'Oh,' I said. Because I didn't know what else to say.

'It's *you* who makes my heart skip a beat when you smile at me,' he said. 'And it's you who makes me want things I haven't wanted before, or ever.'

'Don't.'

'What?'

'Want what I can't give.'

He reached out then, gently taking my chin in between his thumb and fingers. 'You said it yourself,' he said softly. 'We don't control how we feel. And frankly, I'm sick of fighting it.'

Then he kissed me.

26

JACK

She seemed stunned, for a second, and I worried that I'd done the wrong thing. That she *didn't* want this as much as I did, even though I was sure her eyes had been telling me she did. But then she kissed me back and any worries I'd had disappeared. We kissed gently, at first. Soft. Our lips exploring each other's, our noses mildly clashing as we figured out which way the other was going, her teeth sharp against my tongue. Then she moaned, and I felt the vibration of it pass from her mouth to my own, and that was it. My hands were in her beautiful long hair, cupping fistfuls, tenderly pulling her towards me as I probed her mouth with mine, feeling her welcome it, feeling her lean into it just as much as I was.

'Wait,' she said, her voice husky as she pulled away.

'What's wrong?'

'This chair, it's digging into my hip.'

Instantly I was concerned, every protective instinct I had on high alert. 'Are you OK?'

'I'm fine, Jack. I'm not made of china. I just thought maybe we should...' She looked up at me from underneath her long eyelashes, her pupils huge and reflecting the moonlight. She gestured with her head towards the cabin.

I felt my whole chest tighten. 'Are you sure?'

She nodded.

I stood, holding out my hand, and when she put hers in mine I felt like my chest would actually burst from the feeling.

'You don't lock the door?' she asked when I pulled open the screen and then turned the handle to go inside.

'Maybe I've been hoping you'd sneak in one night.'

'I did think about it,' she said. 'The other day, when I was in the shower.'

At the thought of her in the shower I let out a low guttural groan, spinning her until her back was against the wall and I could lean my whole body against hers. Feel her softness yield to my hard, her hands reaching behind my back as she tugged my shirt upwards, her skin against my back, her fingernails lightly digging in as I kissed her with everything I had. With one hand I held her jaw, tilting her face to mine as our mouths opened for each other, tongues meeting, exploring. None of it was enough. It would never be enough. My other hand found her thigh through the slit of her dress. Her skin was smooth and warm, as I ran my fingers up her leg, around to the front, feeling her strain against me.

She moaned again, her hands diving for my belt buckle, tugging at it, sliding it out of my pants and holding it up briefly, triumphantly, like a trophy, before tossing it to the floor. I broke off the kiss and leaned back just far enough to be able to stare into her eyes, where I could see my desire mirrored back at me.

'Are you sure you want to do this?' I asked.

She buried a hand in my hair, pulling my face towards her again.

'You ask too many questions,' she murmured, her head dipped as she planted soft kisses on my neck.

'That has been mentioned once or twice.'

'Then stop talking,' she scolded, nibbling the spot where my neck turned into my shoulder.

I shuddered, and the vibrations rippled through my body. She tightened her thighs around my hand, rubbing against it, and I could feel how ready she was. I was painfully ready myself, straining against the fabric of my clothes.

'You're so beautiful,' I told her. 'God, I want you so much right now.'

'No one's ever said that to me before.'

I drew back in shock, stared down at her in disbelief, with her tousled hair, lips swollen and dark from our kissing, her eyes wide and vulnerable. It seemed incomprehensible to me, what she'd said.

'How is that possible? Your husband... surely?'

She shook her head. 'No.'

'Then he was an idiot.'

'No, that's not fair. It wasn't his fault that it wasn't like this. Or mine.' She swallowed hard. 'He was my first, and the only guy I've been with. We were so young when we got together. Teenagers, playing at being grown-ups. We didn't know any different.'

'I'm so glad he cheated on you,' I said without thinking, and felt her withdraw from me, confused. 'I'm sorry,' I added quickly. 'That sounded awful. I just meant, if he hadn't, we wouldn't be here.'

She relaxed again. 'You're right. *I'm* glad he did too.'

I kissed her, gentler this time, until the intensity built up again, like a glass filling with water, the need, the *desire*, rose inside us both until we were at tipping point, teetering on the edge, the point of no return. I cupped her buttocks with my hands and lifted her. She startled for a second, then submitted to it, wrapping her legs around my waist, and when she did that the cup overflowed, and after that everything was a bit of a blur. I carried her to the bed, collapsing down on top of her because neither of us were willing to let go. She unzipped my trousers, then arched her hips while I pulled off her underwear, feeling my breath catch in my throat when I caught sight of her. She wriggled beneath me, somehow pulling her dress off over her head, revealing her breasts, almost tipping me over the edge again with their perfection. She clutched my head as I buried my face in them, licking, kissing, sucking until she moaned and said she couldn't take it any more, swore she'd die if she didn't feel me inside her right then. It was dramatic, but I felt the same. Couldn't take another second without her. I wanted to savor the moment, but my body betrayed me.

It was everything I thought it would be, and more. We moved together like we were made to do so, in sync, her back arched, hips tilted, her legs around my waist, pulling me in deeper, always deeper. I came with her eyes staring into mine. I never thought I could feel a connection like that with anyone.

27

TAYLOR

The first time was impatient, rushed, urgent. Desperate. I had never wanted Adam, *craved* Adam as much as I did Jack. I needed him with an intensity I'd never felt before. Hadn't realized it was even possible to need someone that much. It got to the point of being unbearable, and I told him I would die if I didn't have him inside me at that moment. It was a ridiculous thing to say, but in that moment, I believed it. I had to have him. And when he entered me, I understood why.

It was as if we were two pieces of the same puzzle. There was no awkwardness, or clumsy, fumbled moments as we figured things out. Only the seamless sense of two pieces coming together.

Afterwards, we lay side by side, facing each other as we tried to catch our breath, staring at each other in wonderment.

'I'm sorry,' he said. 'I couldn't hold out any longer.'

'I didn't want you to.'

'That was incredible.'

'It was.'

For a moment, his contented expression turned worried. 'No regrets?'

I shook my head emphatically. 'No. None.'

He looked relieved. 'Good.'

'You?'

'Hell no.'

I laughed.

'So...' He traced a finger over my sternum, down one side of my breast, along my ribs to just above my belly button, where it lingered. 'What happens now?'

'Now as in, right now? Or now as in tomorrow, and the next day?'

'Both, I guess.'

'Well, for now, we wait for our strength to return, and then, if you don't mind, I'd quite like to do that again.'

'I don't mind at all.'

'As for tomorrow, I can't answer that. And if I'm honest, I don't want to think about it. I'd rather focus on right now, right here.'

He pushed himself up, leaning over me, grinning wickedly. 'Fine by me.'

'What are you doing?'

'It's your turn.'

28

JACK

At some point I awoke and reached for her, finding the bed empty. At first, I was confused; had it all been a dream? But the sheets still smelled like her perfume.

I propped myself up on one elbow. 'Taylor?'

But there was no answer, and the en suite off the bathroom was in darkness. I reached over and flicked on the lamp, checking the time on my phone: 4.36 a.m.

'Taylor?' I called louder, throwing off the sheets and putting my feet on the cool wooden floor. She wasn't in the lounge or the kitchen. A weird feeling settled in my stomach. I hadn't thought she'd be the kind of woman to just take off in the middle of the night. I still didn't think that. Had last night upset her?

Flicking on the light over the sink, I saw it. A note on the fridge, held on by a magnet.

Couldn't sleep. Gone to the beach to watch the sunrise. xx

Relief flooded through me at the sight of those innocuous

little x's on the end. Kisses. She couldn't be that upset if she was leaving me kisses.

I headed back to the bedroom and pulled on a pair of shorts and a T-shirt, then headed outside. The grass was wet underfoot, the air damp and cool. Stars still littered the sky overhead, although the horizon was ever so slightly lighter than the rest of the sky, an indication that dawn was close.

I found her sitting on a rock near the tidal pool, her arms hugging her knees in front of her.

'Hey,' I said softly when I was a couple of meters away. 'OK if I join you?'

She turned her head and smiled. 'Of course.'

'Is that my shirt?' I asked, as I climbed up onto the rock and sat down next to her, our shoulders touching.

'Couldn't find my dress in the dark,' she replied. 'Didn't think you'd mind.'

'I don't. It looks better on you anyway.' And it was true. Even in just the shirt and her underwear, with her hair all tousled, she was the most beautiful woman I'd ever seen, and I couldn't believe how lucky I was to have spent the night with her. To be sitting beside her now. I nudged her with my shoulder. 'How come you couldn't sleep? No regrets, I hope.'

'No of course not,' she replied, leaning her head against my shoulder. 'Last night was incredible. I'm still processing it.'

'Processing?'

'I've only ever been with Adam,' she explained sheepishly. 'And it was nothing like... *that*.'

'Is that a good thing or a bad thing?'

'Oh good. Definitely good. I don't know how else to describe it without sounding corny.'

'I don't mind corny.'

She laughed. 'I guess it's just different, when you have some kind of connection with the person.'

'You didn't have a connection with Adam?'

She reached out and touched my hand, curling hers inside mine and threading her fingers through my fingers. 'Not like this, no.'

Her touch was electrifying. 'I feel it too,' I told her softly.

We sat in silence for a few minutes, then she lifted her head off my shoulder and nodded towards the sky.

'Do you see those two stars over there?'

I followed the direction of her gaze. 'I see a lot of stars. Which two in particular are you referring to?'

'There, see Orion's belt?'

I nodded.

'Follow the line northeast. There are two brighter stars, to the side.'

'Got them.'

'That's Castor and Pollux. The Gemini twins.'

I heard her swallow and waited, sensing, correctly, that she wasn't finished.

'I had a twin,' she said quietly, so quietly I wasn't sure at first that I'd heard her correctly. 'A brother.'

'Had?'

'He died.'

'I'm so sorry.'

'It was a while ago now, when we were teenagers.' She looked around, at the beach. 'This was actually one of the last places I saw him alive.'

'Do you want to talk about it?'

She shook her head. 'Not really. It just hits me sometimes, usually at moments like this, when I'm happy. I had an amazing night and I hate that he never got to experience anything like this.'

I rubbed the back of her hand with my thumb. 'I know what you mean. Owning a restaurant here in Pine Harbor was Alex's dream, and it's not right that I'm the one here doing it, and not him. But I guess that's why they say life isn't always fair, right?'

29

TAYLOR

I shook off the melancholy that inevitably enveloped me whenever I thought of Cal. I didn't want to be sad. Not today. I held Jack's hand, my head resting on his shoulder, and we watched as the sky slowly began to lighten, streaks of pink and orange dusting the sky, chasing away the stars and the dark for another day. It never failed to amaze me, the sunrises over the ocean. The colors were always spectacular when they were mirrored by the water, but today the sky was especially pink, courtesy of wildfires in Canada. There was no sound apart from the occasional bird cry and the waves crashing on the shore.

'It kind of feels like we're the only two people in the world awake at this moment,' I murmured, right before a lobster boat appeared around the point and chugged slowly out to sea. 'Well, it *did* until he showed up.'

Jack laughed. 'I know what you mean. There's just something magical about this place. I come down here often to watch the sunrise. Usually, I bring a coffee with me.'

I moaned. 'Coffee sounds so good right now.'

'Late night?' he teased.

'Yeah, someone kept me up for hours.'

He tutted. 'Some people are so inconsiderate.'

'Oh, I'm not complaining,' I clarified.

'Good to hear.'

I could feel his eyes on me. Not the gorgeous sunrise that was happening right in front of him, but me. It made me feel special.

'I used to come down here a lot as a kid,' I told him. 'When Mom and Cal were still asleep. It was my favorite part of the day. I'd sketch the sunrises with oil crayons. They weren't very good, to start with. But I got better.'

'That's an understatement. I've seen your work. It's incredible.'

I regarded him curiously. 'You've seen my work? Where?'

He had the grace to look embarrassed. 'Instagram,' he admitted. 'I'm not tech-savvy when it comes to social media, but Lucy at work showed me how to find your page. She's very impressed, by the way. Wants you to do her a tattoo.'

'Sure, at the arts festival, or if she comes to New York.'

At the mention of the city his smile slipped a little. 'I'll tell her.'

I nudged his body with mine. 'So you liked what you saw?'

'Are we still talking about your art? Or last night.'

I laughed. 'My art, of course.'

'I loved it. You're very talented.'

'Thanks.'

'You have a way of making the scene come to life. Some of your sunrises and waves were incredibly realistic.'

'That took a lot of practice, believe me.'

'Well, it was worth it.'

'I think so. I know being an artist isn't exactly a reliable career choice, and most artists never find fame or fortune, but it's all I've ever wanted to do.'

'How did you get into tattooing?'

'One of life's serendipitous moments. I met someone at a party who was going to an expo the next day and she invited me along. It wasn't somewhere I'd normally go, but Adam and I were in a bad place and the thought of spending my Saturday in a stadium watching bearded motorcyclists ink skulls onto other's people skin was slightly more appealing than walking on eggshells in the apartment all day, trying not to annoy him or be annoyed *by* him.'

'And? Did you end up getting a skull tattoo from a bearded motorcyclist?'

I laughed. 'No. And I was pleasantly surprised to find that it wasn't like what I was expecting at all. Don't get me wrong, there were definitely big guys, with big beards and even bigger biceps, like I'd anticipated, but there were also other people. All sorts of people. And I realized that day as I wandered around a remarkably clean and well-organized venue, that tattooists are artists too. They just prefer a different canvas.'

'And so you became one.'

'Not overnight. But over the next couple of years, yes. I still remember the first tattoo I did on someone's skin. It was terrifying. Nothing like the pressure of permanently marking someone's body.'

'I'm sure it was fine.'

'It was... acceptable. If I saw it now I'd probably feel awful. I've learned a lot of technique since those early days.'

Jack reached out and touched my cheek, his thumb cool against my skin as he stroked my cheek. 'I find you incredibly intriguing,' he said.

'The feeling is mutual,' I murmured back, my breath hitching in my throat as he stared at me. No one had ever looked at me like that. Then he leaned forward and kissed me, tentative at first, soft, until I kissed him back, feeling a moan vibrate in his throat as he matched my intensity.

When we finally pulled apart, he smiled, resting his forehead against mine. 'I don't know about you,' he said. 'But I'm starving.'

'I have worked up a bit of an appetite,' I agreed. 'Why, are you offering to cook breakfast?'

'If it means I get to keep you with me for a little bit longer, then yeah. I'm offering to cook you breakfast.'

I kissed the tip of his nose. 'Offer accepted.'

30

JACK

'I forgot how kitschy this place was decorated,' she said, wandering around the lounge and picking things up, while I stood in the kitchen and fried us bacon and eggs for breakfast.

'It's not that bad.'

She picked up a lobster lamp. 'No,' she said. 'This isn't tacky at all.'

She was wearing my shirt from the night before, with the sleeves rolled up and the top few buttons undone. It draped down to her mid-thighs. Her hair was a mess, tangled and wild. I had never seen a sexier woman.

'Who decorated it?' I asked her, flipping the eggs and lightly pressing them down into the frying pan with the spatula.

'My grandmother at first, but my mother has added her own touches over the years. Anything with a moose on is probably courtesy of her. They're her favorite animal.'

'Ah. That explains the shower curtain.'

'We have the exact same one in the spare bathroom up at the house.'

'What was your grandmother like?'

She put the lamp down again, and wandered over to the bookshelf, tilting her head to read the spines of the books. 'Um, she was great, apparently. I was only seven when she died of a heart attack. I don't actually remember her very well. But I've been told she was pretty legendary around here.'

'In what way?'

'She was an oyster farmer. The first female one in Pine Harbor.'

'Are you serious?'

'Of course. After my grandfather died, she had to find a way to support my mother. She didn't want to become a secretary or bookkeeper. She liked the outdoors and being physically fit. In this town, that either meant the ocean or the forest. She chose the ocean. Researched the oyster farms that were starting up and down the coast, and started her own, here, in the seventies. It wasn't easy, especially being a single mom, and she struggled to get taken seriously in a male-dominated industry. But she persevered and pioneered the way for more women to follow.'

'That's seriously impressive.'

'I know. I wish she'd lived longer. I would have loved to get to know her better.'

'So that was your mother's mom?'

She nodded. 'Yes. My father's parents were against his marriage to my mother. They didn't have anything to do with us.' She snorted bitterly. 'Apple didn't fall far from that tree.'

'What do you mean? If you don't mind me asking. We don't have to talk about this if it upsets you.'

'It doesn't.' She sat on the couch and tucked her legs underneath her. 'My dad was flighty. Spoilt. His parents indulged him. He and my mother were young, in love, reckless. She got pregnant and he insisted on marrying her, against his family's wishes.' She sighed. 'My mother said he did it because it was the romantic thing to do, and because it gave him a thrill to rebel against his family. My dad had main character syndrome, big time. *Everything* revolved around him, and he thrived on drama. After they married and she had us, he realized exactly what he'd signed up for. Family. Having to *support* that family. Sleepless nights, crappy diapers, the lot. And no one around to see it apart my mother. No one to applaud him and tell him what a hero he was for doing the bare minimum.'

'He sounds like a bit of a dick, no offense.'

She snorted. 'No offense taken. He was a *huge* dick. Couldn't take an ordinary life. Left my mother when we were young and never looked back. He did send her some money every month, at least he did that. But after he died, she was on her own. My grandmother took us in here at the house, and after *she* died, my mother inherited it all.'

I turned the oven hob off and fetched two plates out of the cupboard. 'The oyster farm as well?'

She nodded. 'Yep, sold it in the nineties though, for a good profit. She's been able to live off that money ever since, although she chose to work while we were growing up. Wanted to teach us a good work ethic.'

I plated up the eggs and bacon and sprinkled some salt and pepper on them. 'Was it just you and your brother?'

'Yes. Is breakfast ready yet?' she asked abruptly. 'I'm starving. I think my stomach is starting to eat itself.'

'Can't have that, can we.' I carried the plates over to the wooden table. 'It's ready. Come and get it.'

'About time,' she grumbled, but smiled as she did so. She climbed off the couch and padded over to the table in her bare feet. I sat down on my seat and reached for her, pulling her down on to my lap.

'If you're going to complain, you can cook next time.'

She wriggled in my lap, and I started to get hard for her again. The way her eyes widened told me she felt it. I snaked a hand underneath the hem of the shirt and cupped her breast, running my thumb over her nipple, feeling it stiffen. Her eyes closed as her lips opened and she moaned softly.

'That feels so good,' she said.

'You feel so good,' I rasped back, unable to take my eyes off of her. She was sexy beyond belief, and I couldn't believe how lucky I was. She stood suddenly, and I blinked at her, bereft, before I realized what she was doing. Staring at me intensely, she tugged her underwear down, kicking them off to one side, then she climbed back on my lap, straddling me. I reached for the buttons on the shirt, fumbling with them. Suddenly they were the tiniest buttons in the whole history of buttons, and my hands were all thumbs. Impatient, I gave up, putting my fingers in the gap and pulling it apart, hearing buttons ping off in all directions as it ripped open, revealing her beautiful breasts, right at my face level. I reached for them, enjoying their heaviness in my hands, molding them, loving them, licking at them with my tongue until she couldn't bear it any more, grabbing the back of my head roughly and shoving her whole nipple into my mouth, grinding herself down on my lap as she did.

Reaching between us, she freed my erection from my underwear, maneuvering herself upwards so that she could take the tip of me inside of her. I thrusted upwards, desperate to feel the rest of her, but she pushed my chest to hold me down and tutted at me.

'Nah ah ah,' she said. 'I'm setting the pace this time.'

She lowered herself a little bit more, then withdrew, and repeated. Each time she took a little bit more of me in, teasing me, building me into such a frenzy that by the time she finally slid down the full length of me, gasping as she did, her face contorting with ecstasy, I couldn't take it any more. With a growl, I grabbed her hips and took over, pounding her against me again and again until I exploded inside her like a Fourth of July firework. She came at the same time, her head thrown back, her moans loud. I wanted to spend the rest of my life watching her do that.

'Breakfast is cold now,' I said afterwards in a hoarse voice as she nestled her head in against my neck and I held her.

'Worth it,' she replied sleepily, and for a second, I thought she might actually drift off, right there, but suddenly her whole body jolted and she flew off me, her eyes wide as her hand flew to her mouth.

'What's wrong?' I asked, instantly alert.

She moved her hand and I could see she was biting her bottom lip, her expression guilty.

'Taylor, what is it?'

'Ray,' she said. 'I forgot all about Ray.'

31

TAYLOR

'So, you *are* still alive then,' he said, when Jack and I entered the house.

'Obviously.'

I watched him take in my crumpled dress and messy hair and felt like a guilty teenager caught sneaking into her house after curfew. Beside me, Jack looked clean and fresh, courtesy of the two-minute shower he'd had while I'd got dressed. His hair was damp, and he was wearing a clean T-shirt and a pair of shorts. I felt like a swamp monster next to him, conscious that my body was sweaty and sticky from our night of lovemaking.

'I called all the hospitals,' Ray said. 'When you didn't come home.'

I stared at him in surprise. 'You did?'

'No. Of course I didn't. I'm not an idiot. I figured you and he had... what is it you young people say? Hooked up?'

Jack snort-laughed, as my whole body cringed.

'Can we not talk about this?' I said. 'I'm sorry I stayed out all night and worried you.'

'Oh, I wasn't worried. You're big enough and ugly enough to look after yourself.'

'Thanks.'

'I was, however, hungry,' he complained. 'I had to make my own breakfast.'

I gasped dramatically, clutching a hand to my chest. 'And it didn't kill you? I'm shocked.'

'You will be when you see the state of the kitchen,' he replied smugly.

I turned slowly, surveying the mess he'd left. Pots and a frying pan, plates and cups. Crumbs everywhere, an open butter dish. The milk was even still sitting on the bench with the lid off.

'It's fine, I'll clean it up,' I said cheerfully.

'Really?' His tone was suspicious. 'Why aren't you telling me off?'

'Do you want me to tell you off?'

'I want to know why you're being nice all of a sudden.' Then he looked at Jack and his expression changed. 'Never mind. I can guess what's put you in a good mood.'

'*Life* puts me in a good mood,' I informed him primly. 'So, shut up.'

He gave Jack a look. 'Good luck to you,' he said. 'That's all I can say.'

'Er, thanks?' Jack replied. 'You go and shower, Taylor. I'll clean up the kitchen.'

I smiled at him gratefully. 'Are you sure?'

'Of course.' He smiled back. 'I don't have to be at work until later, so until then, I'm all yours.'

'Thanks.' I tiptoed up to kiss him on the cheek. 'I won't be long.'

'Take as long as you want.'

Ray interrupted. 'Don't listen to him. I need you to take me to the doctor, so hurry up. I've made an appointment for ten.'

'Why? What's wrong?'

He sniffed. 'My leg feels weird.'

I looked at it for some kind of clue, but he was wearing his usual beige trousers. Everything looked normal from where I was standing.

'The one you fell on?'

'No, the other one.'

'Well, what do you mean, weird?'

'I don't know, like it's damp.'

I narrowed my eyes, trying patiently to understand. 'Damp?'

'Damp,' he confirmed.

'You mean your skin?'

'My leg.'

'Yes, but, the skin of your leg?'

'The whole leg.'

'You're not making any sense.'

'I don't know how else to explain it.'

I looked at Jack, who shrugged.

'Do you want me to take a look at it?' he asked Ray.

'Are you a doctor?'

'Well, no, but—'

'Then you can keep your hands to yourself, thank you.'

Jack suppressed a smile. 'Understood.'

I checked the clock on the wall. 'I'd better hurry up, then.'

'Yes, you'd better,' Ray agreed. 'But also, do a good job. I'm not going anywhere with you looking like that.'

I poked my tongue out at him as I headed for the stairs, unable to keep the smile off my face as I ascended. Not even Ray could kill my good mood today. Last night had been the best night of my life. Being with Jack had felt incredible, and my body was sore and aching in all the right places to remind me. There was only one, small niggle. A seed of doubt that was trying to get in, to plant itself, to grow into an entire tree of worry.

Where to from here?

I would still be leaving in a few weeks. And no matter how many times I told myself, or Jack, that we could just live in the moment and enjoy whatever it was between us for just that, whatever it was, it turned out that maybe I wasn't that kind of woman after all. Feelings were creeping in and that would make it harder to walk away. Feelings were definitely a complication I wasn't sure I was ready for.

'What do you mean, damp?' the doctor asked Ray later, in the examination room.

'You know, damp,' Ray replied. 'Wet. Moist.'

'Oh God.' I squeezed my eyes shut. 'Please don't say that word again.'

'What, moist?'

I stood up. 'I'll wait for you out in the waiting room.'

The medical center hadn't changed much since I was a teen. The walls were still plastered with posters, some of them so faded as to be illegible. The building was old and in need of repair, but according to a sign by the front counter, a new medical center was in the process of being built on the other side of town, near the sports fields. I was reading about how this was thanks to community fundraising efforts when someone tapped me on the shoulder.

'Taylor?'

I turned. 'Dawn?'

She squealed, embracing me. 'How are you? God, it's been forever since I've seen you.' She looked over my shoulder. 'Is Adam with you?'

'Uh, no. Adam and I are no longer together.'

'Oh.' Her nose crinkled up. 'I'm sorry to hear that.'

'It's fine, honestly. All for the best, as they say.'

'It seems like just yesterday I was the maid of honor at your wedding. Do you remember?'

'Of course I remember.' Although not, I suspected, for the same reasons she did.

'I still have the dress,' she exclaimed. 'In my wardrobe. Couldn't bring myself to throw it away or donate it to the thrift store. It's so pretty.' She pulled a face. 'Obviously I'll never be able to wear it again though. I'm at least fifty pounds heavier than I was then.'

'You look great,' I assured her, and I meant it. She'd been too skinny back then. Rail-thin.

'So what are you doing back here?' she asked, then clutched my arm and squealed again. 'Please tell me you're moving back to Pine Harbor?'

'Sorry, no.'

Her face fell. 'Damn. That would have been so cool, to have you to hang out with again. We used to have so much fun, all of us together. Before... well, you know.'

'Yes,' I replied in a clipped tone. 'We did. How are you, anyway? Did you become a writer, like you planned?'

'Working on it. It's a lot harder than you might think, actually. Writing a book. And the publishing industry is a tough nut to crack, but I'll get there. In the meantime, I work in the library to pay the bills.'

'You're kidding, you're a librarian?'

'What's so unbelievable about that?'

'Nothing. It's just, the Dawn I remember was a little... wilder than I imagine your typical librarian to be.'

'Hey, for your information, librarians can be freaky too.'

'Remember the night of the festival once, when we all borrowed dinghies and made it a race to row across the bay at midnight? Winner was the first one to ring the bell at the lighthouse on Sandbar Point? That was your idea, if I remember correctly.'

She looked wistful. 'I'd forgotten about that. Remember that cop, Donald? He was so sure it was us but couldn't prove anything.'

'He was a miserable old guy. I don't know what his problem was, anyway. We put the boats back where we found them.'

'Yeah, but Cal and Adam painted faces on some of the marker buoys with glow-in-the-dark paint, remember?'

I stared at her. 'They did?'

'Yeah, that's why they were the last ones back, long after the rest of us.'

'I thought they were just drunk and rowing in circles.'

'Nope. They switched some of the markers around too. There were some pissed-off oyster farmers the next day. My dad drilled me on whether I knew anything about it. I lied. Just like I lied when they put dish soap, food coloring and rubber duckies in the town fountain.'

I smiled. 'God, I'd forgotten all about that.'

'We were little shits really,' she admitted. 'But that's what you get with teens in a small town. We had to find some way to amuse ourselves. The teens these days are the same. They thought it was funny to move all the books around a few months ago. Mix it all up. Took me ages to get them all back in the right places.' She shook her head. 'I couldn't tell them off. We did far worse than that.'

'You weren't even tempted to get out?' I asked.

She looked genuinely surprised at my question. 'Leave Pine Harbor? No. Never. It's home.'

'You don't find it, constricting?'

She shrugged. 'Sure, sometimes it can be annoying, when everyone knows your business, sometimes before you do. But as much as people here love to gossip, you know they've got your back when you need it. Did you hear about Bronwyn?'

I searched my mental memory bank. 'Meecham?'

'Yeah.' She checked to make sure no one was listening. 'She got breast cancer last year. Only thirty-one, with two small kids. It was pretty aggressive when they found it. She couldn't work, had to take time off to go through the treatments.'

'That's awful.'

'She got really, *really* sick. I mean, I've never seen anyone alive look the way she did. It was horrible. Her husband, Ben, was trying to juggle work, with the kids, and ferrying her back and forward to the city for treatments. I organized a meeting at the town hall and so many showed up. By the time we left two hours later, we had a roster and a plan for everything. Filled their chest freezer up with frozen meals and lunches. Washing was picked up twice a week and dropped back clean and pressed. The kids were taken to playcenter; Bronwyn was driven back and forward to her appointments. Even the dog was walked twice a day by volunteers. Ben could carry on working, knowing that everything was taken care of.'

'How is she now?'

'She's doing OK. The treatment regime seems to have worked and she's currently in remission. Very grateful to everyone for helping out while they were in the thick of it. That's why I love this town. You can count on the people here to support you through the hard times, you know? And there's going to be hard times, no matter where in the world you are. I know I'd rather be here if it came down to it. Besides, there's plenty of fun times too. The festival is in a few days; that's always cool. Will you still be here?'

'Actually,' I admitted. 'I kind of got talked into running a tattoo stall.'

She stared at me for a moment, before she burst out laughing. 'No *way* Celia asked you to do that.'

'Oh, she was firmly against it,' I confirmed. 'Tried her hardest to persuade the town it was a bad idea, but sadly for her, she lost.'

'Was that at the town festival planning meeting?'

I nodded.

'Damn, I missed it. I had to work that night. Pity, I'd have loved to have seen her face. I remember when we all used to go over to Adam's house sometimes after school; she'd look at us like we were sewer rats or something. Stuck-up cow.'

'You won't find me arguing with that.'

A door opened and Ray shuffled up to us. 'Done.'

'What did the doctor say?'

'I don't know,' he grumbled.

'Because you weren't listening, or because she said something you don't agree with?'

He glared at Dawn, giving her a quick up-and-down.

'Who's this?'

She pointed at herself. 'It's me, Dawn. We've met before, but it was years ago. I was a friend of Taylor's and Cal's at school.'

'Say no more. Another troublemaker.'

'Actually, she's the town librarian now,' I told him. 'Very respectable.'

He grunted. 'At least one of you grew up and got a proper job.'

Dawn frowned. 'You know Taylor makes way more than I do, right? And has won numerous industry awards, not to mention the fact that she owns her own business. She's accomplished way more than most of our high school year has, so if anyone has a "proper" job, it's her.'

'I'll wait for you at the car,' he said, ignoring her. 'Don't be too long, we need to get to the pharmacy before it closes. And you need to bring me back in two days to get my ears cleaned out.'

'Again? I'm sure Mom told me you had that done not long ago. I remember because it was disgusting, and I told her never to mention it to me ever again.'

'I get a lot of buildup.'

'Do me a favor and never say *that* again, either.'

'Just you wait until you get old,' he complained, shuffling off. 'It's no picnic. My eyes need checking, my ears need cleaning, my hip hurts, and now I'm retaining too much fluid, apparently.'

The complaints continued until he was out the door.

'Man,' Dawn said, shaking her head. 'That guy hasn't changed at all.'

I stared at her, my eyebrows arched, questioning.

'What?'

'How do you know all that stuff about me?'

She shrugged. 'I followed you on social years ago.'

I got a sinking feeling. 'Did I follow you back?'

'No. But that's OK.'

'It wasn't intentional,' I promised her, digging my phone out of my pocket. 'I get a lot of notifications. Half the time I don't even bother checking them, so I must have missed that one. I'm sorry.'

'It's fine. It's not like I post anything newsworthy, anyway. Photos of my cat, mostly. Books I'm reading. Photos of my cat pretending to read the books I'm reading.'

I typed her name into the search bar on Instagram, scrolling until I saw one with a cat for the profile picture. 'Is that you?' I asked, showing her.

'Sure is,' she confirmed. 'That's Ziggy, my calico cat. I know, I've turned into the stereotypical single librarian with a cat.' She brightened. 'But at least I only have one. That's got to count for something, right?'

I clicked the *follow back* button. 'Done.'

'You didn't have to do that just because I'm standing in front of you.'

'I know. I want to keep in touch.'

'You do?'

'Yeah. I'm sorry I didn't.'

'That's OK. I know things weren't exactly easy when you left. I wish things hadn't gone down that night the way they did.'

I swallowed hard. 'I've spent the last fourteen years wishing that too.'

She reached out and gave my arm a squeeze. 'I'm really glad I ran into you. We should catch up for coffee before you go.'

I smiled. 'I'd like that.'

The doctor emerged from the examination room and checked the file in her hand.

'Dawn Porter.'

'That's me,' Dawn said. 'I'd better go.'

'Yeah I'd better get going too. Ray hates waiting.'

She rolled her eyes. 'Ray hates everything.'

32

JACK

'I hate math.'

'Don't say that.'

'But I do.'

I paused from wiping the bar. 'Come on, Oscar, you know this stuff. We covered it last week. Read me the question again.'

He sighed. 'Luke went to Captain's Scoops to buy some ice cream. He ordered two scoops of chocolate, one scoop of vanilla, and three scoops of strawberry. How many scoops did he get in total? And if a scoop costs $1, how much money did Luke spend?'

'OK, so it's basic addition. Think about it. Read the question again if you have to. Slowly.'

I watched his little face frown as he stared at the page in front of him. His mouth moved as he silently worked it out. Fiona, was waiting tables so I'd offered to watch him at a table close to the bar. His grandmother babysat him as often as she could, but sometimes, like tonight, she couldn't, and Fiona was left with no other option than to bring him to work.

'Six scoops?'

'Right.' I beamed at him. 'You got it. Now, how much did he spend?'

He read the problem again. 'I don't know.'

'Don't be afraid to have a guess, Oscar. You won't be in any trouble if you're wrong. It's how we all learn.'

He sighed. Stared at the page for a while. 'Six dollars?'

'Exactly. I told you math is easy when you focus on the problem.'

'No, you said math is fun. And you're wrong about that.'

I laughed. 'You'll get the hang of it. And if you don't end up liking math, that's OK. But you need to know this stuff.'

He rolled his eyes at me. 'Why? That's what phones are for.'

'You can't always rely on technology. What if you were in the middle of the bush somewhere, and you had no phone.'

'Why would I need to do math in the middle of the bush?'

He had me there. 'I don't know, but just trust me. You need to know this stuff. The basics, at the very least.'

'Fine. Whatever.' He brightened. 'Can I have an ice cream now?'

I checked my watch. 'Yeah, go on then. Tell Kevin I said it was OK.'

'Thanks, Jack.' He hopped down from his seat and closed his school exercise book. 'And maybe I could play on the iPad for a little while?' he asked hopefully. 'Please?'

I flicked a tea towel towards him. 'How could I resist that face. If it's OK with your mother, it's OK with me. It's out in the office. But only for half an hour, OK? Any more than that and your brain will rot.'

He rolled his eyes. 'That's not true.'

'Are you sure about that?'

'You're good with him,' Hannah remarked from her perch at the bar after he wandered away.

'He's a great kid.'

Things had shifted between us since the other night. A small shift, almost imperceptible and yet it may as well have been as wide as a chasm. The easygoing familiarity between us had formalized. When we spoke to each other now it was calculated, carefully thought out, checked for possible triggers and flash-points, any unintended innuendo that could potentially be taken the wrong way. It made me sad, and I was glad that Alex wasn't around to see it.

I hated that he was dead. But if he hadn't died I would never have moved to Pine Harbor, and I would never have met Taylor. How could the worst event in my life bring me to the best thing that had ever happened to me? Because that's how I felt about her. She was everything I'd never known that I wanted in a woman. For so long, I'd felt like the third wheel in Hannah and Alex's marriage. I wanted what they had. It was only natural, because what they'd had was pretty special. I couldn't blame Hannah for struggling without him.

'Are you guys all set for the festival tomorrow?' Hannah asked, watching me check the clean glasses out of the dish-washer for water marks and polishing them. 'Is there anything you need me to do?'

'Yes, we're all set, and no, there's nothing left for you to do other than show up.'

She sighed. 'Do you really need me? I'll just be in the way.'

'You don't have to be behind the stall. I've managed to make the rosters work so that both the stall and this place are covered for the whole three days. As long as no one calls in sick we should be OK. But you should be at the festival, even if it's just to meet and greet people out the front. It'll give you a chance to get to know people around here and I think that's important, if you plan on sticking around.'

I was watching her, which meant I saw the face she pulled before she corrected it.

'What was that face for?'

'What face?'

'Hannah.'

'If I tell you, you have to promise not to get mad.'

'Why would I get mad?'

'I'm not telling you unless you promise.'

'Just tell me.'

She took a deep breath and then the words came out in a rush. 'I've decided to sell this place.'

I processed them, staring her. 'Why?'

She threw up her hands, exasperated. 'It's just not me, Jack. We both know that. I've been kidding myself to think I could run this place. Or even live in this town.'

'This isn't because of what happened the other night, is it?'

'No. Not everything revolves around you, believe it or not.'

'Then why?'

She shrugged. 'I've been thinking about it for a little while and now I've made my mind up. This place was Alex's dream, not mine. I'm completely out of my depth.' She pulled another face. 'And, if I'm being completely honest, I'm going out of my mind in this godforsaken town. Seriously. There's nothing to *do* here. I miss the city. I miss my family, my friends. So, I was thinking.' She took another deep breath. 'That if I sold this place, I could reinvest the money into a business back in the city that's more me.'

'Like what?'

'A clothing boutique. Though not just clothing, also shoes, and accessories. The kind of things I like to wear.'

'Sounds like you've given this a lot of thought.'

'I have. And I really think this is the best option. For me and for you. Face it, you don't belong here either. You're only here because you're ridiculously loyal, which is your best and worst personality trait.'

'I'm not sure if that was a compliment or an insult.'

'Don't get me wrong, I'm grateful to you and I always will be. You taking over the running of this place gave me the time I needed to get my head straight. Figure out what I want.'

'Well I'm glad one of us knows.'

'You can get your job back on the force,' she suggested. 'They didn't want you to leave.'

I shook my head. 'No. That part of my life is over.'

'Are you sure? I know how much you loved it.'

'It's one of the few things I am sure about.'

'Fair enough. I'm not going to push you. I'm relieved, actually. After what happened with Alex, I'd only worry about you.'

'It's not your job to worry about me.'

'I'm always going to worry about you,' she replied softly.

I put the glass I was holding down. 'How come you never mentioned you were thinking about selling up?'

'I made you uproot your whole life to move here. I didn't want to disappoint you.'

I walked around the bar and sat on the stool next to hers.

'You didn't *make* me do anything, OK? I offered to take this on for you. That's just what people do when a friend is struggling.'

She smiled. 'Normally, when a friend is struggling you cook them a meal or offer them a shoulder to cry on. Moving all the way across the country to run this business for me was going above and beyond, and you know it.'

'I was happy to do it, for you and for Alex.'

She looked down at her hands, clasped in her lap. 'Do you think he'd be disappointed in me?'

'No. God, no. Not at all.'

'I feel like a failure. Buying this place was such a rash decision, and I was stupid to think that following his dream would somehow make me feel closer to him.'

'You're not stupid.'

'Well.' She shrugged. 'Lesson learned, anyway. Don't make life-changing decisions when you're grieving. It is not the time to make big changes to your life. Maybe I should write a self-help book on what *not* to do when you lose someone you love. Top of the list, don't buy a lobster restaurant in a small town on an island off the coast of Maine.'

'That's very specific advice. I'm not sure how big a market there would be for a book like that.'

She laughed. 'Noted.'

'Look, no one's going to blame you for giving it a shot. You took a risk, tried something new and found out it wasn't for you. That's more than most people do in their lifetime. There's no shame in it.'

'Thanks, Jack. I'm sorry I didn't tell you earlier.'

'It is what it is. I'll figure something out.'

'We'll figure it out together.' She smiled. 'I'm actually looking forward to getting back to L.A., now that I've made my mind up. Back to normal life.' She laid a hand on my arm. 'I know that being in the city is hard for you. It's hard for me too. Memories of Alex everywhere. But as long as we stick together we'll get through it, OK?'

'I don't know. L.A. might not be for me any more.'

'Well you can't stay here.' She laughed as if the very idea was the most absurd thing she'd ever heard.

She had a point. Between her selling the restaurant and Taylor leaving in a few weeks to head back to New York, what was left to keep me here?

33

TAYLOR

I took a step back and checked out my handiwork. 'Is it too much?'

'That depends,' Ray replied.

'On what?'

'The kind of look you're going for. If you're aiming for tacky, you've nailed it.'

I rolled my eyes. 'Helpful.'

'Is that why you dragged me along this early?' he grumbled. 'To be helpful?'

It was still early enough that a sea mist lingered over the water and around the wharf. It was already warm though, the early heat hinting at a beautiful day to come. Gulls screeched down by the returning fishing boats, begging for scraps. All around the town tents were being set up, and I could hear the hum of excited voices, and the sound of bunting flapping in the breeze.

'You said you wanted to come to the festival,' I reminded Ray. 'I have to be here this early to set up, and I'll be too busy later to run back home and get you. You can either suck it up and be helpful, or go away and find someone else to annoy.'

He glared at me. 'Fine. What do you want me to do?'

'Be quiet for a second, while I figure out what's missing.' I squinted at the tent. 'It just needs something else. Something like... ooh, I know.'

I dove into the box of things I'd found around Mom's house that I'd thought might be useful, and pulled something out. 'Perfect.'

'Oh yes,' he said. 'That little bit of crap will make all the difference.'

'Hold the other end,' I said, passing him the end of the lights, small bulbs hanging off a twine string, and pointing to the other end of the pop-up tent front entrance. 'Just keep it there while I fasten the rest of it. Can you manage that?'

'I don't know,' he said. 'It's pretty technical stuff.'

I clipped the lights along the top of the entranceway, reaching the end and relieving him from his duty, flicked the on switch and stood back once again to have a look. 'That's much better.'

Somehow, against all my expectations, I'd been given a great spot to set up my pop-up booth. A high-foot-traffic area just next to the town green, not far from the wharf and the main street. Sandwiched in between a pottery stall and one selling art made from salvaged objects that the artist had beachcombed. Sea glass, driftwood, old buoys and the like. The tent I'd been allocated was navy and white striped, with a little white flag on the top and bunting around the edges. The whole front flap was able to be tied back, which I'd done, so that people could watch if they wanted. But if a client didn't want prying eyes, I had a free-standing white wooden divider that I could unfold to give them privacy.

I'd set up chairs, a portable tattoo bed/table, and the trolley with my tattoo machine and inks, wipes, creams et cetera. Everything was full and ready to go. I'd hung art around the inside of the tent that I'd pilfered off my mother's walls. It was my own artwork. Showcasing my evolving talent over the years. My first rough sketches. Lacking in the finer detail I'd self-taught myself to add over time. Paintings, oils and acrylics. Sunsets, waves. The lighthouse. My mother had proudly framed and displayed them all, and I knew she wouldn't mind me borrowing them for this.

On one end wall I'd hung some of my tattoo designs, and I had folders on a small table out front that contained pictures of tattoos I'd done in the past. I'd spent the whole of the day before coming up and sketching new designs: small tattoos that wouldn't take long and were perfect for the festival. Oyster shells, clams, lobsters, waves, a lighthouse, a sunset, a compass, anchors, sharks, dolphins, seals, and the silhouette of an old fisherman.

Near the entrance, I'd hung a windchime made of shells, hoping that the pretty sound it made in the warm breeze would help attract people to my booth. Despite the fact that I could probably do this in my sleep, if I wanted to, I was nervous. This was my hometown. Somehow it meant more to me that people here liked what I did.

As luck would have it, I already had a wooden sandwich board sign that I'd used at tattoo expos before. Renae, my second in charge back at my studio, had couriered the sign and all my gear to me, arriving two days ago. I opened the sign and arranged it near the entrance.

Taylor Calderwood Custom Tattoo Designs, it said in cursive letters.

I surveyed it all and nodded. 'It's ready.'

'Your boyfriend's over there.'

'He's not my boyfriend.'

'You knew who I meant though.'

I glared at him. 'I thought you were going to go and get breakfast at the café.'

'I thought you were going to go with me.'

'I've changed my mind.'

'Well you could have said that half an hour ago,' he complained. 'Before I sat here and watched you decorate this place.'

'Are you going to be OK to get there by yourself?'

He waved a hand dismissively. 'I'll be fine. It's not far, and my hip isn't as sore as it was.'

'OK. You know my number if you need me though, right? Just ask someone to call. Literally anyone. You're probably the only adult on this planet who doesn't own a cell phone.'

He rolled his eyes. 'Why don't you just tie a note around my neck like a puppy. "Please return to this address if found."'

'If I was going to write a note for whoever found you, it would say, "Free to a good home. He's your problem now."'

'Charming.'

'Thanks.'

'Not a compliment.'

'I know.'

'Ah, what would a morning in Pine Harbor be like without you two bickering,' Jack said, his face amused.

Warmth flooded through me at the sight of him. God, he was gorgeous. 'He started it.'

'Grow up,' said Ray, shuffling off towards Café on Main.

'I will when you will,' I called after him.

'What is with you two?' Jack asked.

'Nothing.' I shrugged. 'It's just the way it's always been. He's been a cranky old bastard for as long as I can remember, and so we spent our childhood trying to provoke him, and succeeding, the majority of the time.'

'You and your brother?'

I nodded, before changing the subject. 'What do you think of my stall?'

He ran his eyes over everything appraisingly. 'Looks good.'

'That's it? Good?'

'I'm not sure what you want me to say.'

'I don't know.' I pouted. 'I guess I just hoped for something more than "good".'

'It's very... festive?'

'It's not Christmas.'

'I know that. I meant bright and cheerful.'

'Where's your stall?'

He pointed. 'Just over there.'

He was on the opposite side of the street, down the other end.

'It's not far from the restaurant,' he said. 'Which is good. If I run out of supplies I can quickly send someone back for more.'

'What's on the menu?'

'Lobster rolls, of course.'

'Of course.'

'Plus, the usual suspects. Anything that's easy to prepare and serve out here. There's a big pot of chowder. Bacon, egg and hash brown sandwiches. Fish and chips, coleslaw, pies, some cake slices and ice cream. A few other things. You'll have to come over for lunch.'

'Maybe. I'll check out the other stalls first. Might be something better on offer.'

He gasped in mock outrage. 'You wouldn't.'

'I might.'

Music started up from the makeshift stage set up over by the water. The live band had set up and were warming up. There was the smoky smell of grilled corn in the air. People were starting to arrive, wandering amongst the stalls. A young couple paused to flick through my folders.

'Oh my God,' I heard the woman say. 'We should totally get matching tattoos.'

'Looks like you're up,' Jack said. 'Catch up later?'

I smiled. 'If you're lucky.'

He checked to see if anyone was within earshot, then leaned forward until his lips were next to my ear. 'I want to kiss you so much right now.'

Heat flooded my insides. 'Not here.'

It wasn't until he turned around and grinned at me that I realized I was still standing there, watching him walk away.

34

JACK

I completely underestimated just how busy and popular the small-town festival would be. By lunchtime, I'd already had to call in Toby, our second chef, from his day off to fire up the stoves in the kitchen and prepare more food.

'I thought you said we'd have enough,' I reminded Kevin during a brief lull.

'We should have had,' he replied, wiping his forehead with the crook of his arm, looking as hot and bothered as I felt. Hot pans sizzled, adding to the heat. 'I was going off the numbers we did last year. This year is already so much busier. I've never seen this many people in town at one time before.'

'It's great,' Hannah said, pausing from buttering the rolls. 'If every day was as busy as this, I'd almost be tempted to stay.'

Fiona looked up at me from where she was demonstrating how to shuck oysters to a small crowd. Her brow was furrowed questioningly.

'I'll tell you later,' I said.

'Just please tell me that I'm not going to be out of a job,' she asked quietly. 'There's not a lot of options in this town for a single mom, especially ones that will let me bring my son to work when I have to, like you do.'

'It's going to be fine,' I reassured her. 'Your job is safe.'

She smiled gratefully, her relief written all over her face, and I told myself I'd do whatever I had to do to keep that promise.

'Would you guys mind holding down the fort for a little while?' I asked, untying my apron and lifting it off over my head. 'I just need to check in on someone.'

'I think we can cope,' Fiona replied.

I fixed a couple of lobster rolls into paper boats and stepped out from the stall, wandering slowly down the street, past an art stall where a bunch of kids were painting old buoys, an impromptu driftwood sculpture garden. A man was drawing live caricature sketches, and I stopped to watch him for a moment. Kids nearby were drawing chalk art on the pavement. Down at the jetty near the wharf they were holding paper boat races. On the other side of the village green I could see a painting class taking place, easels set up to face the lighthouse at the tip of the bay. The atmosphere was joyous and buzzing, and I felt a sense of belonging.

Taylor was just finishing up a tattoo when I got to her stall.

'There you go, Dawn,' she said, straightening up and snapping off her gloves. 'All done.'

The woman, Dawn, sat up and twisted sideways so she could see her shoulder in the long mirror beside the tattoo table. Freshly inked on her skin was a tiny beach scene. A campervan, campfire, some ocean waves, and a couple of surfboards.

'I love it,' she squealed. 'You're so talented, Taylor.'

Taylor smiled modestly. 'Thanks.'

'My first tattoo,' Dawn said. 'And it's even more special because it was done by you. I'm so glad you're back.'

'Temporarily,' Taylor reminded her, and my good mood evaporated.

'Yeah, well, temporary or not, it's just nice to have you back, for however long it's for. Let's have dinner one night before you go.'

'Sounds good.' She looked up and saw me. I quickly pasted on a smile again.

'Hey you,' she said. 'How's the food stall going?'

'Busy,' I told her. 'Insanely so. How's the tattoo business?'

'I haven't stopped,' she said. 'It's been crazy. You wouldn't believe the people who have decided today is the day they get their first tattoo.'

'Like me,' Dawn said, then thrust out a hand. 'Hi, I'm Dawn.'

'Jack,' I said, shaking it.

'You look kind of familiar.'

'He's managing The Cozy Catch,' Taylor told her.

'Oh, yes. I've heard about you.'

I arched my eyebrows at Taylor. 'All good things, I hope.'

'Don't look at me,' Taylor said, holding her hands up. 'I haven't told her anything.'

Dawn looked back and forwards between us. 'Is there something to tell?'

'No,' we both chorused at the same time, which of course only made us sound guilty, like we were, in fact, hiding something. Taylor blushed.

Dawn grinned, backing out of the tent. 'Call me later,' she said to Taylor. 'I want to hear all about this "nothing" you speak of.'

'Great,' Taylor said after Dawn had left. 'That's going to be all around town in about five minutes.'

'What is? She doesn't know anything.'

'I love Dawn, but what she doesn't know, she'll make up.' She eyed the paper boats in my hands. 'Is one of those for me?'

'These? No. Both mine. Why, are you hungry?'

Her face fell.

'Just kidding.' I held one out. 'I thought you might have worked up an appetite.'

'Thanks,' she sighed happily, taking it from me and inhaling its scent with her eyes closed. 'Ohhh, that smells so good.' She took a bite and chewed, her face contorting in ecstasy.

'What is that divine taste?' she asked.

'Lobster?'

'No.'

'Freshly baked bun?'

'No, that's not it either.'

I looked at the one in my hand. 'Oh, I know what it is, it's the seaweed aioli.'

'That is so good.'

'I know. Toby makes it himself, with seaweed from right here in the bay.'

'Toby is a genius.'

'Don't tell him that; he'll want a raise.'

'Here.' She pushed out the other chair with her foot. 'Have a seat.'

We ate our rolls in silence, enjoying the food too much to ruin it by making conversation. While we ate, we watched the festival carry on around us. A man on stilts tipped his hat at us as he strode past, kids chasing after him.

'That,' Taylor declared, licking butter and aioli off her fingers, 'was delicious.'

'You can't get them like that back in New York, can you,' I teased. At least, I meant it to come out as teasing, but in reality, I sounded sad. Wistful. She gave me a strange look.

'Probably not,' she said.

'Where's Ray?'

'Over by the stage. He can see a lot of the live acts and parades over there. I got him a good seat in the shade.'

'Cool. Well.' I stood up, screwing up the paper boat in my fist. 'Guess I better get back to it.'

'Yeah, me too. I'm sure someone will be along shortly.' Her smile turned wicked. 'Unless...'

'Unless what?'

'Unless *you* want to be my next client.'

'I have thought about it,' I admitted.

'Whoa,' she said, eyes wide. 'I was only kidding. Are you serious?'

'Why do you sound so surprised?'

'Because I *am* surprised.'

'Why?'

'You just don't seem like the kind of guy who wants a lobster tattoo.'

'Who said I'd get a lobster?'

'OK, a wave then.'

'I don't want a wave.'

'So what do you want?'

'That,' I said, winking, 'is for me to know, and you to find out.'

'You don't have a clue, do you?'

'Not yet,' I admitted. 'But it'll come to me.'

'You shouldn't get a tattoo just for the sake of getting a tattoo.'

'Have you said that to anyone else you've worked on today? Doesn't sound like advice that would be good for business.'

'I don't care about business. I always make sure people understand what they're getting into.'

'Admirable.'

'I'm just saying,' she said, 'it's a permanent thing. You need to be sure about it. It should have some kind of meaning to you. Some significance.'

'Maybe the significance lies more in who would be doing the tattooing,' I said quietly. 'Rather than in the tattoo itself.'

She stared at me with her beautiful brown eyes, and inside my chest my heart sped up.

35

TAYLOR

The sun was low in the sky but the festival was still in full swing when he came back. I was cleaning up after inking a cute little purple-and-blue octopus onto the ankle of a middle-aged mother, when I heard him clear his throat.

'Have you decided?' I asked, without looking at him. I was worried that if I did, it might betray how I was feeling. I hadn't been able to shake his words and the way he'd said them. It had felt so *intimate*.

'I have.'

'And?'

'I'd like a giant squid, like huge, multiple stories high kind of giant, right across my chest. And I want its tentacles to be wrapped around one of those old-fashioned sailing ships, like a pirate one, pulling it down into the depths of the ocean. And if you could add a few sailors jumping overboard to their inevitable death, that'd be great. The more detail the better.'

I slowly swiveled on the chair and stared at him, incredulous.

'Are you serious? I'm not doing that.'

He grinned. 'Good. Because I was just kidding.'

'You had me going there for a minute,' I scolded him.

'You're so easy to tease.'

He pulled off his cap, revealing his sandy blond, mussed-up hair, and took a seat. He smelled of delicious food and musky male, and I swallowed hard to try and hide my sudden nervousness. It was silly to feel nervous, when I remembered how intimate we had already been with each other. But if anything, it seemed to have made it worse. I knew what was at stake now. What I'd be leaving behind when I left. A few days ago, I couldn't wait to get back to my life in the city. Now, the thought of never seeing Jack again made me feel all hollow inside.

'Can you do it with my sleeve rolled up?' he asked. 'Or do you want me to take my shirt off?'

I rolled my eyes. 'Any excuse to flex your muscles, right?'

He laughed. 'Sleeve it is.'

I turned my tattoo machine on, and starting gathering together what I needed. 'You haven't told me what you want yet.'

He stood briefly, reached into his pocket, and pulled out a small shell. Sitting back down, he held it out in the palm of his hand. 'This.'

I studied it. It was a top shell, a common snail, like you'd find up and down the coast. This was one of the prettier ones though, with iridescent blues and greens along with black.

'Cute,' I said, reaching out and picking it up, admiring the way the colors caught the light when I turned it over in my hand. 'Where did you find it?'

'In the tidal pool,' he said. 'The night we met.'

I stared at him.

'Pathetic, I know,' he mumbled sheepishly. 'I'm not sure why I kept it. I just did.'

'It's not pathetic. It's sweet.'

'Can you draw it for me?'

I nodded, not trusting my words. He sat silently and watched me as I sketched the shell, focusing on all the little details. The imperfections that made it unique. When I finished it and wordlessly passed it to him, he studied it for so long without saying anything that I was worried he didn't like it.

'It's perfect,' he said. 'You're very talented.'

Warmth flooded through me at his words. 'Thanks.'

'Can you tattoo this?'

'I can tattoo anything. Even giant squids.'

He smiled. 'Just this will do. For now, anyway. I've heard that tattoos are highly addictive and once you have one, you usually end up wanting more.'

'There are far worse addictions out there than tattoos.'

I was conscious of his eyes on me while I tattooed the little shell picture onto his arm. He winced when the needle first touched his skin.

'Ouch.'

'Seriously? I barely touched you.'

'I just wasn't expecting it, that's all,' he said defensively. 'I know what to expect now.'

'Just breathe through it,' I told him. 'And try not to move.'

'Don't move. Breathe. Got it.'

There was no sound for a while apart from the hum of the machine, and the music off in the distance.

'Do you always look so serious when you do this?' he asked.

'Shush, I'm concentrating.'

'Sorry.'

I tried not to smile.

'You're very cute when you're concentrating,' he whispered.

'Do you want me to make a mistake?'

'No. Sorry. I'll be good.'

I snorted. 'I doubt that.'

Truth was, I didn't need silence to tattoo. When I was first starting out, I once worked a booth at a heavy metal concert. I was used to noise. Used to crowds, and being watched. Those things didn't bother me. What *did* bother me was his proximity. Touching his skin, I kept having flashbacks to the other night, and then I'd remember the things we'd done, and I'd start feeling a bit hot and bothered.

'You're blushing,' he said. 'Is it because you're so close to my muscle?'

'Oh my God, Jack.'

'I'm kidding. About my muscle, not the fact that you're blushing. You're definitely doing that.'

'We're almost done here; do you think you could be serious for a few minutes?'

'Seriously? That didn't take long.'

I wiped the small amount of ink and blood away and checked the design, adding little bits here and there, little touches. 'It's not very big.'

'Words every man *doesn't* want to hear.'

I laughed. 'What is with you tonight?'

'What do you mean?'

'Teasing, joking around. You just seem, lighter, somehow.'

'Hannah's decided to move back to L.A.,' he told me. 'Permanently.'

'Oh.' I wiped, checked, continued again. 'How do you feel about that?'

'Honestly? I feel... relieved. I think she's making the right decision.'

'What does this mean for you?'

'Are you asking me whether I'm moving back to L.A. too?'

I nodded, wiped, checked, continued. Held my breath.

'No,' he said. 'I'm not. I have no desire to go back there.'

I exhaled again. 'Why not?'

'I don't know. It's just not me. Never was. I didn't realize that though, until I moved here. This place makes me feel, I don't know. More optimistic about the state of the world, I guess.'

'Careful, you're venturing into Hallmark territory again.'

'Is that so bad?'

'I suppose not.' I sat up, wiped for the final time. 'There. All done.'

He sat up and flexed his arm in the mirror. 'It's beautiful.'

'I'm glad you're happy with it.' I pulled off my gloves.

'I am. I love it.' He made eye contact with my reflection. 'Thank you.'

'You're welcome.' I dipped my finger into a tub of Aquaphor, then reached out and gently touched his skin where he now wore my design permanently with him. I rubbed it gently. 'You'll need to wash it with mild soap at least twice daily until it heals, and apply this afterwards. I'll give you a small pot, so you can do it at home. I'm going to cover it, and you'll need to keep it covered for a few days.'

'I think I can manage that.'

'I'll be watching.'

'Is that a promise?' His eyes bored into mine intensely, his tone still jovial but with an undercurrent of seriousness.

I started to pull my hand away but he reached out and caught it in his own, his fingers curling around my wrist. His touch was light, but his skin may as well have been electric. I wondered if I would always feel that way when he touched me. He leaned towards me, his eyes asking permission. I nodded imperceptibly, and emboldened, he closed the rest of the distance between us, his lips touching mine.

This kiss was different to our kisses at the cabin. We had been swept up in our passion then, a physical attraction, a desperate need for each other. This was soft and gentle, lingering.

36

JACK

It was the final night of the festival. A festival that, according to local gossip, had been a huge success. Visitor numbers had been reported to be the highest they'd ever been, and although it was too early to talk about money, rumors swirled around town that a predicted tidy profit meant that next year's festival might not even require external funding at all, something Celia would no doubt be thrilled about.

The Cozy Catch food stand had done extremely well. We'd even had to order in more supplies out of our normal ordering schedule to keep up with demand, on top of the extra stock we'd already ordered in preparation for the festival. More than the money made, though, I considered the festival to be a success because of how many more townsfolk I'd met. Every day, new faces. New stories. New friends.

I finished packing up the last few traces of my stall, helped a few neighboring stalls pull down their gear too, then wandered over to the green where there was a picnic going on. A band was playing on the stage. People were eating, drinking and dancing. There was a bittersweet atmosphere around the square, now that the festival was coming to a close. The smell of kettle corn and cotton candy hung in the air. Children with faces painted on – lions, unicorns and superheroes – ran around chasing each other and squealing, having the time of their lives. I watched them, smiling. You didn't see this back in L.A. At least, I never had.

I'd always wanted a family. Assumed, and hoped, that it would be on the cards for me one day, but it wasn't something I'd actively chased. I figured it'd happen when it happened. But it was why I knew I couldn't go back to being a cop. Not after what had happened to Alex. I couldn't put a family through that, even though they were just a wishful thought still.

Someone nudged my hip. 'Penny for your thoughts?'

I smiled down at Taylor. She looked a little tired and sticky from the heat and a busy three days tattooing half the population of Pine Harbor, but, to me, she'd never looked more beautiful. Her skin glowed in the fading light of the sun and the lanterns that hung all around the square from poles and trees.

I nudged her back. 'All packed up?'

She nodded. 'If by packed up, you mean all thrown into a box to be sorted out and returned to their rightful positions in my mom's house so that hopefully she doesn't notice when she returns that I raided her most prized possessions, then yes. I am all packed up.'

'You're telling me those adorable little lobster fairy lights that you had draped around the top of the mirror aren't yours?'

'Sadly, no. But I'll make sure to go on www.cheapcrap.com to get some of my own.'

'Good. No self-respecting New Yorker should be without lobster fairy lights.'

'Right? I'm surprised they've let me get away with living there for as long as I have.'

We stood in companionable silence for a while, watching people dance on the grass. The band was playing a slow country song.

I stepped in front of her and held out my hand. 'Dance?'

She put her hand in mine, smiling. 'I thought you'd never ask.'

I wove an arm around her waist, my hand on her back, pulling her in against me, and she rested her head against my chest. Her hair smelled like summertime and cherries.

'I can hear your heart beating,' she said softly, tilting her face to look up at me.

'Does it sound like it's beating fast? Because it feels like it's beating fast.'

'It sounds normal.'

'Are you sure? Because I don't normally feel it when it's doing its normal everyday thing. I know it's working because, well, I'm standing, talking and breathing, but I don't *feel* it working. I only feel it when you're around.'

She smiled.

'I thought you were going to tell me off for being too cheesy then,' I said.

'Nah,' she replied. 'I figure you can get away with saying something like that when the whole damn town looks like something out of a Hallmark movie.'

'It does, doesn't it,' I mused. 'The unbelievably green grass. The trees, with their rustling leaves. The water just there, shiny and sparkly and pretty, with all the little sailboats moored, decorated with bunting and hand-painted lobster buoys. Celia might be an annoying pain in your ass, but I've got to hand it to her, she sure can organize a great festival and unite a town. Who knew places like this really existed?'

'I did,' she said softly. 'I just forgot.'

I pulled slightly away so I could see her face. 'Don't tell me you're actually feeling melancholic about this place?'

'Tell anyone and I'll have to kill you.'

'Don't worry, your secret is safe with me. I knew that secretly you liked it here, though. That all that hate was just an act.'

'I never said I hated it.'

'So,' I forced myself to sound casual, unbothered. 'Maybe one day you might, possibly, consider moving back?'

She tilted her head and gave me a look. 'Subtle.'

I opened my eyes wide, a vision of innocence. 'What?'

'Why do you want to know?'

'It's called conversational enquiry.'

'That's all it is?'

'What else would it be?'

She rested her head back against my chest. Her hair tickled my chin. 'I thought you might have been asking because you wanted me to stick around.'

My body stiffened, and I considered my next words carefully, aware the wrong ones now could have the wrong effect. 'Is that even remotely a possibility?'

'If you'd asked me a week ago, not a chance in hell.'

'And now?'

'Now... I don't know. I'm confused. These past three days, the festival, it's been fun,' she admitted. 'I've actually enjoyed myself, which has been somewhat surprising. And it's made me think about when the last time *was* that I had any fun.'

'And?'

'Honestly? I can't remember. Don't get me wrong, I enjoy my life in the city. I like that I can eat a different cuisine every night if I want to. Can take in a show, or go see a movie whenever I want. Visit art galleries. Trendy bars. Get dressed up and dance all night with my friends. There's a place just down the street from my apartment that has *the* best coffee in the world.'

'Really? The whole, entire world? That's a pretty big claim.'

'I'd stake my life on it.'

'Wow. You take your coffee pretty seriously.'

'When it comes to coffee, I'm as serious as it comes. And then there's this place, Veniero's on 11th Street, that has the best New York cheesecake, it's seriously to die for. It's my go-to, whenever I want to treat myself. Or I'm feeling sad. Or tired. Or happy.'

'So pretty much any time.'

'Pretty much.'

'Is cheesecake and coffee enough of a reason to stay living somewhere though?'

'I guess that's what I have to think about. I like my life there. I have my work, friends. A great apartment.'

She hesitated.

'But?' I prompted.

'But being back here...' She looked around. 'Being a part of this. It's reminded me that being part of a community isn't a bad thing. It's easy to feel alone in the city. I don't feel that here.'

I cleared my throat. 'I would never ask you to stay here purely for my sake, but I'd just like to put it on the record that I'd be happy if you *did* stay. Just something to consider when you're making any decisions.'

'You're not planning on heading back to L.A. any time soon?'

I stared at my feet, suddenly feeling nervous about saying aloud what had, until then, been only a thought in my head. A seed, slowly growing. 'Actually, I think I'm going to buy the restaurant.'

'Which restaurant?'

'The Cozy Catch. Hannah's decided to sell it and stay in L.A. for good.'

'Oh!'

I risked a glance at her face. 'That's it? Oh?'

'Give me a second. I'm just processing what you said.'

'Of course. Take your time. I'm still processing it myself.'

She glanced across the town green to where the restaurant and the upstairs apartment were all lit up. The thought of it being mine, and the potential to make it even greater, gave me bubbles of excitement in my stomach. I hadn't felt excited about anything in a long time.

37

TAYLOR

He was staying in Pine Harbor.

'You *think* you're going to buy it?' I asked, to clarify. 'Or you *are* going to buy it?'

'I *am* going to buy it.' He nodded, a slow grin dawning on his face. 'That's the first time I've said the words out loud. I'm going to buy The Cozy Catch.'

'Did you just decide that right now?'

He nodded. 'Pretty much. I mean, obviously I've been thinking about it.'

'That a pretty big, life-altering decision to be making on the spur of the moment,' I said cautiously. 'Maybe you should take some time to think about it.'

'No.' He shrugged. 'It feels right.'

'I don't think bank managers usually recommend buying a business based on a feeling.'

'Maybe they should.'

'At the risk of sounding patronizing, maybe you should do some research. Weigh up the pros and cons. Make sure it's a viable business decision.'

'Don't forget, I've been running the business for the past seven months,' he pointed out. 'I know all the ins and outs, and what I don't know, I'll learn.'

'You make it sound simple.'

'I know it's not, and I know you're just trying to look out for me.' He gave me a look. 'But hey, you run your own business. Did you know everything there was to possibly know about business management before you took it on?'

'Not really,' I admitted. 'Like you, I worked there for a while first. Did tattooing by day and painted at night. Then Pete, the owner, told us he was selling and, well, I liked the location, I liked the staff, and I liked turning up there every day. It was a no-brainer for me. Plus, I'd always thought it would make a great art gallery as well as the tattoo side of it, so it gave me a place to showcase my work, as well as other local artists. I had to get a business loan and Adam was *not* happy about that. There were a lot of long days and sleepless nights, worrying about whether I could repay the loan. But I did it. I worked my ass off. It helped that I have great staff. The best. Reputation is key, and word of mouth, especially on social media, can do more for advertising than actual paid advertisements can.'

'Well there you go. The Cozy Catch already has the best staff anyone could hope for, and with all the tourists it makes a tidy profit. I really don't think it's too much of a leap of faith to take it on.'

I held my hands up. 'At the end of the day, it's not me you need to convince, and it sounds as if you've already convinced yourself.'

Someone cleared their throat discreetly behind him. 'Excuse, me, Jack?'

Jack turned to look over his shoulder. 'It's ready?'

Fiona beamed at us. 'It sure is.'

'Thanks. I owe you one.'

He stopped dancing and took my hand, giving it a light tug.

'What's going on?' I asked. 'Where are we going?'

'Not far.'

'How far?'

He smiled. 'Come with me and you'll find out.'

I allowed myself to be led. He was right. It wasn't far at all. Just underneath one of the big oak trees on the outskirts of the green, where the grass started to slope into a little hill, with the children's playground on the other side. A cozy, pale-blue picnic blanket had been laid out, with a couple of scattered cushions. In one corner there was a basket, and next to it, a mason jar with fairy lights inside. A few scattered pink peony flowers completed the scene. Jack gestured for me to sit, then sank down to the blanket himself, awkwardly tucking his long legs underneath him.

'You arranged all this for us?' I asked, as he opened the basket and peered inside.

'I did. Although Fiona has outdone herself with the little touches. The lights and flowers were not my suggestion.'

'If I didn't know any better, I could swear you were trying to be romantic.'

'Is it working?'

'Maybe.' I gestured with my chin. 'What's in the basket?'

He lifted out a container. 'Oysters, for starters. Don't worry, they're fresh and they've been on ice.'

'Not exactly typical picnic fare.'

'I beg to differ. If you haven't been served oysters on a picnic before, then you've been attending the wrong picnics.'

'What else is in there?'

He pulled out two wine glasses and a bottle of chilled wine.

'From a Midcoast vineyard,' he said, holding it out for me to check the label. 'I hope you prefer crisp and dry over sweet.'

'I do.'

He poured me a glass. 'Here.'

'Thanks.' And I really meant it.

I took a sip. It was delicious, and just what I needed after a busy few days. I moaned loudly as it slid down my throat, refreshing, and started a warm glow in my chest.

'Steady on,' Jack teased. 'We haven't even had the oysters yet.'

My eyes narrowed. 'Wait, is that why you chose them? Because of their reputed aphrodisiac effects?'

He grinned. 'No comment.'

'You don't need to feed me oysters to get me in the mood,' I told him, feeling my heart swell at the sight of him. This big, strong wonderful man sitting on a picnic blanket in a park, wearing the expression of someone who was as proud as punch of his efforts, as well he should be. 'This whole thing,' I said, gesturing around us, 'it's unbelievably sweet. The sweetest thing anyone has ever done for me, in fact.'

He shrugged. 'What can I say, I'm a sweet guy.'

'And so, so modest.'

'Jokes aside,' he said, his face turning serious. 'This is the bare minimum you deserve, Taylor. You deserve to have romantic picnics, candlelight dinners, movie nights on the couch, boat rides at sunset, campfires on the beach, fireworks on your birthday... You deserve to be made to feel special every single day.'

'I feel like it might be unsustainable to expect that kind of romance *every* day,' I told him, though I felt tears brewing at his words.

He scooted over on the blanket, reaching out to tuck a strand of my hair behind my ear.

'Stay with me,' he blurted. 'Here in Pine Harbor. Stay with me, Taylor.'

The intensity in his eyes made my breath catch. 'I thought you weren't going to ask me that.'

'I've changed my mind.' He shook his head. 'Since the moment we met I haven't been able to stop thinking about you. You're the first woman I've ever felt like this about.'

I swallowed hard, overwhelmed by his declarations. By the way he was looking at me. The way his touch felt. 'Like what?' I managed to say.

'Like I've met my match. The person I've been waiting my whole life to find. I'm not going to say my life was on hold until I found you, because it wasn't. I've lived a full life. But everything I've done, every step I've taken, it's all been leading me here to you.'

I opened my mouth to speak but he shushed me with a finger against my lips. I was too shocked and outraged in that moment to argue.

He grinned. 'I know you're mad at me right now for shushing you, and you can kill me for it soon, I promise. But I need you to just listen for a moment. I know that you don't believe in love at first sight and I've never personally experienced it, so I can't say whether it's real or not. But what I can say is that I've felt *something* for you since the moment we met. Even when I could barely see you in the dark, I felt a connection.'

I pulled a face.

'Yes, cheesy I know. But give me a break. I'm an ex-cop, current restaurant manager, soon-to-be restaurant owner, all going well. I'm not a bloody English language professor. I'm doing the best I can with the words I know.'

'You forgot superhero,' I murmured against his fingertips. 'You literally save lives. I think you can add that to the résumé.'

'*Buff* superhero,' he corrected.

I nipped his finger lightly with my teeth and he yelped.

'See what I mean?' he said, nursing it. 'You surprise me, all the time. Every time I think you're going to react one way, you do something else altogether. I love that.'

I sucked in air sharply. Stared at him.

'Yes, I said it,' he said, his face serious again. 'I'm falling in love with you, Taylor Calderwood. If someone had asked me six months ago to describe my perfect woman, I doubt I would have had the imagination to say a dark-haired, brown-eyed, *extremely* sexy, coffee-and-cheesecake-loving woman, who swims under the stars, rides a motorbike in a leather jacket, tattoos her art onto other people's skin, bickers with her uncle *constantly*, stands up in town meetings and argues for what she believes in, not to mention forgoes her own safety to hang off a cliff to comfort another human in their time of need. You are kind, and funny, and caring – stop me if you've heard all this before.'

I shook my head, unable to say anything.

He smiled. 'And you dropped everything to come all the way home to look after your uncle so your mother could still have her holiday. That tells me everything I need to know about you right there.'

I blinked at him, feeling emotional. No one had ever made feel so *seen*.

'You're everything I never knew I wanted, or needed,' he continued softly. 'And now that I've met you, I can't bear the thought of losing you already. Yes, it's sudden. And yes, I know we haven't known each other for that long. But it feels right. And it feels good, and I want to feel good, Taylor. I want to feel like I do when I'm around you, *every* day. But...' He exhaled slowly. 'If being in the city is what's going to make you happy, then I'll accept that. Somehow. I want you to be wherever makes you smile. You deserve to be happy.'

I reached up and touched his cheek. '*You* make me smile, Jack. I—'

I heard a gasp, and my voice trailed off as a figure standing behind him came into focus, just over by the tree. It was Hannah, staring at us, her hand over her mouth.

38

JACK

I turned to see what Taylor was staring at. Or in this case, who.

'Hannah.'

She blinked at me, her eyes glassy with tears. 'You love her?' she said hoarsely. 'How can you love her? You barely know her.'

'I'm sorry you found out this way,' I said, getting to my feet and holding out a hand to Taylor, pulling her up. 'But yes, I'm falling in love with Taylor.'

Hannah shook her head, as if she was trying to make sense of what she'd heard. 'You can't be serious.'

'I am.'

'So what, you're going to move to New York now to be with *her*?'

'I think we should discuss this somewhere else,' I said quietly, conscious that a crowd had started to gather, drawn by her loud and angry voice.

Hannah ignored me, staring at Taylor. 'I knew you were trouble from the first moment I saw you,' she spat. 'Do you enjoy being a homewrecker?'

Taylor gave me an understandably confused look. 'What's she on about? Are you and her...?'

'No.' I shook my head emphatically. 'Of course not.'

'Maybe not yet,' Hannah objected. 'But come on, Jack. How long have we known each other? We both know it was going to happen eventually.'

'I've never said or done anything to give you that idea,' I contradicted her.

'Oh please,' she scoffed. 'I'm not stupid. You've always had a thing for me, even when Alex was alive. Did you think I didn't know?'

'Maybe for a second,' I admitted. 'When we all first met. But you chose Alex, and I accepted that. We've only ever been friends, Hannah.'

'You kissed me.'

'No. You kissed *me*, when you were drunk, and I shut that down real quick.'

'You're only saying all this because of her.'

'She has a name,' I warned, unhappy with her derisive tone. Taylor had done nothing to her and didn't deserve to be disrespected. I felt the urge to defend and protect her.

'If you're really "just a friend", why did you move all the way across the country to this shithole for me, huh?'

'I did that *because* I'm your friend, Hannah. And because I promised Alex I would look after you.'

'No.' She shook her head, losing her balance when she did so, steadying herself against the tree trunk. 'It's more than that, and you know it.'

'Look.' I took a step forward, lowering my voice. When she'd yelled I'd caught the whiff of alcoholic fumes, and realized that her eyes weren't glassy from tears alone. 'You've clearly been drinking and your emotions are running high. This isn't the time or the place to discuss this. Go home. We can talk when you're sober.'

'Don't tell me what to do,' she said angrily, her words slurring.

'Jack.' Taylor put her hand on my arm.

Hannah glared at it venomously. I'd never seen this side of her before, and I didn't like it.

'Get your hands off him,' she spat at Taylor.

Taylor stiffened, but didn't move her hand.

'OK, I wasn't going to get involved, but enough is enough,' Taylor said firmly. 'You two have history; I get that. But you need to listen to what Jack is saying to you, because he really couldn't be any clearer. As far as he's concerned, you're a friend. That's it. And honestly? You're still lucky he sees you as that, the way you're carrying on. Now have some dignity, and walk away.'

Hannah blinked at her, taken aback. Her eyes flicked to mine. 'Are you going to let her talk to me like that?'

'She's right,' I replied. 'You need to get it through your head that nothing is ever going to happen between us. And not just because of Taylor. I don't see you like that, Hannah. I'm sorry, but I just don't.'

She looked around with wide eyes, seeing the small crowd that had gathered. 'But I need you, Jack. I don't know how I'll cope without you.'

'I'm sorry,' I told her, feeling my chest heavy with the words I knew I needed to say. 'But I can't be the one you lean on any more. I'll always be your friend, and as your friend I'm telling you that you need to go home to your family, and lay off the alcohol. It's not helping you heal.'

Hannah stared at me, her face impassive, her blinks exaggeratedly slow as she swayed on her feet.

'Go fuck yourself,' she said. Then she turned and stumbled

away across the green in the direction of the restaurant. I started to walk after her, until Taylor put a hand gently on my arm.

'Let her go,' she said. 'Anything we say now is just going to inflame the situation. Hopefully she'll sleep it off and see things differently in the morning.'

'I'll go,' Fiona said, hurrying off after Hannah.

'Are you OK?' Taylor asked me softly.

I nodded, sighing heavily. 'Yeah, I'm OK. I hate seeing her like this, and I can't help but wonder if I've made things worse since Alex died, by always being there for her. She's come to rely on me too much, and maybe that gave her the wrong idea.'

She reached up and touched my cheek. 'No, this isn't your fault. You were just trying to be a good friend.'

'I promised Alex.'

'I know. But sometimes a bit of tough love is the only thing that works with some people. Who knows, this might be what it takes for her to realize she needs help and to see a counsellor.'

'God, I hope so. I want to help but I think I'm doing more damage than good. I knew she relied on me but not to this extent. I thought when I moved out she'd realize nothing was ever going to happen between us.'

Taylor smiled. 'I can't blame her for holding out hope. You're a bit of a catch.'

'You're not so bad yourself,' I murmured, smiling, before leaning down to kiss her.

'Jack.' Fiona was back, sounding worried. 'I'm sorry to interrupt, but we have a bit of a situation.'

We broke apart. 'What is it?'

She stood close by, wringing her hands, her forehead fretted. 'I tried to take her keys, but she's strong, stronger than she looks anyway. And fast.'

'Hannah?'

'Yes. She took her car. Peeled off into the night.'

'Heading where?'

'I have no idea.'

I swore under my breath. 'She's too drunk to drive. And she doesn't know this island, or these roads.'

'I'm sorry,' Fiona said. 'I should have tried harder to stop her.'

'Hey,' I reassured her. 'This isn't your fault.'

'What do we do now?' she asked. 'We can't just let her drive drunk. She might hurt herself.'

I looked around at the crowd of people that were still gathered on the green. 'Discreetly spread the word to anyone you think might be able to help. I'll get my truck and take the south road out of town, if someone else can cover the others.'

'Are you sure that's a good idea?' Fiona asked. 'She might get mad if half the town are out combing the island for her.'

'Better she's mad than dead,' I told her.

'Or hurts someone else,' Taylor added.

Fiona nodded. 'You're right.'

Taylor touched my hand. 'I'll come with you.'

'No, it's OK. This isn't your mess.'

She put her chin up, defiant, her eyes flashing. 'Don't tell me in one breath that you're falling in love with me and then in the next try and push me away.'

I sighed. 'Is there any point in me arguing?'

She shook her head.

'Well can I at least drive?' I asked.

39

TAYLOR

'We have to find her,' I said, my eyes peeled on the windscreen in front. Jack's headlights were on full, illuminating the road in front of us, sweeping around the bends, briefly illuminating the trees on the sides of the road.

'We will.'

'Where?' I tried hard not to sound as anxious as I felt, although if my voice didn't give it away, my jiggling knee would.

'I don't know,' he admitted. 'But she can't have gone far.'

'What if she's heading back to the mainland?'

'We'll find her before she does.' His phone pinged with a message. Without taking his eyes off the road, he dug into his pocket and passed it over to me. 'Pin is zero, zero, zero, zero.'

'Are you serious?'

'What?'

'It's not exactly a difficult one to hack, is it,' I said, tapping it into the screen. 'I mean, I probably could have guessed that in about four tries.'

'If anyone wants to hack into my phone good luck to them,' he said, shrugging. 'A few sunset photos, some messages from my mother reminding me to call my grandmother for her birthday, and a golfing game I downloaded once when I was bored and haven't played for about two years.'

'How old is your grandmother turning?'

'Eighty-six. Focus. Who was the message from?'

I clicked on the message icon and opened the top message.

'Fiona. She's rallied a few people to help search.'

'Great.' He pulled over, checked his mirrors and did a U-turn. 'I've just remembered the lake. We went there together once. It's probably the only place she'll remember how to get to on her own. Message her back and tell her we'll check it out.'

I did as he said. 'Why don't you seem all that surprised?'

'Surprised about what?'

I flicked him a sideways look. 'You know what, Jack.'

He sighed. 'Because I'm not. Well, not that she's drunk. I've suspected Hannah has a problem with alcohol for a while now, although she hides it well so I doubted my suspicions. But I've never known her to drink and drive before. That *is* a surprise. I would never have thought she'd do this.'

I locked his screen again and put the phone on the console between us. 'She's obviously still struggling with Alex's death. Not that it excuses what she's doing. People lose loved ones every day and don't do selfish, dumb things like this.'

I felt his eyes on me. 'That's a little bit harsh, don't you think? It's not just Alex dying that's upset her. Tonight, anyway. It was finding out about us that tipped her over the edge.'

'I get that she was upset, and I'm sorry she found out the way she did. But do you really think it excuses this kind of behavior?'

'No of course not. That's not what I'm saying.'

'Good,' I snapped. 'Because it sounds like you're blaming *me* for her stupid, selfish actions. And that's not fair.'

'I didn't... I'm not... Who's blaming anyone?' he asked, sounding confused. 'I feel like I've missed something.'

'Jack!' I yelled, grabbing his arm without thinking.

Jack swerved the truck slightly, quickly recovering. 'Jesus, Taylor, what the hell?'

'Turn around. I think I saw something.'

He indicated and pulled over, before performing another U-turn.

'It was back here somewhere,' I muttered, craning my eyes out of the window into the darkness. I could only see where the car headlights illuminated. 'There.' I pointed. 'Broken branches.'

'And brake marks,' Jack said solemnly. 'They look fresh.'

'How can you tell?'

'They're still dark. Haven't had time to fade.' He pulled over, tires crunching on the gravel, and turned his truck off, leaving the headlights on. Opening the glovebox, he pulled out a torch, clicking it on and banging it a couple of times when it flickered. 'Wait here while I check it out.'

'You really should know me better than that by now,' I replied, opening my door. I followed him to the edge of the road, where it dipped down into a gully and darkness. The undergrowth was thick, but as we got close we could clearly see where it had been disturbed. Jack ran the torch over the brush.

'Can you see anything?' I asked, my heart in my throat.

'No.' He moved the torch further to the right. 'Wait. What's that?'

I peered where he was shining the light. Something shiny reflected back at us. Something metallic.

'Oh God, it's a car,' I told him. 'Do you think it's her?'

'Unless she's run someone else off the road and kept going,' he replied grimly.

I froze.

'Go back to the truck and get my phone,' he instructed. 'Gerry's number is saved in my contacts. Call him and tell him we need police and ambulance. I'm going to try and climb down.'

When I didn't move, he touched my arm. 'Taylor?'

I couldn't move, couldn't answer him. Just stood there, staring at the small bit of car we could see.

'Taylor,' he said louder, giving me a small shake. 'I need you to call for help.'

Finally, I looked at him, but it wasn't him I was seeing. 'I can't,' I said shakily. 'I'm sorry. I can't do this again.'

40

JACK

She was pale, paler than I'd ever seen anyone before, and her eyes stared at me, tortured.

'I don't understand,' I said. 'Taylor?'

She shook her head, clearly in shock. 'This isn't happening.'

I gently but firmly gripped her upper arms. 'Hey, look at me. If that is Hannah down there, we need to help her, OK? I need to get down there and I need you to call for help, just like you did when Casey fell off the cliff, OK? Can you do that for me?'

The mention of Casey was like a slap across the face. She blinked rapidly, then focused on my face and nodded.

'Say the words, Taylor, so I know you understand.'

'Yes, I can do that.'

'It's going to be OK,' I reassured her. 'Just stay off the road. I don't need anything happening to you too.'

She nodded, then stood on her tiptoes and kissed me on the mouth, pressing hard, as if imprinting her touch on me. 'Be careful,' she said after she broke away.

'I will.'

Clutching handfuls of the brush to stop myself from falling

down the steep incline, I slowly made my way down into the gully, following the brown branches and dirt until I came upon the wreckage we'd seen from the road. A silver Toyota Camry, latest model. Hannah's car. It had come to rest against a tree, the front bonnet crumpled as easily as if it had been paper. Steam was slowly escaping from the engine, and the front windscreen was shattered.

'Hannah,' I called, shining the torch at the driver's window. There was no reply.

I yanked at the handle, tugging. The door had been warped by the collision, making it hard to open, but after a few solid pulls it gave way with a screech of twisted metal. Hannah was slumped in her seat, blood trickling from a gash on her forehead. Her eyes were closed, and for a brief, heart-stopping second, I thought she was dead. Then she groaned.

I gently touched her shoulder. 'Hannah, it's Jack. You've been in an accident. Help is on its way. Can you open your eyes for me?'

She groaned again. 'Jack?'

'I'm here.'

'What happened?'

'You ran off the road.'

'I don't remember anything,' she mumbled.

'Don't worry about that now. The important thing is to get you out of here. Are you hurt anywhere besides your head?'

She reached up a hand to her head, touching the blood. 'I don't know.'

I reached over and unbuckled her seatbelt. There was an empty bottle of vodka in the passenger footwell, and the smell of alcohol was strong. Anger rose in my throat but I swallowed it down. This wasn't the time for recriminations.

'Jack.'

I jumped at Taylor's voice behind me. 'What are you doing down here?'

'I needed to tell you that Gerry is on his way, and he's organizing help.' She peered past me into the wreckage. 'Is she...?'

'Alive, yes.'

She exhaled audibly. 'She got lucky.'

'I'm not sure I'd call this luck.'

'She could have easily killed someone,' Taylor snapped. 'Or herself.'

'I know, and believe me, I'm upset with her too. But this isn't the time.'

'When would be the right time? At her funeral?'

I could hear how upset she was, her voice raw.

'She needs to understand how badly this could have ended,' she said hoarsely.

'And she will, believe me. If the courts don't drum that into her, her family sure as hell will.' I knew this for a fact. Hannah's parents were conservative and traditional. This would horrify them.

We heard the sound of a vehicle, then red light illuminated the scene. Taylor's face turned towards the source. She looked sad, vulnerable. I wanted to take her in my arms but that would have to wait.

'Sounds like the cavalry has arrived,' I said.

A door slammed, then a man yelled. 'Jack?'

'Down here,' I called back, as we heard the sound of more vehicles arriving.

I ducked my head back into the car. 'Help is here,' I told Hannah. 'They're going to look after you.'

'I'm sorry,' she replied, starting to cry. 'I didn't mean to cause any trouble.'

Gerry and two EMTs arrived beside the car. I knew one of them, a guy named Todd. He did a double take when he saw me.

'Search and rescue get called out to this?' he asked.

I shook my head. 'We just came across the scene and called it in. She has a head wound, and she's intoxicated. Breathing is shallow but she has been responding.'

'She's lucky she didn't kill herself,' Gerry muttered. 'These roads are windy enough when you're sober. She's not the first drunk driver to do herself some mischief on these roads.' He noticed Taylor for the first time and I watched his expression change, the color draining from his face. 'Shit, I'm sorry, Taylor. I forgot you were standing there.'

'It's OK,' she said quietly.

We stood back and watched as Todd and a couple of firemen from the truck who had turned up extracted Hannah from the car and got her onto a stretcher, securing her in place before assessing her.

'What are you thinking?' I asked Todd as the firemen began their careful ascent up the hill carrying the stretcher.

'She'll need a CT to check that head injury, but nothing else seems to be broken and there are no indications of internal bleeding or anything else untoward. You know I can't make any promises, but I think she's going to be OK. Thick vegetation like this, she's just lucky you spotted her.'

'It was all Taylor,' I told him. 'She's the one who noticed the broken branches.' I turned to smile at her but she was gone.

41

TAYLOR

I watched from inside Jack's truck as Hannah was brought up the hill and loaded into the ambulance. Watched it drive away. Jack and the others stood talking on the roadside for a couple of minutes, then they shook hands before Gerry climbed into his patrol car, and Jack walked over to his truck. He climbed in and shut his door. I swallowed hard.

'Are you OK?' he asked gently.

I nodded, staring straight ahead out of the windscreen. 'Yeah.'

'Want to talk about it?'

'Is she going to be OK?'

'Yeah, they reckon so. But that's not what I meant.' He reached over and picked up my hand, giving it a gentle squeeze. 'Tell me to shut up if I'm wrong, but the way you looked when you saw Hannah in the car, and what Gerry said...' He exhaled loudly. 'What happened to Cal, Taylor?'

The mention of his name made my heart squeeze tight in my chest. There was a long silence while I psyched myself up to say the words.

'He died in a car accident,' I finally said.

'Oh Taylor,' he said softly. 'I'm so sorry.'

'Don't be. You didn't know.'

'I wish I had. I would never have made you come with me to search for Hannah.'

'You didn't make me come with you; I knew full well that this was a possible outcome.'

'You don't have to tell me the details, if this is too difficult for you to talk about.'

'It is difficult, but it's... *he*... was such a major part of my life, and I want you to know about him.'

He squeezed my hand again. 'OK. If you're sure. But take your time and stop if it gets too hard. You don't owe me anything.'

'I didn't see Cal's accident scene,' I told him quietly. 'They wouldn't let me. My mother got a phone call from someone who recognized Cal's car, but she made me stay at home. Didn't tell me where she was going in the middle of the night. But I saw his car the next day, at the police yard. I saw his blood.'

'How old were you?'

'It happened the night of our eighteenth birthday.' I looked over at him. 'Cal, Calvin, was my twin. *Is.* I never know what to say any more. Am I still a twin, now that my twin is no longer here?' I shook my head. 'He was my other half. My best friend. We were close, growing up. Especially after Dad left and it was just Mom and us. It was like having my own permanent playmate. A friend who didn't go home at the end of the day but stayed for sleepovers, and midnight pantry raids, and sneaking out of the house.'

'What was he like?'

'He was funny. Really funny. Without even trying. One of those people who had a witty comeback for any situation. He made me laugh, every single day. And he was nice. Genuinely nice. No one ever had a bad word to say about him. You know how when someone dies, people say things like, "He lit up every room he entered"?'

Jack nodded.

'With Cal it was true. He was so vibrant. People couldn't help but notice him.'

'He sounds like a great guy.'

'He was. Never took life too seriously. Always ready to help anyone who needed help, even if they hadn't asked. I mean don't get me wrong, he could be cheeky, too. He and Adam used to get up to a bit of mischief. Normal teenage stuff.'

He frowned, clearly surprised. 'He was friends with Adam?'

'Best friends, actually, since they were six. They just clicked. Thick as thieves, my mom used to say. They had the same sense of humor. Until Cal died. Adam never really laughed much after that. Not with me, anyway.'

'Is that why you got together? Because you were both grieving for Cal?'

I stared at his hand over mine, wondering if I had the courage to say the next bit. Wondering if he would still feel the same way about me if I did. But I had to tell him. The weight of it had burdened my marriage. If I was to have any kind of future with Jack, I had to be honest. 'It was our fault.'

'What was?'

'Cal's death.'

His brow furrowed. 'I thought you said it was an accident?'

'It was, but it was our fault he was on the road in the first place.' I swallowed down a hard lump in my throat, squeezing my eyes shut so I wouldn't see the disappointment on his face. 'Cal and I, we only ever had one rule, and that was that our friends were off limits. We even shook hands on it when we were fourteen. No dating each other's friends. We didn't ever want to have to choose between each other and our friends if, *when*, things inevitably went wrong. I broke that rule. And he died because of it.'

'I don't understand.'

I opened my eyes and stared at him, anguished, tears streaming down my face. The guilt was as fresh now as it was back then. The wound slashed open by the events of the night.

'We had a birthday party down on the beach,' I explained. 'With a big campfire, burgers, alcohol that we'd pilfered from Mom. Music playing out of a big speaker. It was the best night. All our friends were there. The beach, the stars. Anything felt... possible. So when Adam kissed me, I didn't stop him. In fact, I kissed him back.' I could still remember the moment clearly, as much as I'd tried to forget it. 'Cal saw us, and he was angry. Angrier than I'd ever seen him. He stormed off. We chased after him of course, and I begged him not to drive. Even got in front of the car, but he kept revving the engine and Adam pulled me away. I've replayed that moment so many times in my head. Cal would never have hurt me. Adam should have just left me. I could have stopped him from driving away.'

Beside me, Jack exhaled heavily. 'Was he drunk?'

'He'd been drinking. Enough to be impaired, definitely.' My voice shook and I took a sharp breath. 'He ran through a stop sign and T-boned another car. Somehow, miraculously, the other occupants, a couple from Washington, survived with only minor injuries. But Cal was killed instantly. They said the impact severed his neck from his spine. My beautiful, larger-than-life brother was snuffed out in an instant. It didn't seem possible. I still struggle with it.'

Jack exhaled softly, then nodded. 'I know what you mean.

When Alex died, it was a shock, how suddenly someone can go from being here to being gone.'

'I never got to say goodbye. Or tell him how sorry I was that I broke our pact.'

'Is that why you married Adam? Because you felt guilty?'

'Yes.' I stared at my lap again. Wiped the tears from my cheek with the back of my hand. 'We both blamed ourselves, and each other. Everyone who'd been on the beach that night knew what had happened. Why Cal had driven off. It felt like everyone blamed us. The whole town.'

'I'm sure they didn't.'

I shook my head. 'Small town like this. People talk. Even at the funeral, I could hear them whispering. We got drunk again after the funeral and agreed that we couldn't let his death be in vain. He couldn't die because of a stupid, drunken kiss. So, we told everyone that we were in love. It somehow made his death seem less meaningless. Nothing could ever justify it, but it helped to assuage our guilt.'

'Grief and guilt can make us do funny things.'

'It made me marry a man who should never have been more than a one-night stand. It was the least I deserved though. To be stuck in a loveless marriage. At least Adam finally had the guts to end it. I don't blame him for falling in love with someone else, you know. Everyone expects me to be angry with him, but I'm not. I know he blames himself for Cal's death as much as I blame myself. He deserves a shot at happiness.'

'So do you.'

'I wish it was that simple.'

'If Hannah had died tonight, would you want me to spend the rest of my life blaming myself for her death?'

I frowned. 'Of course not.'

'Why not? She drove off because she heard us declaring our feelings for each other.'

'That's different, and you know it.'

'How?'

'It just is.'

'No, Taylor. It's the same. It wasn't your fault that Cal drove. You were eighteen. Do you know how many eighteen-year-olds get drunk and make out at parties every night?'

'But I broke our promise.'

'A promise you made when you were *fourteen*. It was a promise between kids. Look, you need to remember that we *all* have to take responsibility for our own actions in life. Cal and Hannah included.'

'I just wish he was still here,' I said though my tears. 'I miss him so much.'

He leaned over and pulled me in against him. Burying my face into his chest, I cried like I hadn't let myself cry since it had happened. I cried until I had no tears left to cry. Until his shirt was as soaked as if he'd stood in a rainstorm. I cried until my face hurt.

42

SIX MONTHS LATER

Jack

'It hurts.'

'It's supposed to hurt.'

'This much?'

I stopped loading things into a basket and stared at him. 'It's a tattoo, Ray. What did you expect it to feel like?'

He grumbled something indecipherable, studying the freshly inked tattoo on the outside of his bicep. It was a design he and Taylor had come up with together, to represent his life-time on the lobster boats. A sturdy anchor, with a little lobster perched on one of the upper branches of the stock. It wouldn't be my choice, but it was perfect for Ray.

'I need another sherry,' he said, nudging his glass across the bar. 'For the pain.'

I suppressed a smile. 'Of course.'

Moira arrived back from the bathroom in a blur of move-ment and color and noise, and climbed up onto the barstool next to Ray. I was still getting used to her being the mother of my girlfriend, and not just my landlord.

'Where's Taylor?' she asked, leaning over the bar to pluck an olive out of a jar.

I moved the jar out of her reach. 'Those are for the drinks of my paying customers,' I pointed out. 'And you've already eaten half a dozen.'

She pouted. 'I'm hungry.'

Fiona put a menu down in front of her. 'So, order some food.'

Moira laughed. 'Fine. I'll have the landlubber's pie, please, Fiona. I've been meaning to try that. What do you want, Ray?'

'Depends if I'm paying full price or if I get a friends and family discount.' Ray scowled. 'There's got to be *some* perks to your niece dating the owner of the best restaurant in town.'

A warm glow filled my belly at his words, and I looked around the room. The place was busy, the tables and booths packed with people enjoying food, each other's company and the atmosphere. Outside, the December day was gray and chilly. Patches of fog still hung over the harbor, and the road was still slick with the rain that had drizzled throughout the night. Inside, the fireplace in the center of the room was stoked up, its heat permeating right through to the corners of the room. In one corner stood a large balsam fir tree that Taylor and I had picked ourselves from the Everpine Hollow Christmas Tree Farm. We'd spent a wonderful evening decorating it with Moira, Ray, Fiona, Oscar and Taylor's friend, Megan. We'd also hung tinsel, fairy lights and ornaments around the walls. The place looked jolly and festive, like Santa's grotto.

'It is pretty good, isn't it?' I said, agreeing with him.

'All these tourists certainly seem to think so,' he said, scowling again.

'Please don't scowl at my customers,' I told him. *My*

customers. I still hadn't got used to calling them that, but that's what they were, now that I owned the building and business. Hannah had tried to sell it to me for less than what it was worth but I'd insisted on paying full market value. The size of the loan had been daunting, but the fact that I had a business tenant move into the upstairs apartment had helped take some of the stress off.

'Where *is* Taylor?' Moira said. 'The studio upstairs is all closed up.'

'She decided to take her birthday off,' I told her, checking my watch. 'I'm meeting her soon.'

'You guys are still going to come to the house for dinner, right?'

'I think we can manage to walk the hundred yards over from the cabin, yes.'

'Great. I'm cooking Taylor's favorite.'

Ray brightened. 'Blueberry pie?'

'Blueberry pie,' Moira confirmed.

He sniffed. 'Maybe I'll come.'

'Were you planning on sitting on your chair in the next room and ignoring us?' She rolled her eyes. 'Of course you'll come. I hope you've bought Taylor a present.'

He pointed to his tattoo. 'I paid her to do this to me. That's present enough.'

'You love it,' Moira teased.

'I suppose it's not bad,' he said begrudgingly, although it was obvious to anyone with eyes that he was proud of it.

I finished packing the basket and reached for my coat. 'I'll be back in a couple of hours. Fiona, you're in charge.'

'Roger that.' She took my place behind the bar.

I lifted my jacket off the coat stand and shrugged my arms into the sleeves. 'Watch these two don't eat all the olives and drink all the sherry,' I warned her. 'Don't listen to any sob stories they might give you. They might be family, but they still have to pay just like everyone else.'

'So *no* perks then,' I heard Ray grumble as I left. 'That's just great.'

'There.' I stood back to admire my handiwork. 'You'll probably think they're tacky, but I don't care. It's Christmas, Cal, and I wanted you to have some Christmas lights.'

I bought the twinkling star string lights from The Coastal Craftsman. They were solar-powered and waterproof, Jasper had assured me. When I'd told him what they were for, he'd insisted on adding some extra solar lights that poked into the ground for free. One was a Santa Claus light, and the other one a snowman. I knew Cal would have howled with laughter at the sight of them, which made them feel appropriate. I pushed them down into the soil on either side of the headstone, and smiled to myself. 'Just be thankful they're not the lobster ones. Maybe I'll bring those for you in summer. You'd get a kick out them. One of Mom's tackier purchases it has to be said, and as you know, that's saying something.'

I plucked out a weed that was growing next to the concrete headstone, smoothing the grass over the hole it left behind.

'Happy birthday,' I said softly. 'I wish you were here. Mom's cooking lobster mac 'n' cheese and blueberry pie for dinner tonight. Ray will be there, of course. And Jack.'

I took a deep breath and stared out to sea. It was a gray, damp day. Visibility was a few hundred yards, if that. The ocean was a beautiful cold green color, clean and wild. It made a loud swooshing noise as it frothed and broke over the rocks below, clattering over loose pebbles every time it withdrew. I tilted my head up and closed my eyes, letting the salt spray moisture in the air soak into my skin.

I still felt some guilt over Cal's death, but that was never going to change. What I had been able to do in the last six months, since I confided in Jack, was forgive myself. Forgiving myself didn't mean condoning my actions or forgetting about them, but it was step one in letting go of the guilt that had been weighing down my life. It meant accepting that nothing I did or felt could ever change the past, so the best thing I could do was look to the future and live my best life possible, a life that Cal would have been proud of.

It wasn't easy, and I still had bad days, but I had learned to practice self-compassion, to ease up on myself. To remember that I *had* been young, and that I could never have foreseen the consequences that night from an action that, as Jack had pointed out, thousands of teenagers do every single weekend.

Lost in thought, I didn't hear him approach, until he slid an arm around my waist and pressed his lips to the side of my neck. I knew it was him. Didn't need to look. I'd know his scent, his touch, anywhere. Had spent a great deal of the last six months intricately entwined with him. I relaxed back into him, feeling his body wrap around my own. Supporting me. I doubted I would ever get used to how it felt to be held by someone you loved.

Deciding to stay back here in Pine Harbor had been a leap of faith, but one which had paid off. I still owned the studio in New York, only now it was managed by Renae on a day-to-day basis. It had been Jack's idea to turn the apartment upstairs from the restaurant into another art/tattoo studio. I'd been skeptical at first, unsure how much business I'd get in a small town like this, but the stream of tourists wanting souvenir paintings of the harbor or tattoos of little lobsters to remind themselves of their holiday in Maine was constant, and some of my regular clientele from back in the city had even made the trek to see me in the Pine Harbor studio. There had even been a new hashtag created on Instagram, #inkedinpineharbor.

'I thought you weren't going to bring the bike,' he admonished.

'I lied.'

'I'll tell your mother.'

'Go ahead. She has about as much control over me as you do.'

'So... none, then.'

'It's good that you understand that.'

He chuckled, and it reverberated through his chest, rumbling against my back.

'Your mother and Ray are at the bar. She wanted to make sure we'll definitely be at the house for dinner tonight.'

I groaned, wriggling inside his arms to turn and snuggle into his chest. 'Do we have to?'

Since moving into the cabin with Jack, I'd finally understood people who never wanted to leave their houses. It was our little sanctuary. I went to sleep every night curled up in his arms, and woke up next to him every morning. We were insatiable for each other.

'Yes, we do have to,' he said firmly. 'I monopolize you far too much.'

'What if I like being monopolized by you,' I mumbled. 'What if I want to be monopolized by you *more*.'

'Well, obviously your wish is my command. But we're still going to your mother's for dinner. I promised.'

'I didn't.'

'I promised on your behalf.'

'Fine. But *when* she gets sentimental and starts reminiscing, that's on you.'

My words were light, but he understood immediately what I was trying to say. My mother was incredibly resilient. But even she had her limits, and our birthday was one of them. It was the reason I hadn't spent a birthday with her since Cal's death. But that hadn't been fair to her, and I knew that now. She'd already lost one child, and I had been depriving her of both of us by doing that. Now that I lived back here again, we'd slowly started to mend that part of our relationship. After he'd died, any time she'd mentioned him I would shut the conversation down and leave, until eventually she'd learned to speak about him in front of me. But Cal didn't deserve that, and neither did my mother. We talked about Cal all the time now. About the kind of person he'd been. Speculated on what kind of person he would have become. It hurt, but I also loved it.

'I'll be right beside you,' he said, leaning down to press his lips against my forehead.

I spied something out of the corner of my eye. 'What's that?'

He turned. 'That, my love, is your birthday picnic.'

'My birthday picnic?'

He nodded. 'Your birthday picnic.'

'It's raining.'

'Barely.'

'The ground is wet.'

'I have a waterproof blanket.' He grinned. 'You're not going to let a little bit of wet grass stop us, are you?'

'Well, no. But...'

He kissed the tip of my nose. 'We never got to finish our last picnic,' he said. 'The one when I asked you to stay.'

I pulled a face. 'No thanks to Hannah.'

'Yes, no thanks to Hannah. Who messaged this morning, by the way.'

'How is she?'

'Good. Still going to meetings, and counselling. She just hit one hundred and seventy-nine days sober.'

'Good for her.'

'Yeah. Baby steps, but I'm cautiously optimistic. I think being around her family is the best thing for her.'

'The restorative power of love.'

He smiled. 'Indeed.'

'What's in the basket?'

'All your favorites of course.' He released me from his embrace, taking my hand and leading me over to the basket. Pulling out a bottle of raspberry kombucha, he passed me two glasses.

'Hold these for me while I pour, will you.'

When the glasses were full, he recapped the bottle and put it back into the basket.

'We'll have a proper toast with wine tonight, of course,' he explained. 'But I figured this would do for now.' Raising his glass, he smiled. 'Happy birthday, Taylor and Cal.'

I smiled back, tapping his glass with mine. I had never been happier. Never dared to believe I could be this happy. But Jack had shown me that I deserved this and more.

Pine Harbor had always been home, even when I'd lost sight of that. It had taken Jack to remind me that home wasn't a building, a town, or memories. It was found in community, in belonging, in a feeling. Home was love.

* * *

MORE FROM TAMMY ROBINSON

Another book from Tammy Robinson, is available to order now here:
https://mybook.to/NewPineBackAd

ACKNOWLEDGEMENTS

As always, a HUGE thank you to my tirelessly supportive agent, Vicki Marsdon, for her encouragement and unwavering belief in me. Thanks for finding such a perfect new home for my writing, and let's hope this series is just the start of something wonderful!

My eternal gratitude to Emma Beswetherick, my fabulous editor. Working with you again has been such a joy. Thank you for falling in love with Pine Harbor as much as I have, and for trusting me to bring the characters stories to life.

Thanks to my award-winning, innovative publisher, Boldwood. I am blown away by your commitment and dedication to your authors. Thank you to all of the editorial team who worked on this book, the marketing team for getting the word out there, and the design team for coming up with the stunning cover that I'm so in love with.

Thanks, and love as always, to my wonderful readers for sticking with me and enjoying my books. For all your sweet messages and comments and your continued encouragement. Thanks for all your wonderful suggestions when I needed a name for the setting of this series. I hope you all like Pine Harbor.

My gratitude to Sarah Brown and her mum for their entertaining stories about Uncle Ray, who inspired the character Ray in this book.

To Geddy's in Bar Harbor for their live webcam. Before writing, I would log on and watch the locals and tourists going about their day on the other side of the world and find myself inspired. They have no idea they're being spied upon. Guess the cat's out of the bag now.

Thanks to my wonderful friend in the UK, Lorraine Tipene, my first reader and critic for the past twelve years and eleven books. Still hoping to come and visit you one day.

And last but not least, so much gratitude and love to all of my family, but especially my babies (who will hate that I've called them that) Holly, Willow and Leo. You guys are my everything. My world. My 'why'. I love you more than words can say, but I'll keep saying it anyway to make sure you understand. I'm sorry I embarrass you in front of your friends with kisses, but not sorry enough to stop doing it.

ABOUT THE AUTHOR

Tammy Robinson is a novelist from New Zealand. After years spent working her way around the world on cruise ships and for Club Med resorts, she is now settled on a farm in rural Waikato with her husband and three children. After the tragic deaths of her mother and a close friend, she sat down to write a book and hasn't stopped since. She writes heartwarming stories set in small, coastal towns. She is now working on her twelfth novel.

Download your exclusive bonus content from Tammy Robinson here:

Visit Tammy's website: www.tammyrobinsonauthor.weebly.com

Follow Tammy on social media here:

facebook.com/TammyRobinsonAuthor

instagram.com/tammyrobinsonauthor

tiktok.com/@TammyRobinsonAuthor

ALSO BY TAMMY ROBINSON

Summer Nights in Pine Harbor